CASTING THE NET

The Dunbridge Chronicles

BOOK 2

CASTING THE NET

Pam Rhodes

LION FICTION

Published by Lion Fiction
an imprint of
Lion Hudson plc
Wilkinson House, Jordan Hill Road,
Oxford OX2 8DR, England
www.lionhudson.com/fiction

ISBN 978 1 78264 062 2
e-ISBN 978 1 78264 063 9

First edition 2014

A catalogue record for this book is available from the British Library

Printed and bound in the UK, January 2015, LH26

For Tom Sander, the bright young curate who, in sharing his own experience of curacy with me, has helped to shape Neil's story. With inspirational young priests like Tom at its helm, the church we love is in safe hands.

WHO'S WHO
IN DUNBRIDGE

Reverend Neil Fisher – curate at St Stephen's.

Reverend Margaret Prowse – rector of St Stephen's; **Frank Prowse** – Margaret's husband; **Sarah**, their daughter, married to **Martin**, with a toddler son, **Edward**.

Iris Fisher – Neil's widowed mother, who lives near Bristol.

Peter Fellowes – churchwarden; **Glenda Fellowes** – Peter's wife; they have two grown-up children with families of their own: **Christine** in Brighton and **John** in Scotland.

Cynthia Clarkson (Cyn) – churchwarden; husband **Jim** and sons **Carl**, **Barry** and **Colin**, the eldest, married to **Jeannie**; **Ellen** – Colin and Jeannie's baby daughter.

Harry Holloway – elderly widower, Neil's neighbour.

Claire – Harry's great-niece; gardener employed by St Stephen's.

Sam – Claire's young son.

Ben – Sam's estranged father, who returned home to Australia before Sam was born.

Felicity – Claire's mother, who lives with her second husband David in Scarborough.

Wendy Lambert – Neil's keenest admirer; leader of St Stephen's worship group; music teacher at Fairlands School for Girls.

Sylvia Lambert – Wendy's mother; St Stephen's choir leader.

Brian Lambert – Wendy's father; organist at St Stephen's.

Barbara – runs St Stephen's playgroup.

Brenda – Sunday school teacher.

Val – widowed palliative care nurse; regular worshipper at St Stephen's; friend of Peter Fellowes.

Roland Branson – Glenda Fellowes' boss.

Boy George Sanderson – octogenarian leader of St Stephen's bell-ringers.

Madge – bell-ringer.

Clifford Davies – former professional pianist in variety; organist at the local crematorium.

Graham Paterson – Neil's friend at the Wheatsheaf; fellow member of the darts team; Deputy Head of Maths at Dunbridge Upper School.

Debs – lives next door to Graham; policewoman; plays the flute in St Stephen's worship group.

Bob Trueman – local farmer; chairman of the Committee of Friends of St Stephen's.

Garry – pastor of Church of God Evangelical Church.

Shirley McCann – matron of the Mayflower residential care home.

Sylvie – care worker at the Mayflower.

Tom – resident at the Mayflower, who plays the piano.

Victor – previous rector of St Stephen's for more than twenty years.

David Murray – churchwarden at St Gabriel's, sister church to St Stephen's, in nearby village of Minting.

Angela and Keith Barker – worshippers at both St Gabriel's and St Stephen's; live almost next door to St Gabriel's; Angela is a part-time registrar; Keith works in the City of London.

Dr Wynn Jones and **Dr Saunders** – both partners in the local GP practice.

Bishop Paul – head of the team to which both Neil and Margaret belong.

Hugh – retired local minister.

Rosemary – non-stipendiary industrial chaplain.

Mrs Martin – teacher at local church school.

Maria – from Romania.

Lady Romily – chairwoman of St Stephen's Ladies' Guild.

Members of the Ladies' Guild
Beryl – renowned cake-maker; organizes the St Stephen's cake rota group.

Olivia – deputy chairwoman of the Guild.

Penelope – secretary.

Julia – treasurer.

CHAPTER 1

Most of the time he just looked down at his boots, counting each dogged step as he paced, one foot in front of the other. The terrain was becoming more rugged, with unexpected outcrops of sharp rock, and cambers on the scrubland that could easily dislodge his footing or twist an ankle. The straps on his rucksack were starting to chafe his shoulders through his cotton T-shirt, and he could feel a sticky trickle of sweat coursing down his back, even though he'd stripped off his jacket and tied it round his waist a mile down the hill. The sun rose steadily in the sky towards the height of the day.

Three hundred, three hundred and one, three hundred and two, three hundred and three, three hundred and four... Some way back, Neil had begun counting his steps, determined not to slow his pace or deviate from his aim to reach the peak of the hill by eleven o'clock. Then he could stop, unpack his rucksack, and get out his Bible. Until then, he would only let himself think about pausing after each five hundred steps to catch his breath, sip from his water bottle or take in the view. Just a couple of minutes would be allowed to muster his energy and purpose before starting off again. It was a discipline he'd set himself – and God knows, his life needed discipline.

Four hundred and ninety-six, four hundred and ninety-seven, four hundred and ninety-eight, four hundred and ninety-nine, five hundred! Relieved, he bent forward, clasping his knees and gasping for breath. For a few seconds he stayed there, doubled up, as his breathing became more relaxed and regular. Slowly pulling himself up, he reached back into his rucksack for his water bottle and downed the lukewarm liquid in short, frantic gulps. Only then did he look up and around him, his gaze taking in the rolling contours and vibrant summer colours of the Derbyshire Dales.

Last time he and Rob had come here, it had been earlier in the previous year, when there was still a frost in the air and a biting wind. That must have been last April – fifteen months, and yet a whole lifetime ago. They'd both been students then, getting away for a weekend of walking before facing their finals at theological college. They were young men full of academic theory, with high hopes for the life that lay ahead of them. Seeing Rob again over the past week, Neil recognized in his friend a new maturity, honed by the year he'd spent as a curate in a large inner-city church.

Could Rob see a similar maturity in him, Neil wondered. Since the ordination ceremony at the weekend, when they had both taken their final vows of priesthood, had Rob seen him as a man of mission and calling, able to bring wisdom and insight to others as he served his community and led others into a deeper relationship with Christ? Would anyone in Dunbridge think that of him without an incredulous grin on their face?

Neil's shoulders slumped as he thought about his role as curate at St Stephen's Church in the small Bedfordshire market town of Dunbridge. His parishioners might be kind enough to describe him as being fired with Christian purpose to serve the Lord with dedication and skill, but Neil would be the first to admit the long list of failings they might also mention. Who wanted a curate who was naturally shy and hated the limelight? What good was that when the heart of the job was to give inspirational sermons every Sunday? And if he were being brutally honest, his organizational skills weren't brilliant. Of course it was helpful to be quite neat and tidy by nature, but when those qualities were paired with a sieve of a mind that regularly forgot what he'd been thinking about just the moment before, his tidy nature didn't save him from coming across as ill-prepared and forgetful.

And if that sense of inadequacy and muddle weren't enough to overwhelm him, then his complete failure in affairs of the heart would certainly tip him into depression. Some people might think a man lucky to have *two* interesting and attractive women declaring love for him, but not if the man's a priest, for heaven's sake! He could try to excuse himself by recognizing his lack of experience in relationships with the opposite sex, but he couldn't pretend ignorance of the fact that one man was only supposed to share love and loyalty with one woman at a time. Somehow he'd found himself drawn to two very different yet equally remarkable girls.

He could see that Wendy, the music teacher who ran the worship group at St Stephen's, would make the perfect wife for an eager young curate. It was less easy to imagine a future with the other woman who had burst her way into his heart. Claire was his neighbour, prickly, challenging and very attractive in an off-beat sort of way. Quite simply, he'd never met anyone remotely like her – a single mum who described herself as an atheist – and yet, in the year since he'd come to Dunbridge, they'd both been surprised to recognize the unlikely, deeply unsettling connection that constantly sparked between them.

Too much thinking and not enough walking! Stuffing his water bottle back in his rucksack, Neil glanced at his watch, then set off again, singing out loud to give himself a beat to march to.

Onward Christian soldiers, marching as to war,
With the cross of Jesus going on before!

Four verses later, the hill had got steeper, his path less clear – and he was taking the hymn at a much slower pace. By the end of his second rendition, his singing was barely above a whisper, as he no longer had the breath to sing the words out loud.

His thoughts drifted to the music at his ordination service in the abbey the previous Saturday. The glorious harmonies of the opening anthem, and the fullness of the congregational hymns echoing around the ancient walls, which were steeped in centuries of song, prayer and worship – somehow they blended together to fill the huge space of carved arches and curving ceilings with joyful celebration one moment and deeply reverential prayer the next. In some ways, Neil wished he could remember more of the detail of the service. He'd prepared for it for so long, and knew the words by heart, but sadly the whole thing had become a bit of a blur, with just the odd gleaming moment shining in his memory with absolute clarity. Most of all, he could feel again the crackle of energy that seemed to go through him as the supporting group of local clergy stood around him, their hands on his shoulders, while Bishop Paul blessed him and welcomed him into full priesthood. That moment was the culmination of his life's purpose so far, and pointed him towards the path he must follow from now on. He would relive that moment over and over again in years to come – although perhaps not just now, with his lungs ready to explode and a large blister mushrooming on his left heel as it rubbed savagely against the back of his boot.

The summit of the hill loomed clearly into view at last, thankfully not that far above him. Within minutes, he'd got to the top, where he leaned over to get his breath back for a while before lowering his backpack, untying his jacket and spreading it out over the damp grass in front of him. Then he reached into the rucksack to pull out his water bottle, gulping down half the remaining contents. Refreshed at last, he pulled out his Bible and laid it before him as he carefully knelt down on the jacket.

Ouch! His knee made contact with something hard and sharp in his jacket pocket. Pulling out his car keys, he placed them on a flat rock behind him, then settled himself into a position for prayer.

It was a good half hour before the cramp in his knees got too severe for him to stay in that position a minute longer. Pulling himself gingerly to his feet, he stood for a moment to savour the colour and spectacle of the layered hills around him. It had been a good idea to come here, where the wind could blow fresh thoughts into his head, and God himself could whisper in his ear. This walk had served its purpose. He knew now what he had to do.

Quickly gathering his things together, Neil started the downward journey with new energy and commitment. This was how those old-time missionaries must have felt as they ventured out to face unknown dangers in far-flung corners of the world. Now he understood their zeal, their sense of mission, and their certainty that God was with them always. He had joined their holy army! *Look out, world, here I come!*

He didn't even bother to stop for a break on the way down, and forty-five minutes later he was striding across the gravel towards his car. With a smile of anticipation, he peered through the window into the back seat. There it was – the ice box he'd asked the hotel to fill for him before he set out. His mouth watered at the thought of crusty bread filled with home-baked ham and spicy pickle, the crisp salad, and the slice of lemon drizzle cake, all to be washed down with a thermos of hot coffee.

But as Neil fumbled through his pockets, an awful truth dawned on him. Suddenly he remembered where he'd left his keys. He could picture the small rugged outcrop where he'd stopped at the top of the hill, and the low, flat rock on which his car keys were no doubt glistening in the midday sunshine at this very moment.

From his mouth, unbidden and unforgivable, came a very un-Christian expletive – not just once, but twice – and, louder still, three times, four, five – until the sixth completed its echoing journey around the circle of hills in time to smack him in the face like a hard punch.

Ashamed of his language, Neil bent his head in a quick prayer of humble apology. Then he straightened up and grabbed his rucksack to check on his water supplies. Dwindling, he thought miserably, as he shook the water bottle. Still, the sooner he set off, the sooner he'd be back at the car tucking into those ham sandwiches!

Off he marched, chin up, eyes on the horizon, determined that neither the throbbing pain in his heel, nor the bruise he could feel developing on the ball of his foot, would hold him back. Perhaps he should have kept his eyes on the ground, because he failed to notice the cluster of small stones that brought him crashing to his knees.

That word rang out again across the hills – and again, and again, until the hill finally demanded all his breath for climbing.

❧ Chapter 2 ❧

"**A**re you limping, Neil?"

Churchwarden Cynthia Clarkson – "but please call me Cyn" – turned round to glance at him as he hobbled into the church hall kitchen two days later.

"Just a couple of blisters from my walking holiday."

"New boots, were they?"

"The boots were fine. It's me that's falling to bits. I thought I was good at hill walking, but honestly, I'm aching from top to toe."

"Oh dear," tutted Cyn, her eyes sparkling more with laughter than sympathy, "you poor old thing! Not the spring chicken you thought you were, eh?"

"I wouldn't mind," grumbled Neil, "but I'm still in my twenties. I can't believe how out of condition I am."

"What you need," said Cyn, "is a bit of home cooking and good company. You are coming on Sunday, aren't you? I reckon there'll be about forty of us for lunch. I've already started baking. Got all the puds made and in the freezer, so I'll just have the cold meat and salads to prepare on the day. All our own produce, of course."

The mention of food definitely got Neil's attention.

"I wouldn't miss it for the world!"

Neil propped himself against the work surface as she dried the coffee mugs and stacked them neatly in the cupboard while she chatted. She'd been one of the two churchwardens at St Stephen's for more than five years now, deftly combining the demands of that role with the needs of the large, warm-hearted Clarkson family of which she was undoubtedly the matriarch. Neil sometimes wondered if she ever slept, because she seemed so full of energy and purpose that she could be exhausting, humbling company. Mind you, he thought pragmatically, what a blessing Cyn was to all of them there. Every church could do with a Cynthia Clarkson in their midst!

"What wouldn't you miss?" asked Margaret, the rector of St Stephen's, as she joined them in the kitchen, still clutching the papers she'd just been sorting in the office.

"A good meal!" grinned Neil. "Cyn's been telling me what's on the menu after Ellen's baptism next Sunday."

"Did I tell you, Margaret? Ellen's going to wear the Clarkson christening gown that's been handed down through the family for almost a century."

"Heavens! What's it made of? Is it something delicate like lace? Will it stand up to all the youngsters wanting to hold the baby on her special day? Goodness knows what Ellen's going to make of all those boy cousins who'll be bossing her about!"

"Oh, we Clarkson women know how to sort our men out," grinned Cyn. She and her husband Jim had always had an easy relationship with complementary roles: he was the boss when it came to running the farm, but she was in charge of everything else.

"Ellen will have them wrapped around her little finger before they know what's hit them. And you're right, the dress is delicate – and quite small too. I suppose when my great-great-grandma made it all those years ago, babies were baptized when they were only a few days old, in case they didn't last long. That was life then, wasn't it? Of course, Ellen was small when she was born, coming early like that, so it'll fit her OK. Jeannie says she'll just let her wear the gown for the service, then change her into something more practical later on."

"Jeannie seems to have taken to being a mum as if she's done it all her life," said Margaret. "Considering how difficult that pregnancy was, she's just looked better and better every time I've seen her recently."

"That's contentment for you." Cyn turned away from the sink to face Neil and Margaret, wiping her hands on the cloth as she spoke. "They waited so long for that little girl. All those miscarriages – it wasn't just the physical problems. It was hard for Jeannie emotionally, and for Colin too. But they're strong together. Made for each other, those two. And now, at last, they're the parents they've longed to be, thanks to IVF – and God! Our prayers were certainly answered."

"Amen to that," agreed Margaret quietly. "Now, do you need any help with the catering on Sunday? I could always get Frank to knock up one of his fruit cakes."

"What we want is for our new little wonder to be welcomed into the world and the church. And for all our church family to come over to the house and celebrate her safe arrival. It'll be good to treat you for a change, Margaret. You've been great, visiting Jeannie as much as you have, especially when she was so poorly. She was only saying the other day how much receiving Communion meant to her – all those weeks when she was in hospital, and then later when she finally came home with Ellen in her arms. It gave her strength when she needed it."

Margaret reached out to squeeze Cyn's hand, plainly touched by her words.

"It was a pleasure, honestly, and we're looking forward very much to Sunday."

"Good! Oh, I must go," replied Cyn, glancing at the cock-eyed clock on the kitchen wall, which had been hanging at an odd angle for months, too high up for anyone to sort it without the help of a ladder. "I'll see you both at the meeting on Wednesday. Seven o'clock, isn't it? Must go. Bye!"

"You OK for St Gabriel's?" asked Margaret, turning to Neil as Cyn left. "I wonder if a good-looking, newly ordained priest will be more of a draw than I've ever been? If you get more than the usual eight, your name will be down for St Gabriel's every Sunday from now on!"

"Thanks," chuckled Neil. "I'll consider that a challenge."

Margaret laid her papers down on the counter and leaned back comfortably, plainly ready to chat.

"I can't tell you how nice it is *not* to have to cover every service myself after all these years. Every priest I know is stretched to breaking point now, with so many churches to look after in every parish. Last year, of course, you were a bit wet behind the ears..."

Neil grimaced in agreement.

"... but now you've been ordained priest, it's good that we can share the load."

"I hope so, I really do. I don't want to let you down."

Her smile was kind. "Certainly not so far. Your sermon this morning was right on the button, although I can definitely tell you're a bit nervous when you lead the Eucharist..."

"That's an understatement."

"Don't be too hard on yourself, Neil. It's early days. You're still a curate, and your training will continue for at least two

19

or maybe three more years. Just don't beat yourself up if you lose your way or feel uncertain. That's why we're here in this parish together, to support each other. There will be things I'll go off at the deep end about…"

"I've noticed!"

"And so I should, if your lack of knowledge or expertise causes trouble for the church or its members – but that would be as much a lesson for me as it is for you. My responsibility is to support you as you learn, to teach you everything I can, then stand by like a parent and watch you become more than I ever could be."

There was disbelief in Neil's reaction.

"Hardly. You make things look so easy. You're at ease with everyone, wherever you meet them, in church or in the street. But then, I think you're naturally a much more confident person than me. I can't imagine ever being able to get up and give a sermon without writing down every word and reading it verbatim – and I really can't picture a time when my knees won't be knocking together like castanets whenever I stand up to lead the Eucharist. I'd love to be able to talk to people like you do – you're relaxed with everyone. Can you imagine how embarrassing it is to feel myself going bright red the moment I start to think about how I'm probably getting all sorts of things wrong?"

"You'll get there. I have no doubts about that."

Neil fell silent.

"Ask if you're unsure. Sharing is the key. Talk about your worries and concerns – to me, to other Christian friends – to Wendy, perhaps?"

Neil's silence went unnoticed as Margaret continued.

"Wendy's grown up in the church. She understands church life and its challenges. And from what I know of her, she's a practical young woman, good at dealing with most situations. Being a teacher in a busy school probably helps – all those doting parents to deal with! You couldn't have chosen a better partner to talk things through with."

When Neil didn't answer, Margaret looked at him with interest.

"She *is* your partner, isn't she?"

"It seems that way."

"To her, do you mean? What about you? Do you think of the two of you as partners?"

"Well, we do spend a lot of time together. She's great company, talented too. How could music at St Stephen's ever manage without her family – Mum running the choir, Dad on the organ? And Wendy's done wonders with the music group!"

"That's true."

"And she's so pretty, really kind and thoughtful."

"Very."

"She was absolutely wonderful before my ordination. She drove me all the way down to the Retreat House so I didn't have to bother taking my car. That's typical of her. She thinks ahead, sorts everything out so that it all goes smoothly…"

Neil felt Margaret's eyes fixed on him as she spoke.

"She loves you. That's plain to see."

"I know she does. She tells me all the time."

"And you? Do you love her?"

Neil considered the question carefully.

"I think so."

"But you're not completely certain."

"I don't know how to explain my feelings. I definitely fancy her – if I'm allowed to tell my rector that! It's more than just that, though. I enjoy her company. We're good friends. We always have a lot to talk about because we share so many interests and experiences. We seem to make a complete unit, because – well – the qualities I lack are ones she has in abundance. She'd make a fantastic vicar's wife. I know that."

"So let me ask you again – do you love her?"

Neil hesitated.

"If loving is companionship and compatibility and complementing each other in every way, then yes, I do."

"So you've thought it all through and decided this is love – but what about your heart, Neil?"

He groaned. "Oh, I'm hopeless when it comes to affairs of the heart."

Margaret eyed him for a moment before moving along the work surface to stand beside him.

"It's true that friendship can be the very best basic ingredient in a lifelong partnership. But for a marriage to work – if marriage is what you're considering – then friendship alone isn't enough. Don't get me wrong. There's nothing better for riding out the ups and downs of married life than the knowledge that in the end, whatever you throw at each other, your friendship will see you through. But who wants a marriage where things run so smoothly that there aren't any bumpy bits? Believe me, you need a bit of passion in marriage. You need the arguments and the times when you don't speak to each other, because in my experience, what you feel when you hit the depths during any argument is matched by the heights you find in each other when you come together again."

Neil couldn't help the smile that crossed his face.

"Speaking from personal experience, are you?"

"Most definitely! You shouldn't judge a book by its cover, Neil, and that's never more true than when it comes to the feelings between a husband and wife. No one can know for sure what goes on inside a marriage – or any private relationship. That's one of the first lessons you have to learn. I know Frank and I look like an odd sort of couple – me all mouth and orders, and him running along behind, getting the jobs done. That's how it may *look*, but don't be fooled into thinking it's me who has the upper hand. It's the knocks and bumps along the way that forge a relationship. The wonderful thing about Frank is that he faces up to all my emotional outbursts and tantrums, absorbs them and then makes up his own mind.

"Frank is the strong one in our marriage. He's my husband – but he's also my rock, my companion and my love. There's passion in our marriage, always has been – and that passion, that love, comes from the way two personalities constantly spark against each other. It comes from the heart, and sweeps you both along with it. If it's there, you *know* it. And forgive me if I'm speaking out of turn, but from what I can see, that kind of feeling isn't very evident between you and Wendy."

"Well, it may be for her…"

"… but not for you."

"Not yet. Not really. I'm not sure…"

"Not enough, Neil, not nearly enough."

"But what about arranged marriages, where compatible couples are matched together, then years later they talk about the deep love that's grown between them? Compatibility can work. Great marriages can be based on that."

"Don't compromise, Neil. That's all I'm saying. You're talking about your choice of partner for life. In human terms, that's the most important decision you'll ever make, and you'll only make it once. Don't settle for someone who seems right, someone you know you can comfortably live with. Wait for the one you can't live without, the way I can't imagine my life without Frank."

An image of Frank shot into Neil's mind – mild-mannered, compliant, put-upon Frank – and Neil found himself lost for words in reply to Margaret's emotion-charged revelation.

"So," she continued, "you need to have a proper talk with Wendy."

"I know," he agreed. "I'd already decided that."

"You must be totally honest about your feelings. You owe her that. If what you feel right now is not much more than friendship, then be her friend. Don't lead her on to believe there could be more until you're absolutely sure yourself."

"Yes."

"Sooner rather than later. Anything else would be unethical and unkind."

He nodded thoughtfully.

"Right!" Margaret's voice became briskly businesslike. "I hope St Gabriel's goes well. See you at Evensong."

"Yes. And Margaret…"

She turned back on her way to the door.

"Thank you."

With a dismissive shrug of her shoulders and a friendly wave, she closed the door behind her.

* * *

Margaret's advice was swimming in his head as Neil made the short walk down Vicarage Gardens to his house, number 96, towards the end on the left. As he passed, he couldn't help himself slowing down to look towards number 80, the home of Harry Holloway, the elderly parishioner who'd become such a good friend during his year here in Dunbridge. Harry was the first member of the congregation he'd met on the day he took up his post, and when they realized they were neighbours, Harry had welcomed him in every way – which was more than could be said for Harry's great-niece Claire. From the start, Claire and Neil had got off on the wrong foot, which was particularly difficult when Neil realized that she and her young son, Sam, shared Harry's home. But over the months, the tension between them had eased, and although their conversations were always challenging and often confrontational, they'd found themselves increasingly drawn to one another. The unexpected pleasure that crept into their companionship surprised them both.

Not any more, though. Not since the night of Harry's heart attack, when Neil and Claire had spent those long, dark hours at the hospital reaching out to each other in their worry and fear – and the kiss they'd shared that spoke of longing and promise and so much more…

But then came the cold light of day, and the recognition that their relationship could never be. She was an atheist. He was a Christian minister, there to offer pastoral support. She was an unmarried mother. He was in a relationship with Wendy. Instinctively both he and Claire had stepped back. Words weren't necessary. They both just knew. Since then, there had been no communication between them.

There was a car parked in the driveway of number 80. Neil knew that Felicity, Claire's mum, had been staying to help during Harry's illness. Good, that would mean that Claire and her small son, Sam, would be in loving hands. They would need that.

Walking on, Neil was turning in at his own gate when he saw a cardboard box standing in the porch by his front door. On closer inspection he was touched to see it was packed with an array of obviously home-grown vegetables: new potatoes, lettuce, strawberries, raspberries and an oddly shaped cucumber. Tucked down one side was a note:

Neil, I'm home! I wasn't sure if you knew that Felicity brought me back from the nursing home yesterday. I'm feeling much better now, but then they've been very firm with my rehabilitation – all these physio exercises! I'm worn out, but so glad to be alive. It changes everything when you face your own death. I've been there now, so every day for me is a blessing. I don't intend to waste a moment.

This lot is a thank you for the way you were there for us on the night of my attack. Claire told me how wonderful you were, and I am really grateful. As you can see, Claire's green fingers have kept my veg patch blooming even though I wasn't here, and I have to say her spuds are the best I've ever tasted. I know you're not much of a cook, so I've put in the sort of fruit and veg I think you might be able to cope with yourself. But any time you fancy a proper cooked meal, please come and join us. I know you've been on leave after your ordination, but I've missed your company. We all have. Come and see us soon.

Yours,
Harry

Warmed by the gift, Neil carried the box inside and put it down on the kitchen table where he could read through the note again. Harry was plainly on the road to recovery, which was the best of news. His invitation to come and spend time with him and his family was kind and very welcome. It would be good to see him again – and young Sam. Neil got on well with the bright, friendly little boy. And he'd always thought he would like Sam's nan, Harry's niece Felicity, from everything he'd heard about her in the past. He really ought to go and say hello.

But, of course, a visit would mean seeing Claire again. They would keep their distance; he knew that. They would be polite and friendly but, without need of discussion, it was clear they both recognized the danger of being any closer. They were so different. Their view of life was at odds, their paths heading in opposite directions. Better to understand that and nip in the bud anything that might become inappropriate or awkward. That's what they'd do. The first time they met again would be the most difficult, but after that they would simply give each other a wide berth. Easiest all round.

So why did Neil find his heart thumping at the thought of seeing her again? How could the prospect of being in her company seem daunting on the one hand and yet so completely compelling on the other?

* * *

They sat around in the mismatched selection of comfy old armchairs and sofas in the Meeting Room, named by Margaret and Frank more in hope than reality. In fact, it should have been the vicarage dining room, but had only ever been used for the storage of unpacked boxes, old books and the odd pieces of furniture that had, over the years, proved so useful for church gatherings like this one. There were several items on the agenda: individual requirements for the fourteen weddings booked before the end of August; rotas for flower arranging, readings, refreshments, house prayer groups, pastoral visits and charitable collections – and, top of the list, their plans for

"Back to Church Week", a national initiative they were due to take part in during the first week in September.

The two churchwardens were there: Cyn was deep in conversation with palliative-care nurse Val in one corner, while the other warden, Peter Fellowes, sorted through his papers as he discussed an accounting matter with Frank. *Peter looks better than I've seen him for a while,* thought Neil, remembering the older man's gaunt expression when Glenda, his wife of many years, had announced a couple of months earlier that she was leaving him. In retrospect, her defection after more than three decades of marriage, and her decision to set up home with her tie-salesman boss, caused little surprise. It had now become clear that her marriage to Peter had been failing for some years.

All Neil knew from his arrival a year earlier, when Glenda first greeted him by wrapping herself around him in a smothering, choking hug, was that he'd found her overpowering and patronizing towards everyone in general, and her husband in particular. Over the weeks since her departure, Peter had begun to look as if a huge weight had been lifted from his shoulders. He seemed at ease and content – and much of that contentment had to do with the gentle friendship he shared with Val. It was early days, of course, but easy to see that Val was a much more natural companion for Peter than Glenda had ever been.

Brenda, the playgroup leader, was sitting in the bay window settee next to Beryl, head of catering and stalwart of the St Stephen's Ladies' Guild, whose members contributed so much to fundraising. George Sanderson (affectionately known as "Boy George" because he had bags of energy in spite of being in his eighties) represented the bell-ringers, and choir mistress Sylvia and her husband, organist Brian Lambert, sat side by side on single seats near the door. Their daughter

Wendy, leading light of the worship music group, had chosen not to sit beside her parents, but had taken her place next to Neil on a particularly worn two-seater sofa which sagged so dramatically in the middle that she was practically sitting on his lap. Laughing as she sat down, she kissed Neil's cheek and rested her hand possessively on his knee. Remembering both his mountain-top resolution and his earlier conversation with Margaret, Neil gave what he hoped was a suitably warm smile in return, his stomach churning as he tactfully moved her hand so that he could arrange his notes.

"Can you fill us in on Back to Church Week, Neil? How are other churches planning to approach it?"

"Oh," started Neil, a little flustered as he searched for the sheet he knew he'd brought with him, "it seems that a lot of churches will just be encouraging their regular members to consider inviting along a friend who hasn't been to church for a while to come and join them for a special service. From the literature we've been sent, it seems that it's aimed at the sort of person who may have gone to church in the past, but for one reason or another has given up."

"So how can we encourage them to think about coming back again?" asked Margaret. "Are we just going to invite them along to a service and hope they like it?"

"Well," said Neil, rummaging through his notes again, "it's not only us, of course. All the local churches are coming together on this. The suggestion is that between us we organize a week of Christian mission that throws all the doors open. Church members of all denominations can invite people to come and find out what Christians believe, who we are and what we do."

"And how would St Stephen's fit in?" asked Peter.

"Well, I think you all know Garry, the pastor at the Church of God evangelical church in Bridge Street? The idea is that we mix the town's Christians up a bit and share each other's style of worship."

Organist Brian gave a grunt of disapproval, but said nothing.

"So on that first Sunday, Garry and his congregation will be taking over our ten-fifteen service here at St Stephen's."

That was the last straw for Brian. "Have you heard their music, Neil? Do you know what a din their rock band makes, and how long they drag out each worship song, sometimes for over ten minutes at a time?"

"Yes, but that's an approach to worship that a younger generation of Christians seems to enjoy…"

"From what I can tell, they've never heard of an organ! They despise traditional hymns – the ones our congregation loves – and there's no form to the service, no set words. They just go with the flow!"

"That's not strictly true, Brian," Margaret intervened, slightly alarmed as she watched Brian's colour rising steadily with the pitch of his voice. "And we're only talking about one service like this. Later in the week I'll lead our usual Anglican Eucharist when we join our fellow Christians at the Baptist church in town."

Brian huffed his objection. "Well, you can count me out for that!"

"I have to say," said Peter thoughtfully, "I think if we got a bit of publicity for all this, it might have a wide appeal."

"We could even make a bit of a meal of it when everyone comes here," suggested Beryl. "How about we serve tea and home-made cakes after the service, and encourage people to stay on for a chat, or to discuss their own issues for as long as they'd like to?"

"Great idea," said Margaret. "I can see that working. And Brian, your reservations are noted, because we do have an older congregation here, and we don't want to scare them to death!"

"I might have a suggestion there," ventured Neil. "Something we were talking about when I was on retreat the other week – about how a lot of us have found ourselves serving congregations where the age group is mostly over fifty. One of my friends from theological college said that their bishop had suggested offering services which used the old-fashioned wording that people of that generation might find more familiar – from the Book of Common Prayer. It may be full of 'thees' and 'thous', but it's always been thought of as 'the book of the people'. He said that when they introduced Evensong using that wording, their numbers immediately went up. I just wonder if we might consider doing something similar during Back to Church Week to start with – but, if it works, consider it on a more regular basis?"

"Thank you, Neil," commented Brian. "That's the first sensible thing I've heard this evening."

"I'm not sure," said Margaret thoughtfully. "We're trying to make worship more accessible, aren't we, using language that's relevant and meaningful today? That sounds a bit of a backward step to me."

"Well," piped up her husband, Frank, "I think Neil might have something there. I must say I'd love a service like that, with the psalms and readings in their old familiar wording. Call me a sweet old-fashioned thing, but I think it could prove very popular."

"If all you want is a church full of older people…" pointed out Wendy.

Neil turned to her as he spoke. "Well, I'm not an old fogey, but I think I'd like a service like that once in a while. Obviously I enjoy the modern version too, but we already provide that, don't we? This would be something extra, an approach that might ring bells with members of that older age group who've drifted away from church. It could just draw them back in."

Wendy shrugged her shoulders, plainly not agreeing.

"I must admit I'm not certain either, Wendy," said Margaret, "but perhaps we should take a show of hands on it, just to see what the general mood is. Hands up if you think an Evensong service using the wording of the Book of Common Prayer might be worth trying during that first week in September, when we're hoping to encourage people to come back to church?"

Brian, Boy George, Beryl, Cyn, Peter, Frank and Neil all raised their hands, which meant that Sylvia, Val, Wendy, Brenda and Margaret were against the idea. Seven for, five against.

"Well," concluded Margaret, looking intently at Neil, "you've got yourself a job. This is your idea, so run with it. Try it out for that one service in September, and we'll see whether there's enough interest and support to think about offering Evensong using the Book of Common Prayer more regularly. And you'll keep in touch with the other local church leaders, won't you, to co-ordinate who's doing what during Back to Church Week?"

Neil nodded, wondering what on earth he'd started here. He'd certainly have his work cut out.

After that, the meeting went as expected: rotas were agreed, responsibilities shared out and plans made for the fête, prayer groups and pastoral visits. The only time voices were raised was in the discussion about car parking during wedding ceremonies. Wedding guests had drawn complaints from neighbours when they parked on the grass verges in the streets nearest the church. That transgression, combined with the irritation of confetti left all over the churchyard, took up more conversation than any other subject, but within the hour they'd finished their business, had a piece of Frank's walnut coffee cake and a cup of tea, and were all heading home.

As Neil was about to leave, Wendy slipped her arms around him and whispered in his ear that the night was young, and would he like her to come up to his house for a nightcap? Looking down at the loving expression on her pretty face, Neil's heart lurched as he thought again about the conversation he'd had with Margaret earlier.

"Of course, that would be nice," he replied. "Besides, I'd like to talk to you."

"Well, that sounds promising," giggled Wendy. "Hold on while I get my bag, and I'm ready to leave when you are!"

* * *

They walked the short distance from the church to Neil's house with Wendy's hand firmly clasping his. Lights were on behind the drawn curtains at number 80 as they passed, but Neil steeled himself not to look, not to think of Claire or that kiss – challenging, spiky, independent, sensitive, funny, vulnerable Claire. They were no longer in touch. That was right and OK. At this stage in his life he needed to focus on his ministry. Christ had been alone. There could be no better example than that.

"Did I tell you," whispered Wendy, turning to snuggle into him the moment they were through the front door of his house, "how much I missed you when you were away? Really missed you…"

"Yes, it was quite a long time, wasn't it? First the retreat and then my holiday in Derbyshire after the ordination."

"Far too long," murmured Wendy in his ear. "How about I show you just how much I missed you and how glad I am that you're back now?"

"Shall we have a cup of tea?" said Neil, pulling away from her. "I'll put the kettle on."

"Later." Wendy's eyes sparkled up at him. "We may be thirsty later."

"Look, Wendy, I've got a lot to tell you…"

"And I've got a lot to tell you too, like the fact that I'm feeling very warm all of a sudden, so think I should take off my coat – and perhaps my blouse…? Don't you think I'm looking hot?"

Neil looked down at her face in the darkened hallway. Her eyes seared into his as she stretched up to kiss him, lightly at first, then deepening so that in spite of his reservations he could feel his body responding. It took several seconds and a great deal of willpower to pull himself back and set her at arm's length.

"We really shouldn't be doing this," he said at last.

"Oh, for heaven's sake, you haven't minded much before!"

"Yes, but we've never actually – you know…" mumbled Neil.

"Gone all the way, do you mean? No, we haven't – but don't tell me you didn't want to! You can't deny that. I know you want this as much as I do."

"As a man, yes, of course – but as a priest…"

Wendy looked at him in disbelief.

"What are you saying? Because you're now a fully fledged priest, you no longer have a man's needs? That you don't fancy me any more? Because from what I've just felt from standing next to you, nothing's changed there! Do you think that because there's some ancient scripture that says men and women aren't allowed to behave naturally unless they're married, we should behave as if we *don't* want each other? They didn't have contraception back in biblical days, you know. They *had* to make rules like that. You may not have noticed, but we're living in the twenty-first century. Of course we shouldn't be irresponsible and bring children into the world until we're married, but I can't think of one single reason why we shouldn't enjoy each other as God intended!"

"Well, that is the one single reason. God didn't intend it. The gospel tells us that. It's one of the most basic commandments."

"Oh, for God's sake, Neil ..."

"That's right! For God's sake I don't want to do this any more unless..."

"Unless? Unless what?"

Neil squirmed in the face of her angry question.

"Unless what, Neil? Unless we're married? Is that what you mean?"

"I believe that sex should be saved for marriage, yes."

"So unless we're married, I should keep my hands off you?"

"Yes."

"And are we going to get married, Neil?"

Neil fell silent.

"Are we, Neil? Is that in your master plan?"

"I don't know."

"You don't know what? Whether marriage is off your radar altogether? Or maybe what you're trying to say in your typically ham-fisted way is that whatever happens you have no intention of marrying me!"

"Wendy, I really don't know." Seeing the depth of her hurt, Neil's voice croaked with frustration at how badly this conversation was going. "I think the world of you, you know I do."

"I love you, Neil, *really* love you. I've told you that consistently from the moment we got together. I've not made a secret of my feelings for you."

"I realize that, and I appreciate you so much, Wendy, I really do."

"But you've never said those important words, have you?" He saw with alarm that her eyes had filled with tears. "You've never actually told me you love me too."

Neil gave a heavy sigh. "I wonder if I really know what love is."

"Love is what I'm offering you: total commitment and loyalty, help and support in everything you do and care about, a home, a family, a future. That's love, and that's what I know I'm offering you now – my very fondest love for the rest of our lives."

Neil swallowed hard.

"Oh, Wendy, it's not that I don't know what a wonderful gift that is – and what a special and unique woman you are! It's just that you seem to be much further along in your vision of what you want in your life than I am. I admire your certainty. I wish I could share it – but I just don't know what I want, what I need, what I should be striving to have and do. I've just been ordained as a priest, and that's my priority. It has to be, and that's what I want with every fibre of my being."

"And you think that I would hold you back from that? Haven't we always shared our Christian faith, Neil? Isn't that what brought us together in the first place? How could I possibly hold you back? Surely to have someone like me by your side, someone who understands the challenges of church life and mission, could only help you and your ministry?"

"I believe that could be true, yes."

"So? So let's give it a try! Let's make a proper commitment to each other, and step out on this journey together! I love you, Neil. I think in your heart of hearts, however tongue-tied you are, you probably love me too!"

"But I'm just not sure enough. That's what I'm trying to say. I don't want to make a mistake that will hurt or disrespect you. You deserve my certainty. I owe you that."

She took a step back from him then, her mind plainly racing as she glared at him.

"So, let's just make sure I've got this right."

Neil was uncomfortably aware of the coldness of her direct, challenging stare.

"Until you're certain of your feelings, you want us to split up. Believe me, Neil, if that's your suggestion, I'll take it seriously. There will be absolutely nothing between us. I'll avoid you at all costs, because it would be too painful for me to do anything else. So what's it to be? Do we find a way to work through this and face the future together – or is this the end? Your choice! You can be on your own from this very moment!"

Neil's heart ached with sadness for her, for them both. "Wendy, let's not have ultimatums. Please try to understand. I care for you so deeply. I don't want to lose your friendship…"

"Which is it, Neil? Together or apart? There's nothing in-between!"

He looked at her helplessly, words failing him.

Seconds later, she'd scooped up her coat and left the house, slamming the door behind her.

CHAPTER 3

The Sunday of Ellen's baptism dawned bright, with rays of golden sunshine glinting across the stately walls of St Stephen's. Neil couldn't resist stopping for a moment as he made his way up the path in time for eight o'clock Morning Prayer. For a moment, he felt his dad's presence beside him as so often in the past, when father and son had indulged their shared fascination for the discoveries to be made in old churchyards.

"Storybooks of life, that's what churchyards are." His father's words echoed in Neil's mind. "These were real people, dads and mums and sons and daughters as real as you or me. You can learn so much about them from looking at the dates and working out how they related to one another. And even though we never knew them, we can mark their existence, respect who they were and recognize how much we owe them."

Warmed by the memory, Neil turned to gaze at the enclosed family plot under a dark red beech tree in the corner of the churchyard. The graves were lovingly cared for, with small pots of fresh flowers and shrubs in full bloom. Neil read again the names of generations of the Clarkson family who had been laid to rest there. And now there was a new addition to that close, big-hearted clan – little Ellen who would be baptized this morning in the same font that had been used to baptize so many Clarksons before her.

The early morning ritual of prayer and readings in the Daily Office had always made this a favourite time for Neil. Often it would just be him and Margaret worshipping in an intimate circle of shared praise. Sometimes they were joined by other church members, one of whom in the past had regularly been Harry. Neil had a special place in his own prayers for the gentle old man who had become such a firm friend in the year they'd known each other. Until he was fully recovered, Harry's visits to church would have to wait – but Neil knew that wherever Harry was at eight each morning, he would be praying along with them, sharing their worship in spirit.

That morning Neil was joined in the side chapel by both Peter Fellowes and Val, along with two elderly sisters who preferred to make their Sunday visit to church at a time when there were no noisy families, no modern hymns and often no one else at all except the clergy. It had been agreed that Margaret would come along later that morning in time to take the nine o'clock service, which normally drew in a congregation of about thirty to share a shorter, spoken Eucharist with no music. The big family service started at ten-fifteen, when there were often few spare seats. That would be even more true today, when the Clarkson family and friends gathered to celebrate Ellen's baptism.

Knowing there might be a tussle for seats, many congregation members arrived in good time for the family service, and by ten o'clock there was a burble of good-natured chatter as hellos were said, hymn books distributed and Pew Notices (compiled by Neil, the job he struggled with each week) slipped into the service book along with the specially printed sheet needed for the baptismal ceremony.

Neil was acutely aware of Wendy setting up music stands and instruments with the rest of the worship group in the front corner of the church. On one occasion he caught her eye and tried a smile which died on his lips as he felt the chill of her dismissive glance.

"You did it, then?"

He hadn't noticed Margaret quietly coming to stand beside him, her gaze following his.

"It was awful. It just didn't come out right. She was so hurt, so angry…"

"How do you feel now? Do you regret having the conversation?"

"Yes. No."

Neil's expression was full of confusion and sadness. "I had to be honest…"

"Absolutely right."

"… but I hurt her in the process, and I regret that very much because she really didn't deserve it."

"She didn't see it coming, then? It hadn't occurred to her that perhaps your enthusiasm for the relationship didn't match hers?"

"It seemed to hit her like a bolt out of the blue. She was totally shocked – distressed, embarrassed a bit, I think, and then, at the end, absolutely furious. She said that from now on she'd cut me dead, and that's exactly what she's doing."

"Well, don't blame her for that. Perhaps avoiding you is her way of coping with the pain of losing you."

"But she doesn't have to lose me. That's what I was trying to say, but really I didn't get the chance. I wanted her to know that my feelings are uncertain now, but they may not always be. There's so much that's good between us. She's right when she says we make a perfect team. I can see that and I miss it already."

"Well," said Margaret, looking at him carefully, "perhaps absence will make the heart grow fonder. They do say you never really recognize what you have until it's not there for you any more."

"And she is a loss, I know that. What if I've closed the door on the best thing that's ever happened to me?"

"On the other hand, your instinct may be right that you're not certain enough of your feelings for her now. It's better to be truthful and pull back than let her picture a future with you that you aren't ready for."

Neil nodded sadly.

"But," added Margaret as she started to turn away, "don't expect her to wait for you if you've given her the impression there's no hope. If she's wise, she'll get on with her life, as you must get on with yours. And if, further down the line, you decide she *is* the one for you, she may not be there waiting for you. That's the risk you take."

Neil's face was thoughtful as he watched Margaret head off towards the vestry.

* * *

It was a wonderful service. The church was packed with a congregation who were either members of the Clarkson clan, or who knew them well enough to share their joy and thanks that baby Ellen and her mum Jeannie were both doing well after the difficult pregnancy and the complicated premature birth. As Margaret made the sign of the cross on the tiny forehead, watched by close family members and treasured friends who had just become godparents, Neil found himself thinking that miracles didn't only belong to Christ's time on earth two thousand years ago. Miracles happened every day, somewhere and to someone. This longed-for little girl was nothing less than a modern-day miracle for her family and their church community.

Coffee after the service was noisier than ever, with numbers increased by the visitors who'd come especially for the christening. Neil saw little of it as he gulped down a quick cuppa, then hurried off to the nearby village of Minting to take the service at St Gabriel's, a picturesque little church that could trace its history back to Saxon times. As he looked out at the ten parishioners who sat in the ancient pews, he remembered Margaret's challenge that if he managed to attract more than eight people to a service there, he'd get the job on a regular basis! It looked as if he'd be seeing a lot more of St Gabriel's in the months to come.

By the time Neil arrived at the Clarksons' rambling old farmhouse, the lunch party was in full swing. Guests had spilled out onto the wide patio at the back of the house, where picnic tables had been laid out so that they could serve themselves from the buffet in the dining room, then sit in the sunshine to eat their meal.

"You made it!"

Peter Fellowes offered Neil a glass of iced fruit punch. Usually smartly dressed in his role as churchwarden, Peter looked relaxed and informal in slacks and an open-necked polo shirt. Years of running his own estate agency in the town had got him into the habit of never feeling smartly turned out without a collar and tie – but his growing closeness to Val was plainly raising not only his level of contentment, but also his fashion awareness, as Val gently steered him towards a more modern style of dress. She was at Peter's side now, their hands almost, but not quite, touching. The couple were still very discreet about the love they felt for one another, although it was plain to anyone who really knew them. Val had been widowed for years, and it had probably been the cancer that claimed her husband's life which had prompted her to steer her nursing career towards palliative care in the community. Now in her fifties, her small frame, sandy-coloured hair, slightly husky voice and grey eyes gave her a prettiness that belied her age. *That's what love can do for you,* thought Neil, as he considered the tangled mess of his own love life.

"I'm hoping there's still some buffet left," Neil said, taking the glass from Peter's outstretched hand.

"I think the family will be eating the leftovers all week," laughed Val. "They've cooked enough for an army!"

Their attention was drawn to the French doors where Colin Clarkson had just appeared, his wife Jeannie beside him with baby Ellen in her arms. A small group crowded around them to see the little miracle whose birth had brought such joy.

"I don't blame them," said Peter quietly. "There's a lot to celebrate here."

Neil nodded in agreement, his eyes still on the scene near the house.

"Actually," continued Peter, "I'd been meaning to catch you to let you know there have been developments."

"With Glenda?"

"I've heard from her solicitor. She's filed for divorce, citing irreconcilable differences."

Neil almost choked on his fruit punch. "Well, I suppose that's one way to describe your wife going off with her boss!"

"Honestly," said Peter, "I don't care how it happens. I just want the proceedings over and done with so that I can get on with my life – our lives…" he added, looking at Val.

"How long do these things take, do you know?"

"Well, I've no experience in these matters, but my solicitor says that because it's uncontested it could all be sorted in as little as three months."

"You aren't contesting anything? Doesn't Glenda want half of all the assets, especially the house?"

"Oh, yes, she wants any equity she can grab from that – but really, Neil, I just want to make this as quick and easy as possible for everyone concerned. There's no mortgage, and I've got a bit put by. It looks as if we just have to agree on a settlement figure, and that will be the end of it. She can't wait to get shot of any connection with me, and I must say I've got to the point where I share that feeling."

"I know your children are grown up now with families of their own, but has she been keeping in touch with them?"

"She's been down to see Christine in Brighton, but she was tactless enough to take Roland with her, which wasn't well received at all. Christine would have liked some quality time with her mum, just to be sure she knew exactly what she was giving up, and the implications for everyone else of the decision she's making. Not much chance of that with him there! Chris said that Glenda was like a dewy-eyed teenager hanging on his every word."

"And your son – John, isn't it?"

"He's never been that close to his mum. John's more like me, a bit of a Steady Eddie. He simply can't understand her causing all this upheaval when not long ago we were celebrating our thirtieth wedding anniversary."

"I am sorry," said Neil.

"Don't be!" grinned Peter. "I couldn't be happier. Glenda's done me a favour, although that's probably the last thing she ever meant to do. And as far as splitting the proceeds of the house is concerned, Val and I are thinking of pooling our resources anyway, to buy a new home we can choose together."

"We've got our eye on one of the new bungalows being built on the Minting Road," added Val. "We took a look round the show house a few days back, and we were quite impressed."

Peter looked at her adoringly. "It'll make a change being in a new house where everything's finished and working. I've had too many years of sorting out roofs, electrics, plumbing and decorating on our old place. I'm ready to put my feet up a bit now I've got someone I want to relax and unwind with."

Over Peter's shoulder, Neil saw Colin Clarkson raise his arm to beckon him over.

"Look, I'd better go and circulate…"

"… and grab some of that buffet," laughed Val. "We'll see you later."

Baby Ellen was wide awake with an expression of puzzled surprise at the gaggle of people crowding around her. She had been changed out of the family christening gown, and now wore a pale yellow dress that looked as crisp and fresh as summer itself. As Neil got closer, he realized with some alarm that the baby was no longer being held by her mother. It was Wendy who was cooing down at Ellen as she lay in her arms. Hoping he could back away without being noticed, Neil started to move towards the edge of the group – but, as if she could read his mind, Wendy looked up to stare straight at him, her expression cold with disdain.

"You seem to have such a way with babies, Wendy," said Brenda, from the back of the group. "A natural mother!"

Well aware that Neil was looking at her, Wendy let out a sigh worthy of the most saintly martyr.

"Oh, I don't think I'll be having children any time soon – certainly not until I find a man whom I can truly respect.

I only seem to come across empty-headed idiots who aren't much better than babies themselves."

The circle of faces all turned towards Neil, who instantly blushed bright red.

"I'll, um… I'll go and take a look at the buffet, I think," he mumbled, squirming uncomfortably in the chill of Wendy's icy stare as he scuttled off in the direction of the dining room.

Val was right. There was food in abundance, a banquet of meat, pies, salads, rice and pasta covering the length of one table, while a mouth-watering array of fruit flans, mousses, pavlovas, chocolate puddings and lemon roulades was displayed on the opposite side, with an extra section dedicated to cheeses of every colour and description.

Suddenly starving, Neil picked up a napkin and one of the paper plates embellished with Ellen's name. He collected small portions of almost everything he could find on the savoury table – well, they seemed small until he'd piled them up together, at which point they started sliding precariously to one side as the paper plate sagged under their combined weight. Balancing the plate carefully in one hand, he reached out for a knife and fork with the other, which left him with no free hands at all when the plate suddenly folded into a kind of funnel through which a trickle of what looked like beetroot juice combined with meat gravy began to stream onto the floor. Panicking, Neil looked around urgently for a flat surface where he could lay the plate down. In a few moments, as the crowd around him shifted slightly, he spotted an uncluttered space on a small corner table right beside a chair. With the bulging plate dripping profusely, he hurried over, sat down heavily and slid his plate carefully onto the table.

His sigh of relief was short-lived. At first, he couldn't quite work out what was wrong, until he felt a cold, damp sensation spreading across his nether regions. And then he saw it: a bright red, creamy, custardy mess oozing between his legs and all over his best black trousers. Leaping up in alarm, he looked down at the seat of the chair, which was covered in the remains of what had obviously been someone's helping of strawberry trifle and ice cream. But where was the bowl?

"It's behind you!"

A familiar voice had him spinning on his heels to find Claire, her face pink with delighted amusement, observing him from a few feet away.

"Where?"

It didn't appear to be anywhere in the vicinity of the chair.

Trying hard not to laugh out loud, Claire walked calmly up to Neil, turned him round, and pointed at his bottom, where a frothy, multi-coloured mess, was gluing the paper bowl to the seat of his trousers. Appalled and embarrassed, Neil grabbed the bowl, not knowing quite where to put it for safety. Eventually, he squeezed it onto the side table alongside his own lunch plate, covering everything around it in red goo before he finally felt it was safely wedged. He stared down in horror at his rainbow-coloured trousers, and was about to wipe away some of the cream and jelly until he realized that his own hands were now messier than anything else – so he just stood there, his hands waving in the air, his face a picture of indecision and helplessness.

Laughing out loud now, Claire took charge and led him away from the dining room and into the kitchen, which was mercifully deserted.

"Baby wipes!" she declared. "That's what we need to get this lot off. They're sure to have some here with a new baby in the house."

She was right. Finding a pack in a back corner of the

dresser, she grabbed a chair from beside the kitchen table and pulled it over towards Neil.

"Bend over!"

Neil was beyond caring about his dignity. Without a word, he obediently leaned forward to grab the back of the chair. Pulling out a handful of wipes, Claire got down on her knees, her face level with the back of his trousers as she started wiping him just as if his bottom belonged to a baby.

It was at that precise moment that Neil looked up to find Wendy standing in the doorway taking in the scene before her. She didn't have to say a word. Neil could see appalled disbelief written all over her face.

"Look, this isn't quite what it seems…"

Wendy was staring at them both with undisguised disgust. Claire raised her head to see who he was talking to, just as Wendy, with a flounce of her dark brown hair, turned on her heel and stomped off towards the crowd in the garden.

Neil stood up in alarm.

"Oh no, she'll tell everyone! Whatever will they think…?"

But his fear was met by a peal of laughter from Claire.

"Let her tell anyone who's remotely interested, if that makes her feel better. This was just an accident, nothing more. These plates look good, but they really *are* made of paper! It could have happened to anyone."

"But it had to be me," said Neil glumly.

"Actually," smiled Claire, "it was one of the funniest things I've seen for ages – and if you don't dine out on it, or at least weave it into one of your sermons about being able to laugh at yourself and keep things in perspective, I'll be disappointed in you. Come on! It's a bit public here. There's a bathroom on the next floor. Let's finish the job up there."

* * *

"Absolutely brazen! The two of them went upstairs on their own after Wendy saw them, you know!"

"Where the bedrooms are! And he's a minister of the church!"

"He'd taken his trousers off. Did you hear that?"

"Practically naked, that's what I heard. Shameful! Completely shameful!"

Neil didn't need to hear their comments to imagine what people were thinking. In the days that followed "the trifle affair", he became constantly aware of members of the congregation huddling together as they gossiped and stared. Wendy, however, remained aloof with the air of a victim, wronged and wounded. During the choir rehearsal a couple of days later, he tried to find a quiet moment to speak to her, but she was instantly ringed by a protective circle of friends, who glared at him, challenging him to try to approach her. Neil might climb mountains and even cope with his overpowering mother, Iris, but the thought of facing that formidable circle of righteous women around Wendy was just too much for him. He backed away, his dignity in tatters, and imagined yet again what they were saying about him as they sabotaged what was left of his reputation.

Margaret was more amused than sympathetic. She said it would all blow over and that people had very short memories once the next piece of gossip came along. That might be true, mused Neil, but in the meantime it was very difficult to do his job when half the congregation weren't talking to him.

However, talking – very loud and animated talking – surrounded him on the following Thursday evening, as the happy couple who were getting married that Saturday afternoon arrived with their families for their wedding rehearsal. At least, *some* of them arrived. Sophie, the bride, was an English rose who lived just down the road, but her groom, Chris, was a cheerful, laid-back young man who came from a large and loving Caribbean family. Neil had been a bit overwhelmed during the couple's first visit to book the wedding a few months earlier. They'd arrived with both sets of parents in tow, and it became quite clear that all decisions about wedding arrangements were most definitely a family concern. This rehearsal was an opportunity for him to meet the other key members of both families.

The rehearsal was booked for six o'clock. By five to six the bride and her parents had arrived, along with the bridesmaids: Sophie's sister, Sally, and her cousin Jess, whose three-year-old twin daughters were beside themselves with excitement at the thought of the fairytale dresses they would be wearing as flower girls.

A quarter of an hour later there was still no sign of the other bridesmaid, Chris's sister Delia, or in fact anyone at all from the groom's side of the family – not his parents, best man or even Chris himself.

While Rosemary, the bride's mother, marched up and down the aisle tutting with exasperation, Sophie apologetically explained to Neil that being late was all part of the Caribbean culture. They operated on a more relaxed timescale than the rat-race pace at which most other people lived their lives – and, as far as she was concerned, that was just fine. Her explanation didn't stop her glancing anxiously at her watch, though, as the minutes ticked by.

At twenty past six they arrived: a joyous, chattering group of about fifteen people plus two toddlers, who all wandered down the aisle in no hurry to begin the rehearsal until greetings and hugs had been exchanged all round.

It was one of the most chaotic but enjoyable wedding rehearsals Neil had ever tried to organize. The hardest job was simply making himself heard over the babble of excited conversation taking place not just at the front of the aisle where he was trying to give directions, but also among small groups of people nattering or trying to control the tantrums of tired toddlers in every corner of the church.

By seven o'clock, with a semblance of a rehearsal completed, an exhausted Neil raised his voice in the hope of claiming everyone's attention.

"The wedding starts at three o'clock on Saturday afternoon. Please allow yourselves plenty of time."

He nodded in the direction of the groom's thirteen-year-old sister, Pattie, who was going to sing a solo while the register was being signed.

"Please can you be here half an hour before, so that you can run through your song with our organist, Brian Lambert? Ushers!"

At least one of the group of six ushers raised his head to listen.

"Be here at half past two, so that you're ready to greet any guests who arrive early. The groom and best man should be in their places by quarter to three, and all congregation members must be sitting by five to three at the absolute latest. The bridesmaids' car will arrive a few minutes before the hour, so that the bride and her father can make their entrance at three o'clock sharp. OK?"

Sophie and Chris, who were standing in front of Neil, held hands and giggled.

There were sounds of agreement all round, as slowly, very

slowly, ladies picked up babies and handbags, ushers checked their mobiles, and Great Grandma, who'd been propped up comfortably in a corner, was roused and guided back to the car. As Neil finally closed the heavy church door on the last of them, he had the feeling they would be saying goodbye by the porch gate for quite a while.

His stomach rumbled and he realized he was both weary and hungry – not surprising, as his day had begun with Morning Prayer at eight o'clock, and he'd been constantly on the move ever since, with nothing more than a sandwich hurriedly eaten in his car between one location and the next. He thought about the meagre supplies in his fridge and freezer, then made an instant decision to head straight for the pub.

He was aware that some of the older parishioners at St Stephen's disapproved of their curate being a familiar face in the town's pubs. He had long since stopped worrying about that. It was a fact that he mainly went there for a pint of real ale and a decently cooked meal (which definitely had appeal for a man whose culinary heights didn't extend beyond putting a ready-made pizza into the oven), but it hadn't taken him long to realize the positive effect his dog collar had on other locals in the pub. In spite of his natural shyness, he often found himself drawn into conversation with people who saw a chance to unburden themselves of the problems they were facing in their own lives. He welcomed the chance to listen to an outpouring from fellow drinkers of every age and circumstance – dads who were estranged from their children; couples struggling to make ends meet; emotional turmoil; declining health; neighbours from hell; lack of work – and even, once in a while, a spiritual question about prayer or the existence of God. He began to realize that this was an important part of his ministry, to be visible and active wherever people actually were. And, of course, the beer was good…

His local was the Wheatsheaf, an old coaching inn that stood on one side of the market square. He'd wandered in on his first night as curate at St Stephen's a year earlier, and met the man who had since become his best friend in Dunbridge: Graham Paterson, Deputy Head of Maths at Dunbridge Upper School. However, since Graham had moved into the flat of his policewoman girlfriend, Debbie (the girl-next-door he'd known all his life – it had taken years for Debbie to make him realize they were made for each other!), Graham didn't often eat at the pub these days. Besides, Neil remembered that Thursday was Graham's football practice night, so he decided to try a pub he rarely visited, at the other end of the square. The Horseshoe could also trace its history back to coaching days, but its current owner had given it a facelift about ten years previously, installing large screens in the back bar for sports enthusiasts while music videos were constantly playing in the lounge.

Neil was surprised at how busy the Horseshoe was that night, especially in the lounge bar, where a group of about a dozen young women were in high spirits. They were dressed for clubbing in sparkling tops, short skirts and cripplingly high platform shoes. They'd also clearly been downing shots to get into the party spirit for some time before he arrived.

His dog collar attracted their attention immediately, and the moment he settled at the bar, he was surrounded as the girls shrieked at him and about him, their arms on his shoulders, the heady mix of their different perfumes practically bowling him over.

In fact, they were a nice crowd, especially Tash who, with a frilly net veil on her head and a notice saying "I'M GETTING

MARRIED!" pinned to her back, didn't really need to explain that this was her hen party.

"We're taking her out for her last night of freedom!" trilled Bea, who introduced herself as Tash's chief bridesmaid. "She's my best friend, aren't you, Tash? My very best friend! I've known her for *ever*!"

Deeply emotional at the thought, Bea looked near to tears as she threw her arms around Tash's neck.

"He's taking you away from me, that John, and I'm never going to see you again!"

"It's only Portsmouth. Sailors always live in Portsmouth," said Tash soothingly. "There's a train that goes there and I'll come back to visit my mum, so I'll see you then."

Wailing dramatically, Bea was instantly revived by a drink passed along the bar to her by another girl in the group. The tragedy of losing her best friend was soon forgotten as Bea joined in a chorus of "Angels" when the music video of Robbie Williams's hit came on the screen.

"It's here!" screamed one of the girls, who had her nose to the window. "It's here – and it's huge – and so *pink*!"

Curious to know what she was talking about, Neil strained to see what the girls were looking at as they crowded round the window. Seconds later, squealing with excitement, they were all grabbing their belongings and heading out of the door towards the longest, pinkest limousine Neil had ever seen.

"Come with us!" Bea squealed in Neil's ear, giving him one last hug as they were leaving.

Neil laughed. "I'm a fella – and fellas don't go to hen parties!"

"You can come to mine," grinned Tash. "You might keep me on the straight and narrow!"

"I somehow doubt it!" retorted Neil. "It's very kind of you to ask me, but you just have a good time tonight! Take care, and I hope you have a long and happy marriage ahead of you. Bye, girls!"

The Horseshoe seemed very quiet once they'd left. Neil made his choice from the menu, and was making his way over to a free table when he noticed an elderly man sitting alone in the corner, scanning the horse-racing pages of the newspaper. The man looked up at Neil curiously.

"Did they go without you?"

"Who?"

"That other crowd. Going to a Vicars and Tarts party, aren't you?"

Neil couldn't think of an answer to that. He just chose a leather, high-backed seat, took a long sip of real ale, then sat back with his eyes closed.

His was a funny old life…

* * *

Saturday afternoon was glorious, just perfect for a wedding. St Stephen's was playing host to two ceremonies that day. Margaret had married the couple in the morning, and Neil was all prepared for Sophie and Chris's wedding at three that afternoon.

He opened up the church at two, just to make sure there was plenty of time to spare. Rosemary, Sophie's mum, hurried in with her hair in rollers to make a few final checks at quarter past two, then rushed out again. The two ushers from the bride's side of the family arrived bang on half past two. Brian Lambert settled himself at the organ ready to run through Pattie's song – and perhaps it was when Pattie didn't turn up on time that Neil felt the first flutter of foreboding.

By ten to three, the bride's side of the church was completely full. On the other side, there was no one, not even the groom or best man. At three minutes to three, the two bridesmaids from Sophie's side of the family, plus two excited flower girls, had arrived. The other bridesmaid, Delia, was travelling with the groom's family.

With one minute to go, Neil let out a sigh of relief as Chris appeared at the church door. His best man walked in first, hurriedly handing a buttonhole to the groom before checking every pocket in his hired suit to find where he'd put the rings. Apart from them, there were still no guests on Chris's side of the church.

The bride and her father arrived in a horse-drawn carriage at exactly three o'clock. After five minutes of retouching make-up and hair, five minutes of photos, and another five minutes of the bride anxiously biting her manicured nails, Neil suggested they might like to go round the block again.

It was just as the horse and carriage was pulling out that a huge coach arrived, its horn blasting. The doors opened to reveal Chris's family, more than forty of them, a colourful picture in their wedding finery. They tumbled out carrying bags and wedding presents, and waved affectionately at Sophie as they hurried into the church. Neil, who was on the point of calling the whole thing off, couldn't have been happier to see them – and minutes later, once they were all settled, the bridal party glided down the aisle past a beaming crowd of good-natured guests on one side of the church, and a very relieved, slightly disapproving family on the other.

The bride giggled throughout the whole ceremony and the groom fluffed his vows, but when Neil announced that they were man and wife and Chris could kiss his bride, the church erupted with applause and cheering. This was obviously a very popular couple.

While Chris and Sophie signed the register, Brian's fingers hovered nervously over the keyboard as Pattie stepped up to the mike having had no proper rehearsal. With a confidence beyond her years, she started to sing a love song that had climbed the charts after being featured in a recent film. Everyone in the church fell silent under the spell of her haunting, compelling performance, and their appreciation was more than clear when they whistled, stamped and pleaded for more once the song was over. Having just given the performance of a seasoned professional, Pattie became a girly teenager again as she acknowledged their praise, then went over to join her friends in one of the front pews.

The bride and groom had chosen a piece of recorded music to be played as they walked down the aisle and left the church. The sunshine of the Caribbean wafted into Dunbridge as Bob Marley's rendition of "One Love" filled the church. The congregation on both sides of the aisle danced out of St Stephen's on a euphoric cloud.

Just as Neil was about to head back to the vestry to de-robe, Chris's sister Delia hurried back in to search for Great Grandma – who was found still snoozing gently at the end of one of the pews. How she could have been overlooked while she was wearing such a vibrant orange suit with a matching feathered hat was a bit of a mystery, but Delia scooped her up and propelled the sleepy matriarch towards the door. Then, to Neil's surprise, as Delia drew level, she stopped, smiled sweetly at him, then threw her arms round his neck and kissed him full on the lips. Neil stared after her in delighted astonishment – just as Brian walked by.

"Your lipstick's a bit red."

Neil rubbed his lips furiously, knowing he'd been caught

on the back foot yet again by the Lambert family. He knew exactly how Wendy would react when her dad reported this to her. From now on, she could add "wearing lipstick" to her growing list of his misdemeanours.

⇒ CHAPTER 4 ⇐

"*H*ow's your mother, Neil?"

Neil was just coming through to the vicarage kitchen with a tray full of used supper dishes. Frank had cooked. Frank always cooked – and thank goodness for that, because he was not only an excellent chef, but Margaret would probably fade away from hunger if meals in their household were left entirely to her.

In spite of the delicious meal, the mention of Iris wiped all sense of contentment from Neil's mind.

"Oh, her sciatica is playing her up. Her neighbours are a nightmare. Standards at her local shops have gone down, while the prices have all gone up. Her only son is a great disappointment to her because he's chosen to be a minister rather than an accountant – and to add to her despair, he's not planning to marry any time soon and give her grandchildren. Apart from that, she's fine."

Frank's laughter was joined by Margaret's as she came into the kitchen, obviously searching for something she'd lost.

"OK," said Frank, "I know that look. What's gone missing?"

"That Back to Church schedule for next week, the one Neil gave me yesterday. I know I put it somewhere safe…"

59

"You just can't remember which particular safe place that was."

There was no reply as Margaret disappeared under the kitchen table to rummage through the boxes that stood haphazardly underneath.

"Not on top of the table, is it, dear?"

"Can you see it there?" was Margaret's curt answer.

As one, Neil and Frank looked across at the table, which was piled at least a foot high with a disorganized array of books, boxes and papers.

"Not immediately, no."

"Well, that's where I put it." Margaret's voice wafted towards them from under the table.

"And someone has moved it?"

"They must have – and that someone, dearest Frank, can only be you!"

"Hold on!" interrupted Neil. "Didn't you have that on the lounge table earlier on?"

"Why on earth did you move it there, Frank? I do wish you'd leave any papers to do with church business alone. It's so frustrating if I can't find them where I left them."

Frank shot a wry smile in Neil's direction. They both knew that Margaret was the untidiest person they'd ever come across – which made it all the more difficult for Neil to understand why Frank was so long-suffering and willing to take whatever blame and flak Margaret chose to lay on him.

"Anyway," said Neil, digging into his briefcase, "I've got another copy here. I think it's all settled now. It's got all the details we need – about worshippers from all the different denominations being actively encouraged to go along to services at churches other than their own, and how we hope the different styles of worship might encourage lapsed

Christians, or even potential new believers, to come along and experience Christianity for themselves."

"And we're all set for the big opening service at St Stephen's on Sunday morning?"

"I think so. I've been talking to Garry, the pastor of the evangelical church, all week about what they need. We've never had a television screen right at the front of the church before, so it'll be interesting to sing words from there rather than the hymn books."

"And they don't need any printed order of service?"

"Apparently not. I gather they don't plan too much in advance, but prefer to wait for the Spirit to move them."

"Hmm." Margaret looked thoughtful. "I can just imagine the reaction of some of the more traditional members of our congregation to that!"

Neither man felt the need to reply; they shared Margaret's reservations.

"So that's Sunday. Are we all sorted for our Evensong service on Wednesday evening using the Book of Common Prayer?"

"It's been well publicized," responded Neil, "and I've had a surprising number of people ask me about it. I was even stopped in the market square the other day by an elderly lady who said that the last time she'd been to church, the Book of Common Prayer was all they used. She may have disliked it then, but it's plainly enough of a draw now to entice her back into a church again."

"And you're still happy to lead that?"

"I'd like to, yes – unless you'd prefer to do it."

Margaret's face brightened. "Actually, what I'd prefer is for you to do all the work that evening, so that I can just sit in the body of the church as a normal congregation member, worshipping along with those wonderful old words I grew up on."

"That's settled, then." Neil caught sight of the kitchen clock. "Heavens, I didn't realize it was so late. I said I'd drop the service schedule round to Harry tonight. He's getting quite excited about the Back to Church idea. I'm still not convinced he's well enough to do much chasing around, but he's certainly keen to come to the two services at St Stephen's."

"Then give him our love and I'll see you in the morning, Neil. Eight o'clock sharp!"

It only took Neil a few minutes to reach Harry's house, and he hesitated for a few seconds before opening the front gate. He hadn't seen Claire since her starring role in the "trifle incident", and the mere thought of that embarrassment still gave him nightmares and had him breaking out in hot and cold sweats.

That thought was still in his mind when the door was opened by Claire herself. Her instant smile when she saw him was quickly followed by a formal invitation to come through to the lounge where Harry and her mother were chatting.

"Neil, you've met Mum, haven't you?"

"Felicity," greeted Neil, his hand outstretched towards her. "It's good to see you again."

He was struck by how alike mother and daughter were. Claire had plainly inherited her sandy blonde hair, creamy skin and light green eyes from her mum.

Felicity smiled back at him. "Yes, I'm back in Dunbridge until the end of the week anyway, because Claire's so busy with work. I don't like the idea that there might not be anyone here to keep an eye on Harry."

"And Sam too!" added Harry. "I'm not the only big kid who needs looking after in this house!"

"Where is Sam?" asked Neil, looking around.

"Sound asleep, I hope," replied Claire. "He's completely exhausted every night now he's at school."

"Will you say hello to him for me?" Neil's head was practically touching hers as they stood together. "Tell him I'm looking forward to hearing all about big school."

"I will."

Claire held his gaze for just a second or two before Neil broke the spell by reaching for an envelope, which he drew out of his jacket pocket.

"For you, Harry," he explained, offering it to the older man. "It's the leaflet about the evangelical service we're having instead of our normal Family Worship at St Stephen's this Sunday. I don't know if you fancy coming?"

"If he does, I'll take him up in the car," said Claire.

"Or I might walk," added Harry. "The doctor says I need to get plenty of exercise."

"Then I'll walk with you," said Claire firmly.

"And stay at the service, do you mean, until I need to go home again?"

"If need be, yes."

"In that case," said Harry, his eyes twinkling as he turned towards Neil, "you're definitely not to bother yourself with how I'm going to get there. You'll have a lot on your plate that morning, and I can't think of anything nicer than knowing that Claire – who, incidentally, professes to anyone who'll listen that she doesn't believe in God at all – will be sitting alongside me in the pew. That's worth being ill for!"

After that, goodbyes were said, and Neil left the house warmed, just as Harry had been, by the thought that Claire might actually come along to a service, albeit for Harry's sake rather than her own. So Neil would see her again on Sunday. That would be nice.

Later that evening, when Harry had taken himself up to bed, Claire was stretched out on the sofa watching television as her mum came in with a couple of cups of hot chocolate. Settling herself comfortably into the armchair, Felicity clearly had something on her mind.

"What?" asked Claire, putting her cup down on the table beside her. "Something's bugging you."

"Neil. He's nice."

Claire eyed her quizzically. "Yes."

"You seem close."

"Not particularly. We hardly see each other."

"But you'd like to."

"For heaven's sake, he's a vicar, in case you hadn't noticed. Not really my type, is he?"

"Isn't he?"

"Well, what do you think? If it weren't for Harry getting me the gardening contract for St Stephen's, I'd never choose to set foot in the place. I'm not a Christian. I can't believe in any of that mumbo-jumbo about God and the Holy Trinity. So, no, he's not my type!"

When her mother didn't respond, Claire kept talking to fill the silence.

"Look, we're mates. He was the best possible friend to me the night that Harry was taken ill. He's a nice man…"

"I can see you like him."

"Yes, I like him. I don't *like* him in the way you mean."

"So how do you feel about him?"

"Mum, this is madness. He's nice. He makes me laugh. He's great with Sam and Harry. He's caring and supportive. But there are loads of ways he drives me mad, because he's completely hopeless at looking after himself and is so disorganized sometimes. But he's good fun. He makes me think. I enjoy his company."

"You *like* him…"

Claire's shoulders dropped as she took a deep breath to think for a while. Finally, she said, "Yes, I like him. I really like him."

"Does he know how much?" asked Felicity gently.

"We've spoken about it."

"Does he feel the same way?"

"Perhaps. I'm not sure now. We both know we couldn't be more incompatible, so it's not something we choose to take any further. We're friends. Good friends."

Felicity picked up her cup to take a sip of hot chocolate. Claire seemed too absorbed in her own thoughts to remember she had a cup too. Cupping the steaming mug in her hands, Felicity studied her daughter with interest.

"I got a letter a couple of weeks back," Felicity said at last.

Claire looked up then. "From?"

"Ben Stone."

"What! How did he know where to write to you?"

"He's always known. I made sure he had our address when he went back to Australia."

"And this is the first time he's bothered to get in touch in more than five years?"

"No. I've heard from him a couple of times before."

"And you never told me? You didn't think I should know that Ben was in touch with you – the man who got me pregnant but cared so little that he scuttled back home to Australia without a word before Sam was even born?"

"I wasn't sure what to do. That whole situation hurt you so badly. You always seemed really angry about him. I didn't quite know what to do for the best – and in the end, because he wasn't saying much that was likely to help you, I decided it was best to keep it to myself."

"You had no right to decide that."

"Maybe not, but it was me he was in touch with, not you. I just dropped him the odd card and photo every now and then at his parents' address. Sam's his son. His mum and dad have a grandchild. It seemed right they should have the chance to know about him."

"Ben has no rights! He ran out on me and Sam like a scared little rabbit – not the man and father we needed him to be."

"He was young and immature, not ready to be a dad…"

"I was young and immature too, but I had to get on with being a mother. I didn't get pregnant all by myself. He played his part just as much as I did, but he couldn't wait to put half a world between us when he thought he might have to act like a responsible adult."

Shocked at the strength of Claire's anger, Felicity fell silent. Minutes ticked by, until eventually it was Claire who spoke again.

"Why are you telling me now? What was in this last letter?"

"Can I show you? I have it here."

Pulling out an airmail envelope from the pocket of her dressing gown, Felicity held it out. Reluctantly, Claire took it, and Felicity watched as shock registered on her daughter's face at the sight of Ben's handwriting for the first time in five years.

> *Dear Felicity,*
>
> *Mum gave me your last letter with the photo of Sam in the garden. I can't believe how tall he is. He's a proper little man.*
>
> *It's good of you to keep in touch. Not many people would in your situation. Does Claire know? How does she feel about you sending me photos of Sam?*

*Seeing how grown up Sam is now makes me
realize just how much I've changed too. Life is
very different for me these days. I've started my
own car repair business, and it's really taken off.
I've got proper premises and even employ another
mechanic, so I'm quite the entrepreneur – well,
I'm working on it anyway!*

*It's made me think that it's time I started
supporting my son. I'd like to set up a regular
payment arrangement to make sure Claire has
everything she needs for Sam. How do you think
she would react to that? Should I write to her?
Would it be better if you sounded her out for me?*

*I just know I should take more responsibility.
As I live thousands of miles away from
Dunbridge, I can't do much, but I would like to
do this.*

What do you think?
Yours,
Ben

"No, definitely not." Two red spots had appeared on Claire's cheeks as she read the letter.

"You could do with some proper financial support for Sam…"

"I could have done with his support five years ago. How dare he think he can swan in now and play Lord Bountiful with his money! I don't want a penny. I don't need anything from him!"

"But what about Sam? Like it or not, Ben is his dad. Doesn't he have a right to know he cares?"

"He doesn't care!"

"He wants to show his care in a practical way – with money."

"Easy come, easy go; that's what money is to him. Where's the care in that? Where was Ben when I was nine months pregnant and terrified? Where was he when Sam didn't sleep at night for the first six months? Where was he when his son woke up with nightmares, or had chickenpox, or fell off his bike? If he thinks money makes him a parent, he should be ashamed of himself."

"I think he is ashamed, and he does regret the way he let you and Sam down. I also think he wants to make amends in the only way he can from the other side of the world."

"The best thing he can do is to keep his regrets and his suggestions to himself in deepest Australia. Sam and I are managing very well without him, thank you."

"Claire…"

"Mum, just drop it, will you!"

Claire got up suddenly and headed for the door.

"I'm going to bed."

And with that, the door slammed behind her.

* * *

"Remind me," muttered Peter as he and Neil stood at the door welcoming people into church for the first Back to Church Week service on Sunday morning. "Why are we letting the evangelicals take over our Family Worship this morning?"

"Because," replied Neil under his breath, managing to keep smiling towards the newcomers while continuing to speak, "there is one God, one body, one church. We're all Christians. We just have different *styles* of worship."

"And what exactly made you think happy-clappies waving their arms in the air would fit alongside the conservative crowd here at St Stephen's?"

There was no hesitation in Neil's answer. "It's just what we need! They'll shake things up a bit. Yes, our lot are a conservative crowd, but if they're confident and joyful in their faith, why not have a bit of clapping, arm waving and *happiness* in their worship?"

"Right," laughed Peter as he started to move away, "see you at the other end – if you live that long…"

Neil took a deep breath, hoping he was coming across with a semblance of confidence, even though that was far from how he felt. His name was all over this week of events, and he knew he was taking a tremendous gamble. He looked around at some of the familiar faces from St Stephen's, who were sitting stoically in their usual places as the church filled up with visitors. And there was Harry back in his usual seat, with Claire at his side. *Dear God, please don't let this all fall apart with her here!* With trepidation, his eye moved along the row to find the one person whose presence he probably feared most: Lady Romily, the elderly wife of the largest landowner in the area, who was not only a staunch Anglican and regular churchgoer, but the formidable chairwoman of the St Stephen's Ladies' Guild. Her lips were strained and tight, her eyes narrowed and her expression one of appalled indignation as she surveyed the scene. *Oh heck*, thought Neil, *we're in for a bumpy ride!*

"A word, please, Neil?"

Neil turned to find Brian Lambert at his side.

"You know they've brought their own musicians?"

"Yes. You thought that would be OK, didn't you?"

"But they've not brought any music, so how exactly is our worship group supposed to join in?"

"These are all quite familiar modern choruses, aren't they? And they're in the books we've got here. I checked."

"Yes, but in a different key."

"Oooh!" sighed Neil, running his hand through his hair. "Can't we find copies of their music, perhaps on the internet? It wouldn't take long in the church office…"

"But then," continued Brian, "they now tell me they like to busk their own thing at the start of the service *as the Spirit moves them* apparently."

"I see," said Neil, who was completely unmusical and really didn't see at all. "What can I do to help?"

Brian looked straight into Neil's eyes. "Whenever there's anything to do with music here at St Stephen's, you need to ask *me* to organize it. I am Director of Music here. You don't let complete strangers come in and impose their ideas without talking to *me* first. Do you understand?"

Neil nodded humbly. "I'm sorry, Brian, I thought this was all arranged. Garry assured me that his music man, Rick, was in touch with you."

"Well, he wasn't."

"I see. I'm sorry. Where does that leave us?"

"It leaves you, Neil, with a complete mess on your hands."

"For heaven's sake, Brian!" Neil voice was hoarse with exasperation. "Love your neighbour – isn't that what Christ taught us? We're all Christians. You know these songs – and even if you don't, you know how easy they are to learn. Just do your best, please. You're brilliant at what you do. Our worship group's really talented, and Wendy's made them so versatile. You can do this, I know you can!"

Perhaps it was the note of desperation in Neil's voice that brought a slight glimmer of satisfaction and appeasement to Brian's face.

"OK," he agreed, "but don't say I didn't warn you."

"Ready?" asked Margaret, appearing at Neil's side. "About five minutes to go. I'll just say a few words of welcome at the start, then hand straight over to the visiting pastor, shall I?"

"Fine," agreed Neil, noticing as he spoke that the pastor was making his way towards them. "Margaret, you know Garry, of course."

"Welcome to St Stephen's," said Margaret smoothly. "We have high hopes for this opening Back to Church event. It's good for us to welcome so many new faces here."

A tall man, Garry stared down intently into Margaret's eyes as he clasped her hand in both of his own.

"We are here in his name, Margaret; here in his holy name. Now, before we start, shall we pray?"

Garry's arms went round both Neil's and Margaret's shoulders, drawing them into a tight circle.

"Father God," began Garry, suddenly lifting his face heavenward, "we just want to worship you, praise you and lift your holy name on high! You know us. You have held us in the palm of your hand. You know our hearts. You know our failings. We just ask for your presence with us today, Lord. Father God, pour out your blessing on our worship here. Just bless us. Be with us, Lord, now and always. Father God, we just ask this in your blessed and holy name. Amen. Amen."

"Amen," came the muffled response from Neil and Margaret, their heads bowed down with the weight of Garry's arms on their shoulders.

"Show time!" said Garry. "You start, Margaret. We'll take over from there!"

The muscles in Neil's stomach twisted into painful knots as he picked his way through the combined musicians of both St Stephen's and the evangelical Church of God, and headed for his usual seat at the front of the church. He caught Wendy's eye, but found no friendly reassurance there. In fact, what was it he could see in her expression? Pity? Triumph? Suddenly he felt like a naughty five-year-old in one of her music classes – beyond hope. He bowed his head, closed his eyes and tried to quieten his mind enough to pray. It didn't work. Whatever happened from now on, he knew the next hour was one he'd never forget – and if it went completely wrong, he also knew that no one else would ever forget his part in it either.

Silence fell as Margaret moved to the front to make her brief welcome and to introduce Garry, who was greeted by a ripple of applause as he stepped up to take over.

"Let's stand and praise God!" Garry's arms were spread wide in invitation. "You'll see the words on the screen at the front here. Even if you aren't familiar with these choruses yet, just let the prayer in the words and the beauty of the melody wash over you. Father God, we pray that your Spirit will be the wind beneath our wings!"

And with that the music, which had been throbbing quietly beneath his words, took over with an urgency and volume that seemed to shake the old walls. The Church of God singers, who were seated alongside the St Stephen's choir, got to their feet immediately, swaying to the rhythm, their arms in the air, faces lifted high. With uncertainty and a little embarrassment, one by one the St Stephen's choir stood up too, as they fumbled to find the song in their regular hymn books.

Feeling he should lead the way, Neil quickly got to his feet and started singing, hoping the rest of the congregation would follow his lead. Peering out towards the body of the church, he could see a wide range of reactions, from some of the visitors who were joining in with enthusiasm, to the most conservative of the St Stephen's worshippers who were either sitting doggedly in their seats, or looking around at people they knew so that they could decide whether or not to join in.

But if the service started shakily, Neil wasn't the only one to realize that the whole atmosphere gradually changed from uncertain to positively electric within the first quarter of an hour. Perhaps it was because the choruses, with their lilting melodies, soon became more familiar and easy to sing. Maybe it was the words, which were pithy, current and steeped in praise and deep belief. Or was it simply because, without a doubt, God was with them? As the service continued with its flowing mix of readings, inspirational teaching, prayer and praise, a sense of fellowship drew that congregation of diverse souls into one body, the body of Christ. Tears pricked at Neil's eyes as the last chorus was followed by a blessing that brought a sensation of pins and needles throughout his whole body. He was moved, touched, inspired – and more relieved than words could say. Surely the experience must have been as compelling for everyone else in the church as it had been for him?

Joining the queue for coffee and cake in the church hall ten minutes later, he felt a huge weight lift from his shoulders as he realized that the overriding opinion was that the service had been an unexpected and thoroughly enjoyable success. One by one, the parishioners of St Stephen's came up to congratulate him for his foresight in organizing such a joyful outpouring of faith and praise. Most heart-warming of all was the enthusiastic endorsement he got from Harry when Neil went to sit beside him at the edge of the hall.

"I'm an old man," said Harry. "I have old-fashioned tastes. I like doing things the way they've always been done. If I'm honest, Neil, I only came along this morning to support you because I was worried you might come a cropper. I certainly didn't expect to enjoy it. But I did, I really did!"

Neil couldn't hide his pleasure at hearing that, and the two men were still busily discussing the service when Claire came over carrying a tray of coffee and cake.

"I brought you some lemon drizzle cake, Harry. You too, Neil. I seem to recall it's your favourite."

"Fancy you remembering that!" replied Neil, moving up a seat so that she could sit between them. "Thank you. I appreciate the coffee as well."

"White, one sugar," she said with a wink. "You see, I remembered that too."

"Well?" asked Neil. "I'm longing to know what you thought of the service today."

"It was..." Claire hesitated. "It was surprising."

"Why?"

"I didn't expect it to be like that. It was fun. I enjoyed the singing. I liked the atmosphere. I just didn't expect it."

"And? Would you come again?"

She grinned at him. "To their church perhaps. To yours, probably not."

"How hurtful!" he retorted. "Should I take that personally?"

"No. This morning I got a sense that there could be something in this God business, but that was because of the way they led the service. I just don't get that at St Stephen's."

"I do," interrupted Harry. "But I can see that perhaps your generation needs a different approach from the one that suits an old codger like me. In the end, everyone's relationship with God is personal. I think it's got less to do with what goes on in church and more to do with what God does in your life all the rest of the time."

"Maybe," conceded Claire. "Anyway, as soon as you've finished your cake, I think I ought to get you home to put your feet up after all this excitement."

"Well done, lad," said Harry, shaking Neil's hand. Then his attention was claimed by Brenda asking how he was feeling, and he turned aside.

"Well done, lad," echoed Claire so that only Neil could hear. "I know you were nervous, but it went really well. I'm pleased for you."

"And I'm glad you came. Any time you fancy coming along…"

"Which I probably won't…"

"Understood, but you're always welcome."

"Don't hold your breath."

"So I suppose I might just see you when I pop in to visit Harry."

"That's true."

"And if you were there…"

"… with a lemon drizzle cake in my hand…"

"… that would be very nice."

"It would."

"No rush, though."

"Definitely not. Whenever you're passing…"

"I'll see you, then."

"Probably."

"Take care."

"You too."

And with that, Claire took Harry's arm and led him towards the exit.

"Reverend Fisher!"

Neil turned to the commanding figure striding up to him.

"Lady Romily, how are you?"

"In need of a conversation with you – soon."

"Right. Of course. About anything in particular?"

"Many things in particular. I can't fit you in until Tuesday week. You will come for tea."

"I will?"

"You will."

"I'll have to check my diary…"

"You will come at four o'clock sharp." Lady Romily was already turning away from him.

"Sharp!"

Dismissed and slightly shaken at her obvious displeasure, Neil sat down again to finish his coffee. If he had looked up then, he might have noticed the interest Wendy and her best friend, Debs, were taking from the other side of the hall.

"How are you feeling about him now?" asked Debs.

"He's an idiot, but quite endearing at times."

"Could you ever forgive him?"

"Certainly not."

"No chance of you getting back together, then?"

"Oh, I didn't say that! He just needs to stew a little bit longer first – but of course we will, just as soon as I make up his mind for him."

➣ CHAPTER 5 ➣

A s Neil walked through the churchyard to the car park on the other side of the wall, he found himself smiling with the same enthusiasm he'd felt every year as a child, when he noticed the first few conkers on the ground beneath the horse chestnut trees.

Mind you, he was nervous. Margaret reassured him that he shouldn't be, that Lady Romily was a real sweetheart once you got to know her, but that didn't stop the sense of foreboding he'd felt since her poker-faced summons. Being busy with the rest of the Back to Church Week events around the town, he'd seen her only once since then, when he'd spotted her in her usual seat in St Stephen's for his Evensong based on the Book of Common Prayer. From his seat at the front, he could see that she was upright and expressionless. His mouth went dry at the memory. Yes, he was definitely nervous.

Romily Hall could trace its ancestry back to the Middle Ages, which would normally have fascinated him. Neil had always enjoyed an enthusiastic interest in history, encouraged by his father. Today, however, not even the gracious old house with all its turrets, elegant windows and the impressive coat of arms over the door could lift his spirits as he stretched out towards the bell pull. He half expected a butler to open the door, but instead it was Beryl Turner, a bustling, friendly woman, renowned in church circles for her pastry skills. She greeted him warmly and showed him through to an elegant drawing room with French doors looking out over a beautifully kept rose garden. A clock ticked loudly on the mantelpiece, counting out several minutes before Beryl came back with a tray carrying a silver teapot, milk jug, strainer, bone china crockery and crisp linen napkins. She returned almost immediately with a three-tier cake stand laden with an array of tiny sandwiches, pastries and cakes, and it was just as she was finishing laying everything out neatly that Lady Romily entered the room. Taking a seat in a chintzy cushioned armchair, she didn't acknowledge Neil's presence until Betty had poured out two cups of Earl Grey, then left the room, closing the door quietly behind her.

"Help yourself, Reverend Fisher."

"You first, Lady Romily. Can I pass you anything?"

"I never eat at this time of day."

Neil, who had been considering loading two dainty sandwiches onto his plate, thought better of it and took just one. Balancing the plate on the occasional table beside him, he decided against reaching out for a lump of sugar for his tea, and instead sat back on the uncompromising high-backed chair he'd been shown to.

"I have a list."

For the first time, Neil noticed the sheet of paper she held in her hand.

"Oh?"

"A list of suggestions for you."

"How helpful!"

"It will be."

Steadying the silver spoon, which seemed to be rattling against the cup and saucer on his lap, Neil watched as Lady

Romily perched gold-rimmed glasses on her nose, then lifted the paper with an air of authority.

"Firstly, St Stephen's is an ancient place of worship. It should be used with the highest reverence and decorum." She raised her eyes to look intently at Neil over the rim of her glasses. "That service last Sunday was a disgrace. It must not happen again."

"Excuse me, Lady Romily, but that's not the opinion of most of the—"

"Please do not interrupt me until the list is finished. Do you understand?"

Neil swallowed the words on the tip of his tongue, and sat back in chastened silence.

"Point Two. Waving arms in the air during worship is common, theatrical and totally unnecessary. That must not happen again within the walls of St Stephen's."

In spite of his growing indignation, Neil knew from the challenge in Lady Romily's stare as she finished her sentence that no argument would be tolerated.

"Point Three. For centuries, St Stephen's has been a high Anglican church following, both in word and spirit, the liturgy celebrated throughout the Anglican communion. It betrays our tradition and faith to deviate from that course in any way. Since you have been taking services at St Stephen's, I have noticed the small changes you have been introducing here and there hoping, no doubt, that most members of the congregation are too stupid to notice. There are certainly some very stupid people associated with the church, but I am not one of them – and I represent a significant and powerful group of church members. You ignore us at your peril, Reverend Fisher. You may think you're a new broom here to modernize the old guard in Dunbridge, but we have no need of your half-baked ideas in this parish."

With curiosity rather than anger, Neil watched in fascination as a vein in Lady Romily's neck throbbed visibly with passion and mission.

"Point Four. The Peace." She paused dramatically to allow the subject to register. "This idea of worshippers giving each other the Sign of Peace during the Eucharist has crept in much against the wishes of many lifelong Anglicans. Now the whole ridiculous idea is being allowed to extend until people are actually walking from one corner of the church to the next, hugging strangers and getting into long conversations with them – right in the middle of the service! It is unseemly. It is intrusive to our privacy. It is irrelevant to our worship. It has to stop!"

Neil opened his mouth to butt in, but she didn't draw breath before going on to her next concern.

"Point Five. You are introducing far too many of these modern choruses, which have no substance at all compared to the great traditional hymns that have served the church for centuries. These new pop songs have no place in Christian worship, and should be banned from St Stephen's.

"Point Six. It seems our organist, Brian, is only able to play at one tempo: fast. The majority of our most beautiful and inspirational hymns should be taken at a quiet pace, which allows us to consider the full meaning of the words. If Brian doesn't understand that, he shouldn't be allowed to spoil the enjoyment of others. Get someone who actually knows what they're doing."

Neil stiffened with frustration. Was he imagining the almost manic gleam in her eye as she read?

"Point Seven. Children. If they are to be in church, they must be seen and not heard. Parents are so lax on discipline these days. There's no control, no consideration for those who

80

wish to come to church for quiet contemplation. Children should be excluded at all times but one – during the Family Service at which children are encouraged to attend, which you insist on holding once every four weeks."

At this point, she leaned a little nearer to him to look him straight in the face. "And now, a few points that relate to you personally, Reverend Fisher. Firstly, I was shocked and dismayed to see that you were wearing trainers under your cassock last week. Black shoes, clean, well-heeled and polished, are the only possible footwear at all times! I am sure they taught you that at theological college, and if they didn't, their standards are slipping. Yours must not, do you understand? And one last thing – show me your finger nails!"

Too surprised to refuse, Neil laid his hands out flat while she scrutinized each one of his nails.

"They are very short."

"Yes," he agreed.

"Do you bite them?"

"I do not."

"Then why are they so short?"

"Because they really don't grow much. They never have."

Studying his hands closely to check for signs that he was being less than truthful, she finally released her grasp and sat back with an air of finality.

Suddenly furious at her cold-hearted dissection of the style and ministry of the church he loved, he breathed in deeply before letting rip.

"Lady Romily, you have made your views and preferences very clear, and I have listened patiently to them all. Now you must listen to me, because, as you didn't include Margaret in your invitation here this afternoon, I represent the ministerial team of St Stephen's.

"The style of worship at our church reflects the mix of tastes, age groups and experience of all those who form our congregation. While traditional hymns and wording appeal to many, there is a new generation that wants a more relaxed, spontaneous and modern form of worship. We are committed to bringing the word of God to them, just as we are to you and any others who prefer a more conservative approach. That's why we vary our worship style from week to week throughout each month. Christ came – and died – for us all. In his name, our church must welcome everyone. That is our role!"

This time, it was Lady Romily who was staring at him wordlessly.

"I don't think God minds if I wear black shoes or red carpet slippers. I think he cares most that I do his will faithfully, and bring others to knowledge of him through my ministry. I believe that Christ welcomes us all with loving, open arms. I fail to see either a loving spirit or an open mind in your views when you dismiss the choices and feelings of your fellow worshippers in the most high-handed manner!"

There, he'd said it! His raised voice faded away to leave a deafening silence resounding around the elegant room. Suddenly fearful that he had completely overstepped the mark, he was surprised to see the twitch of a smile at the corner of Lady Romily's lips.

"Well, well, well," she mused, sitting back comfortably in her armchair. "I never put you down as a man with backbone, Neil, and now I see you have some fight in you after all. Thank God for that!"

"Lady Romily, I–"

She hushed him with a wave of her hand. "You will need that backbone, Neil, if you are to make your mark on this church. Of course things must change with the times, but

I urge you not to throw the baby out with the bath water. Take your time. Change is dangerous unless it is well considered. Be careful when you are thinking about taking a sledgehammer to traditions that have lasted for centuries. And Neil, if you had remained silent long enough for me to finish, you would have allowed me to say how wonderful I thought the Evensong was the other night. Margaret told me that the idea of using the age-old words of the Book of Common Prayer came from you, and I wish you to know that was an inspired and very wise decision. Did you notice how full the church was?"

"We had more than two hundred there that evening."

"Why do you think it worked so well?"

"Because those words are embedded in the mind and experience of most of us."

"You're right. It was immensely moving, almost sentimental in its familiarity."

"We can't always have services like that, though."

"Of course not. I realize the church has to cater for all comers – but please be fully aware of the reason for the success of that Evensong. For most of us, faith is rooted in our past, with its familiarity and sense of homecoming in the words we have heard and spoken all our lives. That's why it worked."

He was still mulling over her words when she suddenly stood up, the conversation plainly over.

"Food for thought, Neil. Thank you for coming. Good afternoon!"

And with a whiff of rose-scented perfume, she swept past him and left the room.

Neil picked up his briefcase and let himself out of the front door, his mind racing at the curious lecture he'd just received. And it wasn't until he'd driven half a mile down the road that he realized that not one dainty sandwich nor a sip of Earl Grey had got as far as his lips.

* * *

When Neil arrived at the church office on the day before the barn dance, he realized immediately that he had walked into an intense conversation going on between Margaret and churchwarden Cyn. Tactfully he withdrew to the church hall, where the children's playgroup was just coming to an end. Ten minutes later Margaret joined him.

"Everything OK?" he asked.

"Probably," replied Margaret, her expression thoughtful. "Baby Ellen isn't at all well. Cyn thinks it's because she was born so prematurely and has a lot to catch up on."

"But Colin and Jeannie think it could be more than that?"

"They waited so long for her. It was a miracle she was ever born. Who can blame them for being overprotective?"

"What does the doctor say?"

"Well, he's not exactly encouraging. Jeannie noticed that one of Ellen's eyes seemed to have a bit of a squint, and when the doctor took a look, he sent her straight off for tests."

"Tests?"

"An ultrasound scan, Cyn said, and I know she's been beside herself with worry. I don't know what the results were, but I get a dreadful feeling the news isn't good."

"Then we'll all pray for Ellen and the whole family. Shall I add her name to our prayer list for Sunday morning?"

"Not yet. Let's just keep this to ourselves for now. She'll certainly be in my prayers though."

"Mine too. It's good that you know the family so well."

"In some ways that makes it harder. Frank and I are parents

too, and we know the mere thought of anything going wrong with your children's health is terrifying."

Margaret suddenly spotted a stack of cardboard boxes full of glasses in various sizes and shapes.

"Good, they're here! I was worried those wouldn't be delivered in time for tomorrow night. How are the tickets going?"

"Looks like we're going to have a full house! It's handy that the committee chairman of the Friends of St Stephen's just happens to be a farmer with a barn that's perfect for our dance. I popped over to Hill Farm earlier this morning, and Bob was there lining the sides of the barn with straw bales. It feels quite cosy now, in spite of its size. The school's come up with some staging and lights we can borrow – and that's it really, because the caller will do the rest. It's just him and his sound set-up, and we'll be do-si-do-ing like cowboys!"

At that moment, Neil's mobile rang. He groaned as he mouthed silently to Margaret that it was his mother.

"Oh, please give Iris my love, and tell her I hope to see her soon!" And with a chuckle and not one ounce of sympathy, Margaret left him to it.

"Mum," Neil began, hoping to keep the weariness out of his voice. "How are you?"

"Waiting for you to ring me back from my two calls already this week! Don't you ever look at your phone?"

"Sorry, it's really busy here with the barn dance coming up tomorrow night."

"Well, I'm glad I'll miss it. It sounds very vulgar to me."

Neil stiffened. "It's a sell-out and we're hoping for a delightful evening."

"Hmm. Well, there's no accounting for taste. I certainly hope for a quieter week during my stay."

"You're staying? When?"

"I arrive next Thursday. Pick me up at Paddington at half past three."

"I'm always at the hospice on Thursday afternoons."

"Then you'll have to go earlier in the week. I'm sure they'll understand that your mother must come first."

Argument was futile. Neil had had enough years of experience with Iris to know when to give in gracefully.

"How long do you plan to stay?"

"My heating's playing up. My man says it's the boiler. It seems I need a new one, and I can't possibly stay in the house without heating, not at the end of October with winter closing in. My neighbour says she'll keep an eye on everything, so there's no need for me to hurry back. I can stay as long as I want!"

What about what I want? How about a day trip? The thought struck Neil so quickly that he wondered if he'd actually spoken out loud – but if he had, it was wasted on Iris, who was still in full flow.

"Please make sure I have my own flannelette sheets on my bed, and it would be a good idea to keep the electric blanket on for twenty-four hours before I come so the bedding's properly aired. Oh, and pop a casserole in before you start in the morning so it'll be ready when we get back. Have you got all that?"

"Got it."

"By the way, how's Harry?"

"Surprisingly well. He's been coming along to church every now and then, and I've seen him in the garden a couple of times."

"Nice man. There aren't many gentlemen like him around these days."

"Right then, Mum, I must go. See you on Thursday."

"And run the vacuum over before I come. You could do with a feather duster too. I'll bring mine, if I remember."

"Bye, Mum."

"Half past three. Did you write that down?"

"I've got it. Bye!"

Neil ended the call and stared at the phone forlornly.

His mother was coming for an indefinite stay. Oh, joy!

* * *

"Neil, mate, it's not going to be awkward, is it?" Graham's voice, when he rang later that evening, sounded uncharacteristically anxious. "Only with Debs and Wendy being best friends, it's natural that we'll all team up to go to the barn dance together."

"And I'm glad you're coming! Who else is likely to volunteer to lend me the fashion item from his extensive wardrobe that is exactly what I need – a check shirt old enough for Roy Rogers himself to have worn, and in just the same style?" teased Neil. "Of course you must come, and of course I understand that you'll be in Wendy's party. It's shaping up to be a great night. You'll have a good time."

"Right." Graham still sounded a bit doubtful. "Um, I'm not sure if I'm supposed to be telling you this, or if you already know, but Wendy's bringing a partner along with her."

Thump! That bit of news winded Neil like a punch in the chest. A new partner?

"Aah," he managed to say at last, "no, I – I didn't realize that, but it's fine. We're not together. She's a free agent."

"So you're all right about it?"

"Absolutely. A lovely girl like her won't stay alone for long, will she? I realize that, and I want her to be happy."

"Uh-oh, I've put my foot in it, haven't I? You *are* upset. I can hear it in your voice."

"No, not at all. Just took me by surprise, I suppose."

"He seems a nice bloke. In fact, I know him a bit. He's the deputy head of the school she teaches at. You might even like him."

Neil grinned. "Perhaps not! He'd better be good to her, that's all I need to know."

"Yes, well, it's early days. Debs says they've only been out a couple of times, so they may just be friends for all I know."

"A couple of times? That sounds a bit serious to me."

"But you broke off with her, so even if it is, you don't mind, do you?"

"No," was Neil's firm reply. "I'm very pleased for her, for them both, and I wish them well."

"That's OK, then. Look, I'll drop that shirt into the church office when I drive past in the morning. I've got a pair of old cowboy boots too. What size are you?"

"Ten."

"Like me. They should fit a treat. I should warn you, though, they're bright orange. I bought them years ago when I went on holiday to Nashville. I don't know what they do to the leather there, but these boots seem to look more like satsumas every year."

* * *

"You're here! I didn't think a barn dance would be your thing."

Claire looked up from where she was stacking glasses beneath the makeshift bar they'd set up in the barn.

"This is my Uncle Bob's barn. He's got twin boys a year older than me, so I grew up playing Cowboys and Indians on this farm."

"Whose side were you on?"

"The winning side every time! Whether I was a cowboy or an Indian, the boys were always too scared of me to let me lose."

"Scary, huh? What did you threaten them with? Your black belt in karate?"

"No, I just knew too much about them and told them I'd spill the beans to their mum if they didn't do exactly what I wanted."

"Claire Holloway!" laughed Neil. "I'm shocked that you'd stoop to blackmail!"

"Neil Fisher!" she grinned in return. "This is a charity evening. Are you just standing at the bar trying to look decorative, or you going to buy me a drink?"

"Are you allowed to drink on duty?"

"I'm told I mix much better drinks when I've had half a pint myself, but not tonight! I might allow myself a quick shandy – half an inch of bitter and lots of lemonade."

"You're right. We don't want any tiddly bartenders or curates at a sophisticated church do like this! So a shandy it is for me, barman – and have one yourself!"

At that point, Claire's attention was taken by another customer, so Neil turned round to survey the scene. The barn looked amazing, like a film set straight out of a John Wayne movie. Bob had done a terrific job in decorating it with horse tack, pitchforks and shovels, and the subdued lighting created a cosy atmosphere, especially now the nights were drawing in. Bales of hay were set out around tables made of wooden crates, each with a flickering candle in the middle – well, what looked like a candle, but was actually a small bulb powered by battery, in deference to Health and Safety.

People were beginning to pour in now, many of them dressed in blue jeans, denim shirts, neck scarves and a variety of footwear that ranged from flashy cowboy boots to the odd pair of wellies. *None of them have boots as orange as mine,* thought Neil wryly. *Still, no one's going to lose me in the crowd!*

Just then, a small group approached the bar: Margaret and Frank, looking splendid in their cowboy hats, and Peter and Val, who had really got into the spirit of the evening in matching check shirts with ornate brass buckles on their wide, patterned belts. They were just ordering their drinks when the caller started inviting everyone to take their partners out onto the floor to form circles of eight.

"Coming?" said Margaret almost coquettishly to Frank. He didn't hesitate, and the two of them were the first couple to find their places.

"Coming?" copied Val, holding out her hand to Peter. There was just a moment of panic in Peter's eyes before he grabbed her hand to follow Frank and Margaret, who were already some way ahead of them. Neil watched them go, thinking that the old Peter who'd lived under Glenda's thumb for thirty years would have been far too inhibited to join in with something like this. No one could take pleasure in the collapse of a marriage – and Peter had definitely done his very best to keep his going – but when Glenda left him so suddenly and cruelly, anyone who was his friend had to feel relieved to see that a burden had clearly been lifted off his shoulders. Peter was a new man. That's what the love of a good woman could do for you.

At that moment, bang on cue, Wendy entered the barn, linked arm in arm with a tall cowboy who was immaculately dressed in a smart check shirt, and jeans with pencil-sharp creases down the front. They looked relaxed and happy, sharing a joke as they picked their way through the crowd to where Graham and Debs were laying claim to a table they'd spotted in a nearby corner. As she took off her coat, Wendy glanced over towards Neil for just an instant. She looked beautiful. Wherever had she found that Wild West saloon-girl dress that went in and out in just the right places? Her hair was swept to one side in shining ringlets – the Doris Day of Dunbridge!

The moment was broken as Mr Immaculate Jeans said something that made her lean across to whisper in his ear. Neil's stomach lurched at the intimacy of the movement – until he gave himself a stern talking-to, determined not to take any notice of Wendy and her partner for the rest of the evening. It was nothing to do with him. He should mind his own business and perhaps overcome his natural shyness and find his own partner to dance with. Suddenly he spotted someone who seemed a safe option. Barbara was walking towards the bar, so before the astonished playgroup leader had time to refuse, Neil grabbed her hand and marched her onto the dance floor.

If Neil had been anxious about tripping over his two left feet once the music started, he needn't have worried, because it soon became clear that enthusiasm and a good sense of humour counted for a lot more than any dancing skill. The caller tied them all in knots by making them think they were moving one way, when suddenly he barked at them to turn tail and head the other. Two dances later, gasping for breath but laughing along with everyone else, Neil led Barbara off the dance floor and returned her to her husband, who was sitting next to the large table surrounded by members of the Clarkson clan. Neil was delighted to see that Jeannie and Colin were among them. Spotting an empty seat next to Jeannie, he sat down to join her.

"It's good to see you out. Haven't seen much of you since Ellen's come along to take up your time. How is she?"

As Jeannie turned to greet him, he was shocked at how drawn she looked, her thin face dominated by the dark circles under her eyes.

"She's poorly, Neil. Very poorly."

Without even thinking, Neil covered her hand with his. Jeannie's eyes became instantly glassy with unbidden tears.

"Sorry," she mumbled, "just ignore me. This is a night out. I've got to stop being like this."

"Why? How? You can't help what you feel."

Rubbing her eyes with her free hand, Jeannie looked down towards her lap to hide her embarrassment.

"Do they know exactly what the trouble is?"

"Well, it's got a name now. Retinoblastoma. That's the enemy. That's what our beautiful daughter's having to fight."

"I've never heard of it."

"You're not alone. Neither had we. There are only about eighty cases a year in the whole of the country – and it had to pick her."

"What is it?"

"Eye cancer. Did you ever notice that she seemed to have a slight squint? Perhaps you didn't, but it started to become clear to me when she was just a few weeks old. I wasn't really worried then, because babies often have squints when they're very young. But then, in quite a lot of the pictures taken during the christening, we could see that the reflection of the flash looked different in her left eye to the other one. When the doctor saw that, he sent her for tests straight away."

Neil squeezed her hand as tears threatened again.

"It's taken a while to pin it down, but now we know for sure. It's a cancerous tumour behind her eye."

"What triggers something like that?"

"Mostly they're hereditary, but this one isn't – and that's very rare apparently. As unlikely as Ellen being born against the odds in the first place. What are the chances of one little girl having to cope with two completely different sets of impossible circumstances like that? Millions to one! But it's happening to her – to us."

"What do the doctors say? How will they treat her?"

"They've mentioned chemotherapy, radiotherapy – even surgery. The trouble is, the tumour's huge already. It may be too late."

"Oh, Jeannie, I'm so sorry…"

"Colin and I don't know what to do. They want us to decide. Should they go ahead and operate? Do we want them to try? *Of course* we're desperate for them to try anything that might save her life. But then they tell us about the potential dangers. She might be brain damaged. She might end up blind or deaf. And in the end, after all that trauma and pain, she might just die anyway."

She stopped to pull out a tissue from her sleeve, looking down again in the hope that no one beyond Neil could see she was crying.

"I watch our beloved little girl sleeping in her cot, and she's just beautiful with her perfect little fingers and her soft skin and that downy fair hair. You'd never believe there was such evil lurking inside her. Then I think of the surgeons cutting into her, ripping her apart, and I don't know what to do. Could they cure her? Could they give our darling baby back to us? Or will she die anyway? If that's the case, I don't want to cause her one moment of suffering or pain that could be avoided. I'd rather she just faded away, having only ever known the warmth and security of a loving home and family.

Not hospital wards, with tubes and chemicals being pumped into her."

"What does Colin think?"

"He's just as wrecked as I am. It's impossible for us to know what to do for the best. The trouble is that the doctors can't say for certain how things will go. Their only answer is that we should try every option modern medicine can offer. But what will that be like for Ellen? We're her parents. We adore her. We want what's right for her – but what if that means putting her through torture? The facts at the moment seem to suggest that she'll die anyway, so should we put her through painful, frightening treatment, or just let nature take its course, with all the pain-control she needs to have a reasonably comfortable life?"

"Either way is heartbreaking."

"But we have to make the decision right now. If the treatment's to have any chance of working, we've got to start straight away. We've talked about it endlessly. We've sat for hours reading up about the prognosis and deciding once and for all that we have to give her a chance by letting the doctors try to save her. And then we hold her in our arms, and look down at that trusting face, our perfect little girl – and we change our minds again. No wonder the doctors are losing patience with us! What sort of parents are we?"

"The most loving mum and dad who are faced with an intolerable situation."

Jeannie looked up straight into his eyes.

"And what's God up to? What cruel trick is he playing on us? After all those years of praying for Ellen, he gives her to us knowing he plans to take her away again. You know all that rubbish about him being a loving God? Don't believe it!"

"I do believe it, Jeannie, because I know it's true."

"You would say that. It's your job and nothing really awful has ever happened to you. You can afford to have a rosy view of God. We're beginning to realize he's actually heartless and cruel."

"We can't know the bigger picture, Jeannie. We can't understand why Ellen had to be born, and why perhaps God may take her back to be with him again. All we know is that in his care she'll be safe, with no more pain or illness."

"I don't know that. All I know here and now is that the tumour in her head is killing her."

"There's a school of thought that says we're put on this earth to learn the lessons in life we need to know, and when someone's only here for a very short time, that's because they've reached perfection and don't need to stay any longer."

Looking down at her tightly clasped hands, Jeannie was silent.

"I don't know all the answers, Jeannie. None of us can. But I do know without a shadow of doubt that prayer has power. God listens and he cares. We pray every day for his will to be done – but we have to allow that to happen, even when we can't understand."

"If his will is that Ellen should have to go through unbearable suffering when she's done nothing to deserve it, then I've got lots of doubts, I'm afraid."

"Well, we'll be praying for you – for your pain and fear as well as your doubts. And Ellen is constantly in our hearts and prayers, Jeannie. You're all very loved in this community. If there's any practical help you need, remember there are plenty of loving friends around you, longing to lend a hand in any way we can."

Jeannie's smile was weak but warm. "Thanks. I do know that and we may well need to take you up on that offer. And

Neil, thank you for listening. I've believed in God all my life. I've never questioned his love for us even once – until now. Now I feel as if I'm not just losing my daughter, but I've lost my dearest friend. Where's God when I need him? How can I trust him when I know he could cure her but probably won't? Oh, I still believe in prayer and I know he doesn't need to hear our endless, desperate pleadings to know exactly what we're going through, but I can't help feeling that Ellen's illness is his decision. He's allowing it to happen, and our prayers feel irrelevant."

"Illness, accidents and tragedy are facts of human life, Jeannie. There are so many things that just happen, and we can't stop them. I don't think that makes them God's doing. They're just part of the life we've created over centuries in this world we share. Selfishness, lethargy, greed – they've prompted people's actions since life began, because God gave us the free will to do just that."

"I'm not selfish! And there couldn't possibly be anyone more innocent than Ellen!"

"But our world's been shaped and influenced by the actions and reactions of others down the years. The way we live, what we eat, how we relate to others – that's created a modern-day malaise in which conditions like cancer seem to flourish. Is that God's fault, or, collectively, is it ours? I don't think God wants even one second of pain or suffering for any of us. After all, his own son faced the ultimate in human suffering, so he does understand exactly what you're going through and he is in this with you, Jeannie. Whatever the outcome, please keep that knowledge in your heart."

"It's not easy."

"No, of course not. Bless you, Jeannie. God bless you all."

And against a backdrop of laughing, thigh-slapping dancers, the two of them sat in their own circle of shared sadness.

Much later during the evening, after the fish and chip supper, the raffle, and eventually the news that the barn dance had raised nearly £1,000 for the Friends of St Stephen's Fund, Neil was hardly listening as the caller announced that the next dance was a Ladies' Excuse Me.

"Grab your partner, girls! Don't take no for an answer!"

It wasn't until Neil looked up to see Wendy making a determined line towards him that the significance of that invitation got through to him.

"Well, cowboy?" she challenged as she stopped in front of him, her hand on one hip to allow the best possible view of her costume as an extremely glamorous saloon girl. "You dancing?"

"You're asking?" gulped Neil.

"I'm asking!" was the firm reply as she grabbed his hand to pull him to his feet.

Then I suppose I must be dancing, he thought in a panic, suddenly aware that many pairs of eyes seemed to be focused in his direction.

This dance was slower than most of the previous ones, and instead of constantly changing partners, the caller explained that in "The Lovers' Stroll" you stayed with the partner of your dreams. Acutely aware of his lack of dancing skills, Neil allowed himself to be guided by Wendy, who drifted round and past him, floating in and out of his arms in a fragrant cloud of swirling fabric. One moment she would be dancing apart from him, her eyes flashing and seductive, and the next, she was up close, with her lips almost touching his. The feeling of her in his embrace brought back a host of exciting and evocative memories. She was so beautiful, so hard to resist…

As the music drifted to an end, Wendy twirled around beneath his outstretched arm, fixing her eyes on him as she gracefully dropped into a curtsey. Then, before he could draw breath, she turned on her heel and walked away without a backward glance. Her point was made – and they both knew it.

"Need a shandy?" whispered a voice in his ear.

Claire was beside him, watching as Wendy walked away. Grateful for her company, Neil still felt decidedly weak at the knees after the experience he'd just been through.

"You're not over her, are you? And she's definitely not over you."

"I thought I was. I knew I couldn't lead her on when I simply wasn't sure enough of what I felt for her."

His eyes still on Wendy as she disappeared into the crowd on the other side of the hall, Neil leaned towards Claire so that their shoulders touched.

"And there was you. Why did I find myself feeling so much for you if it was Wendy I wanted?"

With the slightest of motions, Claire's fingers brushed against his own.

"I think…" Her voice was so soft that he could hardly hear her. "I think Wendy's right for you in many important ways. You've got a lot in common. She's bright and gregarious, and she's grown up in the church, with the same faith that's at the very heart of you."

He turned towards Claire.

"Yes, she would be the perfect life partner for a vicar, and I know that's my vocation and calling rather than just a job. But as a man – the rather feeble, uncertain person I know I am inside – there's something about her confidence that she knows exactly what's best for me that I find rather overwhelming."

"A bit like your mum?"

He chuckled. "Exactly like my mum! That's probably my problem."

Claire's fingers tightened gently around his own.

"Neil, there's nothing wrong with you exactly as you are. Life isn't certain. No one knows all the answers, so no one has the right to decide what *you* need. You have the kindest heart I've ever come across. Trust it. Trust in you. I do."

In the depths of her green eyes, Neil glimpsed the same warm understanding and genuine care that had swept them both away on the night of Harry's illness.

It was Claire who broke the moment.

"I've seen what they do in Wild West movies to barmen who desert their thirsty customers. Come on, I'll make us both another shandy. I think we deserve it!"

≋ CHAPTER 6 ≋

November roared in with dark nights, high winds, whipping rain – and Iris. His mother arrived with two full suitcases plus copious other bags, which Neil obediently dragged across Paddington Station towards the car. Once at the house, she grumbled about the heating, said the place needed dusting, muttered about the state of all the cupboards and commandeered his favourite armchair. The tirade of criticism continued as they ate the casserole he'd prepared, as per her instructions, before leaving. It was bland. He'd used the wrong meat. He should never have added garlic – and how could he ever think a decent casserole could be made without butter beans, which had always been her personal favourite? It was when she said that during her stay she would obviously have to take personal charge of all culinary requirements in the house that the non-cook in Neil breathed a sigh of relief and thought that perhaps every dark cloud did have a silver lining.

"Harry's invited you for tea tomorrow, if you'd like to go."

Iris's expression brightened. "How charming. Of course I'd love to take tea with such a delightful gentleman. What time are we expected?"

"Only you, I'm afraid. I'm at a planning meeting tomorrow afternoon for the Remembrance service at the weekend. The

British Legion always organizes a special gathering, but this will be the first time I've led the service, so I'm anxious to get everything right."

"Harry will go to that, surely?"

"I expect so. I haven't asked him."

"Then I shall. We'll go together."

"And I'm out first thing in the morning at the local church school, so I'll have to leave you to your own devices then, if that's OK."

"I'm used to being on my own, Neil, since your father died. Being alone is a way of life for me. How on earth do you think I manage at home?"

"It's different when you're in someone else's house, though, isn't it? I hope you can find everything you need."

Iris sniffed delicately.

"I doubt that very much. I think I need to do a bit of stock-taking in this house of yours and sort it out once and for all."

"Mum, please don't. I like it just as it is…"

"Neil, you always were badly organized. Heaven only knows what you ever learned in all those years in the cubs and scouts, because you've never been properly prepared for anything!"

"Look, you came here for a rest. Please have one. I really don't want you rearranging anything here. This is my home, *my* home!"

Her eyes widened with disbelief at his outburst.

"There's no need to take that tone, Neil, when I'm simply offering help you plainly need. That's one thing you've never understood – that if you don't take good advice when it's offered to you, then you can blame no one but yourself when things fall around your ears."

She stood up abruptly.

"I'm going to have a bath. The heating is on in the bathroom, I take it?"

Neil nodded wearily.

"And the water's hot? Then I'll bid you goodnight, Neil. I prefer my own company to yours – and the book I'm reading will be a great deal more interesting."

And as she swept upstairs in a haze of her favourite Lily of the Valley perfume, Neil watched her go before burying his head in his hands with a heavy sigh of sheer exasperation.

* * *

If Neil found a congregation of adults daunting, that was nothing to the fear he felt when faced with an audience of junior-school children. He went in to talk to two different classes during his monthly visit to the local church school, and on the whole he found the younger pupils in the infants' class much easier to cope with. They listened as if he were a wonderful storyteller, generally not questioning the logic or truth of anything he told them. It was when he got to the older pupils aged eight and nine that he began to find the whole experience quite a challenge.

That week, he decided to take Remembrance as his theme. He explained that there had been two world wars, which had torn Europe apart and probably involved and maybe even cost the lives of many of their great-grandads. He told them how, during the Great War, so many thousands had been killed that everyone said that was the war to end all wars. And yet just over twenty years later, there was another even more devastating war which had claimed the lives of millions, and touched almost every family from here in Dunbridge to right over on the other side of the world. He added that it was important never to forget the lessons learned in war, so that we could all make sure nothing like that ever happened again. Then he finished by explaining the significance of the services on Remembrance Sunday when people could pray and remember those whose lives had been lost in war.

The reaction of the class ranged from the shocked and interested to the downright bored, but they all perked up when he took round a box of bright red poppies with detailed instructions about how they could pin them onto their school sweatshirts without stabbing themselves or each other.

"Does anyone know why we remember people who have died in war with poppies?" he asked.

One hand went up. It was David, a ginger-haired boy who always seemed anxious to answer any question he was asked, even if he had no idea of the answer.

"Because they're red?" he suggested hopefully.

"What's the significance of them being red?" asked Neil.

David's arm shot up again.

"Because you can see them when you pin them on yourself?"

"Yes, I suppose so, but what about the colour? What can you think of that's red?"

"Ketchup?"

"Yes, you're right, but that's not what I'm after," continued Neil, wondering if he was fighting a lost cause here. "Think about war. Think about men dying in the trenches when they've been shot at or bombed."

"I don't like to think about things like that." Sitting near the front, Janice's eyes looked enormous in her pale face framed with a thatch of dark curls. "I don't like war films and I don't like the games my brother has on his Play Station either. They're always about fighting and killing, and there's

103

lots of blood and gore. I hate them! And I hate him for making me watch them."

"Well, I'm sorry to hear that, Janice, and I think that's a very sensible way to feel – but you've hit on the reason for a red flower to help us remember. Blood is red, isn't it? So the red flowers remind us of the blood that was shed when the soldiers died."

"Euck!" said Janice. "I think I'm going to be sick."

"But," Neil persevered, "why poppies? Why not roses or tulips? Because they're red flowers too."

"Sir! Sir!" David's hand was waving above his head again. "Because that's the sound the guns made: pop, pop, pop, pop, pop!"

"Good idea, David, but not quite right. The idea of using poppies dates back to the First World War a hundred years ago now. As the soldiers were fighting in the trenches, they could see great big patches of poppies growing wild over the ground between where they were and the other side where the enemy were hidden in their own trenches. Because the poppies were the colour of drops of blood, they became the symbol of remembrance for people everywhere who have sacrificed their lives in service of their country."

The class fell silent as they considered this. Suddenly David's hand shot up again.

"You're a vicar. You believe in God, don't you, sir?"

"Very much, David."

"I don't. If there's a God, things like that wouldn't happen."

"But was it God's fault or was it the fault of people – like the leaders of the countries who decided to go to war in the first place? Was it God who invented guns and bombs? Was it God who wanted one group of people to hate another to the point where they were prepared to kill their enemies? Don't you think we need to take responsibility for our part in all this? Because I think God's heart is broken when we behave that way."

"I still don't believe in God," retorted David.

"Does anyone know the word that describes someone who doesn't believe in God?" asked Neil, thinking that a change of subject might be helpful. He was faced with a sea of blank faces, even from David, who was plainly struggling to come up with some sort of answer.

"It begins with the letter 'A'," hinted Neil.

"I know! I know, sir!" David was almost jumping off his chair in his enthusiasm. "Is it an *arsonist*, sir?"

Neil had to smile. "Not quite, David, but that's a good try because the word you need sounds a bit like that. It's *atheist* – and it means someone who doesn't believe in God. Has anyone heard of that word?"

"I have, sir! I have! That was the word I meant!"

"OK, well, here's another question for you. There's another word that also begins with the letter 'A' that is used to describe someone who isn't *sure* whether they believe in God or not."

Again, a row of blank expressions stared back at him for several seconds before David practically leapt to his feet in his determination to answer first.

"I've got it, sir. I've got it!"

"Right, David, what is the word to describe someone who doesn't know if they believe in God or not?"

"An Anglican, sir?"

I give up, thought Neil. *I just give up.*

* * *

On the whole, with a year and a quarter now under his belt since he first came to Dunbridge, Neil was beginning to feel a great deal more comfortable with the cross section of people who made up the busy life of St Stephen's. There was, however, one group who struck him as so formidable that he literally felt his knees knock when one of them approached him. He'd already had his audience with Lady Romily, Chairwoman of the St Stephen's Ladies' Guild, but she was supported by a clique of equally daunting ladies: Olivia, Penelope and Julia, who were Deputy Chair, Secretary and Treasurer respectively.

Margaret had impressed upon him from the start that it was important to keep on the right side of the Guild committee because, as a group, their main responsibility was to raise money for the curate's expenses. That always made him feel awkwardly beholden, especially as it soon became clear that they expected him to sing for his supper! He was regularly summoned to their afternoon meeting, held on the third Thursday of each month, where he found himself grilled by the Treasurer, made to sign a variety of paperwork by the Secretary, measured up for socks and pullovers by the knitting team, stuffed with sandwiches by the catering ladies (led by the talented Beryl who, everyone said, should go in for *Masterchef*) and generally bossed about and fussed over by this group of grandmothers. They plainly thought he'd not had a square meal for weeks, definitely needed some style advice when it came to his choice of clothes, and could certainly do with a bit of matchmaking to find him the perfect wife to sort him out.

Meekly following orders, Neil found himself holding up his hands so that a skein of wool could be hung around them while one bespectacled knitter, working at terrific speed, wound neat balls of wool from it. As the skein of wool disappeared, he tried to keep count of just how many times they dropped Wendy's name into the conversation. He'd got the message. The Ladies' Guild thought Wendy was the girl for him: accomplished, beautiful, a leading light in the church community, brought up in a well-respected Christian family – she fitted the bill perfectly! Neil could feel his face getting redder by the minute as they bombarded him with questions about why he and Wendy had broken up and what he planned to do to make matters right. Just when he thought he could dodge their questions no more, Lady Romily unexpectedly stepped in to rescue him.

"Ladies!" she announced in a voice that could cut through all conversation and probably panes of glass too. "As you know, our Annual Baking Competition will be taking place in the church hall next Saturday. Entries are invited not just from members of the Ladies' Guild, but from anyone who feels they would like to try their hand at whipping up something special. There will, of course, be the usual fierce battle to produce the best classic Victoria sponge. The Rich Fruit Cake category is also very popular, and may I remind you that those two categories stand alone in that there is a separate winner for each of them? However, the most coveted prize is for the Best in Show, and for that there is no limit whatsoever to the kind of baking masterpiece you might choose to enter."

There was a hubbub of conversation as this information was noted and commented upon by just about every lady in the Guild.

"We do, of course," continued Lady Romily, raising her voice to ensure absolute attention, "need an independent judge. I have been giving this role some careful consideration, and I have a suggestion to put to you. I have noticed that our young curate, the Reverend Fisher, not only has a very sweet tooth, but over the year or more that he's been joining us at our meetings,

I feel he's developed an eye for knowing a good cake when he sees one. What do you think, ladies? Could he be our judge?"

To Neil's surprise, there was a murmur of approval, together with a smattering of applause as all eyes looked at him. Before he could answer, Lady Romily spoke directly to him.

"We recognize that your expertise is limited to taste rather than any in-depth cookery skill, and for that reason, we won't ask you to judge the specialist areas of Victoria Sponge and Rich Fruit Cake. As usual, by popular demand, I will do that myself. That means, young man, that you will have responsibility for judging the most important category of all, Best in Show. Do you think you could manage that?"

"You do realize that I don't know a thing about baking, don't you?" Neil pointed out. "Nothing at all. Apart from being sure about what I like to eat, the science of cooking is completely lost on me. Now, if you were to ask me about the winners and losers in the local take-away establishments, then I'm your expert!"

Beryl led the chorus of reassurance.

"An enthusiastic consumer is exactly what we need to judge the skill of the chef. You're definitely the man for the job!"

"Well, if you're sure…"

At this point, Lady Romily regained control of the conversation. "So I'm proposing that the Reverend Fisher be officially named as judge of the St Stephen's Annual Baking Competition. Do I have a seconder?"

Practically every hand in the hall went up.

"Carried, then," concluded Lady Romily, as Penelope reached for her pen to make an official note that the motion had been passed.

"The event is next Saturday here in the hall," Lady Romily continued. "Doors open to the public at two for a tea party, plus the chance to taste and hopefully buy not just the competition cakes, but all the other culinary treats our ladies have conjured up. You, Reverend Fisher, must be here at one o'clock precisely. You will observe and learn as I judge the two main cake categories, after which you may make your choice for Best in Show."

"Does that mean I get a bite of every one of the cakes?" asked Neil hopefully, definitely warming to the idea.

"Naturally, as judge, you are welcome and, in fact, encouraged to sample any entry that seems promising." Lady Romily's voice was icily cool. "I stress, *only* those that are promising. Needless greed will not be appreciated. Remember our bakers are anxious that their offerings remain in good order for public display."

"But every cook who's entering cupcakes or biscuits will be trying to tempt you to take a taste," laughed Beryl. "There's hot competition here, you know, and none of us is above a little bribery and corruption to get round a judge known to have a penchant for fancies and fairy cakes!"

* * *

Beryl's words echoed in his mind as he stepped into the hall the following Saturday to find it ringed in beautifully dressed tables covered in cakes and confectionery of every kind. There were scones (plain, sultana and cheese), fruit tarts and flans, fluffy meringue pavlovas covered in cream and strawberries, sticky shining chocolate fudge cakes – and an alarming bright green concoction that Neil read was a Key lime pie. There were cupcakes that were nothing short of works of art standing alongside homely coffee walnut cakes that had Neil thinking longingly of his gran, who'd made them specially for him when he was a child.

"Oh, there you are, Reverend Fisher!" Lady Romily was bearing down on him from the far end of the hall. "You've cut it very fine to observe me judging the Victoria Sponge and Rich Fruit Cake categories. Follow me!"

For the next twenty minutes, Neil dutifully stood two paces behind Lady Romily as she inspected and sampled one cake after another. To be honest, they all looked practically identical to Neil, but to a connoisseur like Her Ladyship, every detail of shape, density, jam spread, cream thickness, surface decoration and general presentation was minutely scrutinized and assessed. Finally satisfied, she made a note of the entries that had gained third, second and first place, handing the sheet to Penelope, who also stood at her side ready to organize the appropriate rosettes to be presented later to the winners, as well as the certificates recording the glory of the moment forever.

Once her deliberations were complete, and the results of the Victoria Sponge and Rich Fruit Cake secreted into gold envelopes so they could be dramatically revealed at the opening ceremony, Lady Romily turned to Neil.

"For your eyes only, Reverend Fisher, here is a note of the two winners in the categories I've judged. These two cakes are obviously superb specimens, expertly made. It is not unusual for one of these winners to be judged Best in Show. I have no wish to influence your decision in any way, but I thought a word to the wise might be useful."

"Come on, Neil!" Beryl had suddenly appeared at his elbow. "Let me show you round."

For years afterwards, Neil was to treasure that meander around the tables as one of his very happiest memories. Beryl guided him towards cakes of every shape, size, colour and level of expertise, pointing out shortcomings on some and glorious finishing touches on others. She wheeled him round plates of cupcakes decorated in everything from Union Jacks to baby's bootees in delicate blue and pink. There was even one inspired iced creation that had his own photo on the top! When it came to getting the judge's attention, Neil thought, that probably took the biscuit.

"And I really can choose whatever I like here, can I?"

"Your choice, yours alone," confirmed Beryl. "Don't take any notice of Her Ladyship. She'd like you to pick one of the two category winners because it would endorse her own opinion, but honestly, you can award the title to whichever of all these platefuls you most fancy!"

Neil wandered along the tables thoughtfully until he had narrowed his selection down to just three. Which would he most like to eat right now? That question was soon answered in his own mind – and the winner's fate was sealed.

At two o'clock precisely, the doors were unbolted to reveal a queue of people eager to come in.

"Best day of the year this, Vicar," trilled Edie Brown, one of the St Stephen's elderly regulars, as she pushed her way through the crowd. "You'll never find a spread like the one you get here on cake competition day. Can't stop! I'm losing my place in the tea queue!"

In minutes the hall was packed with a chattering crowd, all eager to inspect the entries and make up their own minds which should be winners and losers.

"Your attention, please!"

The Ladies' Guild Secretary, Penelope, had commandeered the microphone, which squeaked into action.

"Silence, please, for our esteemed chairman of the St Stephen's Ladies' Guild, Lady Romily, who is ready to announce the first winners of the day."

A sense of inadequacy swept over Neil as he listened to Lady Romily speaking for some minutes about the qualities of the perfect sponge and fruit cake with the precision of a nuclear scientist. It was a master class in baking after which he was left in no doubt that she was an expert on the subject. Her first announcement of the winner of the Victoria Sponge competition was greeted with approval all round because, as usual, Beryl took the honours on sheer merit rather than any form of favouritism. It was also no surprise when Mary Morris won the rosette for best Rich Fruit Cake, because she reckoned she'd had about seventy years' experience at making and icing them. In her case, it was generally agreed that practice made absolutely perfect!

"And now," announced Lady Romily, "I would like to introduce the Reverend Neil Fisher, who's had the onerous responsibility of selecting the Best in Show winner. Reverend Fisher!"

As Neil climbed the stairs at the side of the stage, he thought again of the choice he was about to announce. Was he certain he'd got it right? Yes, he decided. Of all the plates on show that afternoon, this was definitely the one he'd fight to grab. Tapping the microphone to be sure it was still working, Neil cleared his throat to make his announcement.

"Ladies and gentlemen, the winner of the Best in Show prize has come up with an absolute favourite of mine, which makes my mouth water just to think of it. The baker is Stephanie Walters, and the winning entry is her plate of cornflake chocolate crispies!"

The silence in the hall was deafening. Suddenly uncertain, Neil stared down at the crowd as they turned to each other in a mixture of surprise and shock. Puzzled, Neil looked towards Lady Romily to see her expression darken to black anger.

"Cornflake chocolate crispies!" she spat at him under her breath. "Cornflake chocolate crispies that any half-witted five-year-old could make! You've chosen *that* as the Best in Show winner?"

As she spoke, a smattering of applause began when a young girl, probably little more than five herself, was guided up towards the stage by her obviously delighted mother. Penelope appeared at his side to hand him a silver cup and certificate, which he bent down to present to her, turning the little girl round to face the crowd as her proud father took their picture.

With the microphone still in his hand, Neil asked her to let the audience in on the secret of making her lovely cornflake chocolate crispies.

Her voice was surprisingly loud and clear as she replied. "Mummy helped me melt down the chocolate, then I stirred in the cornflakes, then put them in cases with Smarties on top."

"That's it?" asked Neil. "Nothing else?"

"That's it."

You're right that's it, thought Neil, as Lady Romily swept past him the moment the prize-giving was over, without even a backward glance in his direction. Feeling a barrage of disapproving looks heading his way from just about everyone in the hall, Neil slipped out to the side of the stage to keep a low profile behind the curtains. Minutes later, that's where Beryl found him.

"You said I was free to make my own choice!" he wailed. "I love cornflake chocolate crispies!"

"So do I," grinned Beryl. "Everyone does."

"She wanted me to pick something really complicated, didn't she? I should have chosen one of Lady Romily's winners. Why on earth didn't she make that clear?"

"Because it wasn't her place to say such a thing. She's full of her own importance, that one – and she really doesn't know much about baking at all."

"But she sounded so knowledgeable…"

"Neil, if you promise not to breathe a word about this to anyone, will you allow me to tell you a story?"

Intrigued, Neil nodded.

"Years ago, when I was quite new to baking, the Ladies' Guild organized a Bring and Buy cake sale, and I agreed to make something along with everyone else. Well, I was still working then, and with Jack and the kids to look after, time was tight. In the end, I knocked up a cake really quickly and baked it very late the night before. But you know what they say about more haste, less speed. The next morning when I came to ice it, the cake had sunk so much in the middle that there was just a big round dent in the top of it. I didn't know what to do, because I had to go to work that morning and didn't have time to make another one, so I came up with a plan. It still makes me go red to think of it all these years later. I turned the cake upside down, dug out the middle, and stuffed it with screwed-up sheets of kitchen roll. Then I turned it back up the right way, did a bit of fancy icing and decoration, put a ribbon round it – and called my daughter. The cake sale started at ten in the morning, so I made her promise that she would be first in the queue so that when the doors opened, she could whizz in, buy back the cake – and save my bacon!"

In spite of his misery, Neil was chuckling.

"So all was well?"

"My daughter rang me at quarter past ten to say she had been the first in, but the cake was nowhere to be seen! She didn't want to draw attention to the fact I'd made it by asking anyone outright, but it had definitely disappeared."

"Well, if no one knew it was yours, you could just forget about it, couldn't you?"

"That's what I thought – until the next day, which happened to be our Ladies' Guild Annual Charter Lunch, organized by…"

"Don't tell me – Lady Romily?"

"Right! It was a three-line whip that we all had to go, and to be fair it was always a really lovely occasion. She got caterers in to serve up a wonderful spread. The moment I walked into the room, though, I saw it. My cake was the centrepiece!"

"What on earth did you do?"

"Well, one moment I thought I should own up, and the next I just wanted to say I had a headache and get away from there as soon as I could. In the end, though, my conscience started to prick me. Suppose Lady Romily was publicly embarrassed when the cake was cut? I knew I just had to find a chance to own up. I was terrified, I can tell you."

"She has that effect on me too."

"So I was just thinking about making my way over to see if I could have a quiet word with her, when suddenly one of the ladies over in the other corner called out across the room to her so that everyone could hear. She said that the cake looked absolutely beautiful, and asked who'd made it."

"Oh no! What did you do?"

"I had to own up, didn't I? And I was just trying to work out what on earth I was going to say when, cool as cucumber, Lady Romily stood up and announced that *she'd* made it herself!"

Neil gasped in disbelief.

"So," said Beryl with a satisfied smile, "I sat right back down again and thought, *There is a God!*"

⇒ Chapter 7 ⇐

By the beginning of Advent, it seemed as if the shops had been full of Christmas tinsel and gift suggestions for weeks, but for the people of Dunbridge, the highlight of early December was the switching on of the market square lights. In spite of an icy chill in the air, several hundred of them turned out to see the captain of the local football team do the honours and announce that the travelling fairground was open for business. Neil hadn't particularly intended to be there for the occasion, but he had arranged to join Graham earlier in the evening for a pint in the Wheatsheaf. When they heard the speeches ringing out over the loudspeakers, they wandered out with their pints in time to see the square become a twinkling fairyland as thousands of white bulbs sprang to life.

"Did I tell you Debs and I have decided to get our own place?" asked Graham, emptying his glass.

"You're not planning to stay in your house after all?"

"Debs says it's a bachelor pad. She's not impressed with my motorbike in bits in the back room…"

"No, I can understand that."

"And she says she's offended because I've had other girlfriends while I've lived there."

"Well, that's fair enough too. Where are you planning to live?"

"That new estate going up where the old mental hospital used to be – have you looked around it at all? Those places were awful; hundreds of patients kept there sometimes for years, often for no good reason. It's not surprising they closed it down years ago, but it's getting a new lease of life now. They're making a good job of keeping the old style of the building even though a brand new estate is going up around it. Debs has got her eye on a terraced house she thinks will suit us."

"And you're quite happy about that?"

"Hmm, I reckon so."

"Thinking of getting married, then?" Neil added with a twinkle in his eye.

"Debs may be. I'm not."

"Because…?"

"Because I don't believe in marriage. I don't think you need a bit of paper and a ring on her finger to know you're committed to each other."

"And Debs is happy to go along with that?"

"Don't know. I haven't asked her."

Neil finished his pint in silence.

"Another?" he asked at last.

"Just a half and a couple of packets of crisps, please. Debs is trying to put me on a diet, for heaven's sake. She's got this new cookbook where she measures everything out to make sure I don't have a calorie over what it says I should have."

"Hence the crisps?"

"And the bacon butty from the van just down the road from the school in the morning, not to mention the sandwich and biscuits I have in the staff room at lunchtime."

"Not doing well with the diet, then?"

"I'm not on a diet at all. I just haven't told her."

Neil laughed, and went to fetch the drinks.

"You eating at the Wheatsheaf tonight?" asked Graham when he had returned.

"Honestly, I'd love to, but my mum is still staying with me. Four weeks now, and there's no sign of her leaving."

"Nagging you to death, is she?"

"To hear her, you'd think there's nothing about me at all that she likes. It's wearing me down."

"Is she still going on about you being home at the exact time she puts dinner on the table?"

"In my job? I keep telling her that's just not possible, but I get it in the neck every time."

Graham glanced at his watch.

"Well, you'll be in trouble tonight. It's gone nine."

"She's out! She's gone with Harry to a bridge tournament, so she's left a casserole in the oven – with butter beans…"

Graham looked at him quizzically.

"I hate butter beans. I've always hated butter beans, but they're her favourite, so they go in just about every meal."

"Nice not to have to cook for yourself, though."

"Yes, there is that."

The two men fell silent for a while as a rather noisy rock version of "Hark the Herald Angels Sing" drifted towards them from the fairground in the square.

"Busy time of year for you, eh?"

Neil almost spluttered into his beer. "You could say that. It's great, though. I love seeing the church used by the whole community. We've got seven extra carol services this week. All the schools, of course. Yours is on Friday week, isn't it? Local businesses too."

"Sick of singing carols yet?"

"No, honestly, I like them!"

"That's more than I can say. Ask any school teacher. We start getting geared up for Christmas somewhere around September, what with rehearsals for end-of-term productions, the Christmas fayre and trips out. Anyone would think we've not got anything else to think about – like national exams, for example."

"Bah, Humbug!" laughed Neil. "I bet you like the mince pies, though."

"Oh, yeah!" Graham's eyes lit up.

"If only you weren't on a diet…"

"Oh, yeah," agreed Graham glumly, downing his half. "Better get off then. She'll have my lettuce-leaf salad ready. See you, Neil!"

Neil stayed in the square for a while to chat to several parishioners who were there with their families. Half an hour later he was thinking about getting home to have a hot shower, a cup of tea and a plate of his mum's casserole in front of the telly, when he felt his mobile phone buzz in his back pocket. For a few seconds, the music from the fairground made it difficult for him to hear the voice at the other end, but when he did, his blood ran cold.

"Neil," said Margaret, her voice strange and choked, "I'm glad I caught you. I just wanted to warn you before you come in tomorrow morning. Cyn Clarkson called just now. Baby Ellen died at home an hour ago."

And in the middle of the square, with its cheerful flickering lights and loud Christmas music, Neil slumped against a wall, bowed his head and wept.

* * *

With Christmas looming, the date for Ellen's funeral was arranged very quickly. Margaret spent a lot of time with the family during the days that preceded the service. The Clarkson clan were well known and much loved locally, and an air of sadness permeated the whole St Stephen's community. The church was busy, as schools, clubs, charitable organizations and business groups filed in day after day for their annual carol services. The congregation was surrounded by the trappings and tinsel of Christmas, but the sense of helplessness and frustration at the loss of such a longed-for and adored baby sent shockwaves into every heart.

Neil was at his desk in the church office on the day before the funeral when a quick knock on the door made him look up to see Claire standing in the hallway.

"You're busy. I won't disturb you."

"No, come on in. It's good to see you."

"I just wanted to drop off the key for the padlock on the back gate. I've been putting in some new bulbs under that red beech tree down in the corner of the churchyard – you know, where the Clarkson family plot is. They should be out by Easter."

"That's thoughtful. The family will like that."

"Neil? You look awful. Are you OK?"

With a sigh, he leaned back in his chair.

"It's been a hard week."

Claire came across to perch on the corner of his desk.

"I saw Cyn yesterday morning," she said quietly. "She's always seemed such a tough, larger-than-life person, you know, able to cope with anything that comes her way. But it was as if she'd shrunk, like a big weight had crushed not just her body but her spirit too."

"It has."

"How's Margaret coping? She and Frank have always been close to that family."

"You know Margaret. Sometimes it's hard to know exactly what she's feeling, because she just knuckles down and gets on with things."

"It's her job to provide pastoral care, though, isn't it? Is she good in situations like this?"

"I've often been with her when she's been talking to bereaved relatives. I admire her so much because she always knows just what to say, which line from the Bible to quote, what prayer is most appropriate. While I'm sitting there thinking I just want to put my arms round them and give them a hug, she keeps her cool – which is absolutely how it should be. It's at moments like that I realize I still have a lot to learn."

Claire reached out to cover his hand, and his fingers moved to entwine with hers.

"I'd give them a hug too."

He almost smiled.

"Yes, you would."

"Softies of the world unite!"

He said nothing for a while, gazing down at their joined hands before he spoke.

"Tell me, do you find yourself thinking about that night?"

A stillness settled around them as if, just for a moment, they were blanketed from the world beyond the office walls.

"Yes."

"So do I. More than I should."

"Was it just the worry about Harry? Was that what drew us together, because we were both scared of losing him?"

"Perhaps – but it felt like more than that."

"You were the first person I thought of when I found him," said Claire. "I knew if you were with me it'd be OK – I'd cope."

"I remember at the hospital looking down at you while you were sleeping." Neil stroked her hand as he spoke. "You were so exhausted, there was hardly any colour in your face, and I found myself thinking that, in spite of everything you were going through, I'd never seen anyone look lovelier. I wanted to lean down and kiss away those dark circles beneath your eyes, take away your worry, make things better…"

"You prayed." Her voice was soft. "I'd never prayed before. I'd never wanted to. But you drew me into your prayers, and it felt good, as if I was part of something that had the power to help. And it did…"

"Yes, thank God."

"I'm not there yet, Neil. The God thing. I can't get my head round it at all, but I do know that something very deep and wonderful happened that night – to Harry and to me…"

"The next morning – do you remember the word you used?"

"Love. I said I loved you. You said it too."

Neil drew a deep breath before he answered. "It *had* been an emotional rollercoaster of a night. It's easy to get swept along when your feelings are all over the place."

Gently and deliberately, Claire drew his hand up and pressed it to her lips, her eyes burning into his.

"I know what I felt. I said what I meant. And it wasn't just a spur-of-the-moment thing, because I still feel it now. I've never stopped."

"Claire…"

Suddenly he was on his feet, pulling her to him, clinging to her as their lips met in a passionate kiss of longing, waiting and loving. No words. No need, except for each other. The questions, the what-ifs, the reasons why they shouldn't, all fell away in their desperate, exciting, unwise, illogical, compelling, overwhelming, soaring need for one another. Their bodies, their separate souls were moulded into one, a single unit, whole and complete.

Sometime later they drew back, breathless and euphoric, staring at each other in glorious disbelief.

"I love you, Claire. I've never been more certain of anything in my life."

"I'm not what you need…"

"… but you're what I want…"

"… and I want you, so very much…"

The sound of the outside door banging brought them back to earth. Guiltily, they pulled away from each other as Frank walked in carrying a pile of carol sheets for the civic service at the end of the week. If he noticed their heightened colour and flustered expressions, he made no mention of it.

"Oh, Neil, just the man! Margaret was hoping you'd call in this afternoon. She wants to make sure everything's organized for tomorrow."

"Of course." Neil was surprised that his voice sounded so normal, bearing in mind that his life, his world, his whole being had just been turned upside down by the events of the last few minutes. "I can pop in after this."

"How are you, Frank?" asked Claire. "You're very close to Jeannie and Colin, aren't you? Their loss must have hit you hard too."

The mask of businesslike efficiency dropped from Frank's face.

"It's awful, Claire. Thank God they're such a strong and devoted family, always there for each other, particularly at times like this. Jeannie's wrecked, of course. She's not slept or eaten properly for weeks. Colin's different. He's trying to carry on as usual, keeping work going and everything, but now Ellen's gone, well, he's in pieces. It's dreadful to see lovely people suffer like this."

"And Margaret?" enquired Claire. "I know she's got a job to do, but this must be affecting her too. How is she?"

Frank shrugged. "You know my wife. Practical, stoic. She's just getting on with what needs to be done."

"I admire her for that," commented Neil. "Envy her, really. Every time I think of that dear little girl, loved so much by that family who waited years for her, I find myself welling up. It's tragic."

"Margaret doesn't wear her heart on her sleeve, but she does feel things very deeply."

"Well, I'm anxious to help in any way I can. I'll go over to the vicarage now."

"Thanks, Neil."

"I must get on too," added Claire, catching Neil's eye. "Harry and I would like to come to the funeral tomorrow, Frank. That will be all right, won't it? It's not just for family?"

"Anyone involved with St Stephen's *is* family as far as the Clarksons are concerned. Of course you must come. It'll be good for them to know how much they're loved and supported."

"I'll ring you…" called Neil as Claire headed for the door. With a nod of mutual understanding, she disappeared from view.

* * *

"I am the resurrection and the life," says the Lord. "Those who believe in me, even though they die, will live, and everyone who lives and believes in me will never die."

As she spoke the ancient words, Margaret led the sombre procession down the central aisle towards the front of the church. St Stephen's was packed: the congregation had turned out in full force to stand alongside the Clarksons in their grief. All eyes turned towards Colin and Jeannie as they came behind Margaret, carrying between them the small white coffin that contained the body of their beloved daughter, Ellen. Neil followed next, leading the way as Cyn, her husband Jim and their other sons Barry and Carl with their wives and children silently found a place in the front three rows. From there they could watch the tiny box being placed lovingly on the stand in front of the pulpit.

Jeannie had chosen the opening hymn herself, a Charles Wesley favourite from her own childhood, which she had slightly reworded with her little daughter in mind:

> *Gentle Jesus, meek and mild,*
> *Look upon this little child.*
> *Pity her simplicity,*
> *Suffer her to come to thee.*
>
> *Fain she would to thee be brought,*
> *Dearest God, forbid it not;*
> *Give her, dearest God, a place*
> *In the kingdom of thy grace.*

The sound was thin and ragged in spite of the presence of the choir and the large congregation. No one had the heart for singing, especially not such poignant words on an occasion as sad as this.

Hand in hand, Jim and Cyn made their way up to the pulpit to read from the Bible about how Christ himself had said, "Suffer the little children to come unto me." Jim did the reading, clutching the hand of his wife, who simply let the tears slide down her cheeks as she stood beside him, her head held high. The church was hushed in unnatural silence as the congregation sat, some staring ahead, some with their heads bowed, dabbing their eyes and noses as they listened.

Most moving of all was the moment when Ellen's father, Colin, walked stiffly up to the pulpit and laid out the sheet of paper on which he'd written the words he wanted so much to read without breaking down. He nearly didn't make it. Several times he stopped mid-sentence, gulping for breath as every person in the church tearfully willed him to find the strength to carry on. As he came to the end, he turned towards the coffin.

"Goodbye, little one. We made you. We cherished you. We adored you. We worried for you. We hurt with you. We will love you always. God alone knows why you had to suffer so much, but he has taken you home again and we know you are with him now. Ask God to bless your mummy. She loves and misses you with all her heart. So do I. We all do…"

And the tall, strong man crumpled with grief as he stepped down from the pulpit and walked across to lay his hand on the white coffin. Cyn's arm went around Jeannie's waist as Colin allowed his father, Jim, to lead him back to his seat.

Margaret took over then, drawing raw emotions together in a series of prayers for Ellen, each member of her family, all who knew and loved her – and finally for anyone in the church who might be feeling their own grief at that time. After several minutes of silent, personal prayer in which quiet sobs could be heard around the church, Wendy's clear, sweet soprano voice rang out as she started the sad, soft anthem with which the choir brought the service to a close. Asking for God's blessing on them all, Margaret then suggested that the majority of the mourners might like to make their way over to the church hall while just close family and friends walked to the Clarkson family plot in the graveyard. There Ellen would be laid to rest alongside generations of her family who had gone before her.

As Neil stood at the back of the family group, watching the tiny coffin disappear into the ground beneath the red beech tree, he found himself thinking about his father. He remembered the times the two of them had wandered among old gravestones, reading the names and dates, trying to imagine what had brought these people to their final resting place. They had often commented on the number of very young children who'd died in years gone by, but Neil realized that until that day, until that moment when Ellen's body finally disappeared forever, he'd never truly recognized the bleak despair that had probably marked the loss of every single child.

The sky darkened as a cloud of drizzle soaked them through, but no one was anxious to leave. They just stood there, looking towards Ellen's final resting place, hearts heavy, heads bowed.

* * *

The wake in the church hall after Ellen's funeral was surprisingly lively and warm-hearted, as if the sadness of the service had to be replaced by hugs and smiles that somehow represented the pleasure Ellen had brought to them all during her short life. Old friends of the Clarkson family had come from far and wide, some of them former members of the Dunbridge community, and over the sumptuous buffet lovingly provided by Beryl and her team, many neighbours got reacquainted as memories were shared.

At one point, Neil turned to see Wendy standing alone just a few yards away from him. He knew that Colin and Jeannie were special friends of hers, so, after a moment's hesitation, he went across to stand by her side.

"You sang beautifully today."

"Thank you. It wasn't easy."

"I'm sure it wasn't, but you sounded wonderful."

"I can't believe she's gone. I keep thinking about how excited Jeannie and Colin were when they knew she was finally on her way, after all those years they'd waited. Three attempts at IVF, that's what they went through. Lesser couples would have been crushed by that, but those two just grew closer than ever."

Wendy drew a white hankie out of her jacket pocket.

"Sorry. I'm OK really. I've just got to stop thinking about it."

Neil reached out to touch her shoulder.

"No, you haven't. There's no time limit on grief. You just have to let it take its course."

To his surprise, Wendy moved forward to lean against him, resting her head on his shoulder as if she were a small child. For a moment he stiffened, embarrassed at her closeness, but then he gave in to his instinct to close his arms around her, wanting to give her comfort and strength. Her whole body sagged as she relaxed into his embrace, sobbing quietly – and the two of them stood with their arms around each other as they had so often in the past.

"I'd forgotten how good this feels." Her voice was muffled and wretched, almost a whisper, as she spoke. "I've missed you, Neil."

An image of Claire crept into Neil's mind and he was uncertain of what to say. Fortunately the need to respond was removed as Wendy's mother, Sylvia, noticing her daughter's distress, called over to her. With a wan smile, Wendy allowed herself to be drawn away.

"I've got some news for you."

Neil turned to find one of the churchwardens, Peter, standing beside him.

"Hello, Peter. A sad occasion today."

"Very," agreed Peter, "and this is probably not the best of times to say this, but I just need to tell someone! My decree nisi papers came through this morning. In six weeks' time my marriage to Glenda will be over, completely and absolutely!"

"I'm glad for you, Peter. Six weeks, eh? That's around the end of January."

"And Val and I have something to ask you. We'd like to book ourselves in to get married – in April, perhaps, just after Easter?"

Neil couldn't help but return Peter's delighted grin.

"I'm sure that can be arranged. Have you spoken to Margaret yet?"

"She knows what we're planning, but I haven't had chance to tell her about the timing, what with everything going on today. Val and I need to book a proper chat with her, because it's important to us that we actually marry in church, and that all our vows are made in St Stephen's, which is our spiritual home. We don't just want a blessing. That wouldn't feel right for us."

"No, I can see that. Of course, it's always an issue when there's been a divorce, but the decision to allow a full marriage service is at the discretion of the minister. I know Margaret feels that decision must be based on the Christian understanding and commitment of the people involved. I'm sure she'll be glad to help – and if she won't, I will!"

"Thanks, Neil."

Much later that afternoon, after the buffet had disappeared and the crowd dwindled away, Neil and Margaret arrived back in the church office at the same time. Margaret looked tired.

"I'll put them away for you," offered Neil, taking a stack of papers out of her arms. "You're all in. Not surprising after all that's happened today."

Margaret sat down heavily on the seat by her desk.

"It was a tough one. It's never easy when you know the family involved, when they're your friends."

"You led the service with great sensitivity today. I couldn't have done that."

She looked at him steadily.

"Not yet, perhaps, but in time you will. You're still learning your trade – but you'll find that when it comes to helping families through their grief, and trying to make sense of it all for them, you learn what you need to know."

"Really? I mean, I know what you're saying. There's so much in Christ's teaching to reassure us of life after death, and God's comfort and constant love. But surely every loss is different, so everyone's grief must be different too."

"That's when you have to be firm, Neil. In life there is death. That's the pattern of things. But as Christians we don't fear death, because Christ promised us that he's gone to prepare a place for each one of us in heaven. People need to know that. In grief, more than ever before, they have to be reminded that whatever they feel now, this is God's will, and that God is with them in their loss. They need to hear the gospel, remember Christ's promise and recognize God's constancy and love."

Neil pictured the bleak despair he'd seen in Jeannie and Colin earlier that day, and wondered whether, in spite of their lifelong Christian faith, that thought was cold comfort to them as they lowered their baby daughter's body into the ground.

"You don't doubt that, do you, Neil? It's the heart of what we believe. Our lives are God's will, our death too. We live. We die. And throughout it all, Christ walks with us on earth, and in everlasting life after death."

Neil felt suddenly very weary. It had been a long day. Tidying a few papers on his desk, he turned to grab his coat from the back of the chair.

"I understand what you're saying, but sometimes, like today, I want to shout at God for letting such a thing happen. And even if he did need to take Ellen back to be with him, why did she have to suffer so much? She was an innocent. She'd never done anything to harm a soul, and yet she lived in pain for the few weeks she had on earth. Where's the love in that? How can a loving Father let that happen?"

"Because he gives us free will, and Ellen's illness wasn't caused by God, but by human living. You know this, Neil. You must know it right at the heart of you – or you're in the wrong job."

He nodded.

"I'm just tired. I'll head off home. See you in the morning."

"It's the civic carol service in the afternoon. You'll need to be on the ball by then."

"OK. I'll be fine. Sleep well, Margaret."

And as Margaret stepped out in front of him, Neil switched off the lights before closing the door.

≫ CHAPTER 8 ≪

To Neil's surprise, his mother decided to head back to Bristol before Christmas. He had to admit she'd mellowed a bit over her six-week stay in Dunbridge: not towards him, of course, because she never let up on her tirade of criticism and correction of her only son, but certainly towards others, especially Harry, Claire and Sam. Iris had spent a lot of time with Harry, ostensibly to help him in his recovery, but Neil and Claire shared the view that somehow Harry's gentle company was helping in *her* recovery too. She smiled more. She nagged less. She even relaxed once in a while, which had Neil chuckling when, on several occasions, he caught her stretched out sound asleep on the lounge settee, her mouth wide open as she snored contentedly. So her sudden decision to return to Bristol was a surprise – and a double-edged sword of concern for Neil. On the one hand he was delighted to have his home back, but on the other he worried about what was actually going on in that complicated mind of hers.

"David is far from well," she announced when Neil dared to broach the subject. "He's my brother, the only living member of my immediate family apart from you. He needs me – which you don't, as you make abundantly clear at every opportunity."

"Well, if you're sure. You know Harry and everyone else at the church would be glad of your company over Christmas."

"Not you, though, Neil. It's plain I've outstayed my welcome."

Neil started to object.

"No, don't argue! I've made up my mind. You can take me to Paddington first thing in the morning."

And with that she went, leaving Neil's house at 96 Vicarage Gardens feeling oddly quiet and empty, although, to be fair, he was rarely at home. Pastoral visits to the local hospital and hospice, and to congregation members at home or in residential care, preparation for funerals, marriages and christenings, his weekly services at their nearby sister church of St Gabriel's, plus the organization of the weekly Evensong service using the traditional words of the Book of Common Prayer that had proved so popular with church members young and old – all this kept him very busy. And beyond work, he longed for the company of one person above any other: Claire.

The passion they'd rekindled before Ellen's funeral had stayed with them, and they tried to spend as much time together as possible, often late at night when Neil had finally finished work and both Harry and Sam were tucked up in bed. They had decided to keep their relationship discreet for the time being – partly because Claire was naturally a private person, but mostly because they both recalled how the eyes of the whole congregation had been incessantly on Neil as he and Wendy had got to know each other the previous year. Although Claire pointed out that the pastime of match-making among the older ladies of the St Stephen's community probably suited Wendy's purpose very well, she recognized that it had left Neil feeling exposed, vulnerable and pushed into decisions he simply wasn't ready to make at the time.

Harry knew of the growing closeness between his two favourite young people, of course. He said nothing, but the twinkle in his eye betrayed his understanding and delight. As for Sam, with the simple logic of a six-year-old, he treated Neil as if he were just another member of his family, there to tell stories, play card games, read books and listen to his chatter without any sign of boredom. No question. No problem.

Being the only child of a dominating mother like Iris, who had deliberately sent her beloved son to an all boys school because she thought it would toughen him up for whatever manly career he chose in adulthood, Neil knew he'd had woefully little experience of being comfortable in the presence of women. It wasn't that he didn't like them, or even that they didn't feel drawn to him, but his clumsy shyness in social situations, especially in his younger years, had made him doubt that any woman would look at him twice.

"Perhaps that's why Wendy swept me off my feet?" he confided to Claire one evening.

Claire shook her head. "I've known her a long time; enough to know that what Wendy wants, Wendy gets. She's grown up in a Christian community. Her whole family spend just about all their time and energy in developing the music and worship at St Stephen's. It's only natural that the idea of being a vicar's wife would appeal to her. You fitted the bill perfectly. No wonder she made a beeline for you."

He grinned sheepishly. "So it wasn't just that I was devilishly attractive and she couldn't resist me?"

"More like wet behind the ears! You didn't stand a chance once Wendy spotted you."

He pulled Claire to him. "Good job you rescued me, then!" And the next few minutes were happily filled with the pleasure of being in each other's arms.

However, their decision to keep their exciting new relationship to themselves for the time being meant that they both had to watch their words when they were in the company of others who knew them well. Neil became acutely aware of that when he met up with Graham for a quick game of darts one icy January evening. From the start, it didn't take long to see that Graham was in the mood for celebration.

"We've got the house! The sales team for the new estate moves like greased lightning, as my mum would say. We get the keys for number 32 Snowdrop Close this coming Saturday!"

"So soon? Has Debs got you organized? Are you all packed up?"

Graham guffawed at the very thought. "Not a thing! I'm still trying to work out what to do with the motorbike in the back room."

"She won't let you keep it in the *new* back room then?"

"She won't even let me have it in the garage. Debs has got some quaint idea that the *car* should be in there!"

"Huh, how unreasonable!"

"Exactly, which is why I'm on the scrounge. Is there any chance I can put the bike in your garage – just for a while, you know, while I work out where else I could put it?"

"I don't see why not, as long as you remember I'm only a curate for three years, and I'm halfway through that already. I'm definitely not keeping it, before you even ask."

"Neil, mate, you're a pal! Can you come and help me move it on Friday night?"

"I should think so."

"And what are you doing on Saturday fortnight? The second weekend in February?"

Neil's mind was racing as he tried to remember what was in the diary for that weekend.

"Can you come over to help us move? Bring your car, any cardboard boxes you've got, and every ounce of energy you possess."

"I'll need to check, but I think that should be OK – as long as you've finished by Sunday morning! I'll be taking Morning Prayers at eight."

"Debs and I will be tucked up in our new home then, thanks to great friends like you – and Wendy! She's helping Debs pack up her stuff at her mum's house, then the plan is that the four of us go out for a pizza when we've finished."

"Right," said Neil, trying to think on his feet. "I'm sure I'll be able to lend a hand during the day, but the evening might be more difficult."

"Why? You've just said you're not busy until the next morning."

"Yes – but, er …" Neil struggled to find the right words. "It's just probably best if I don't come out with you all that night."

"Why ever not? Come on, Neil, spit it out! You're being very mysterious!"

"Um, well, it's just Wendy being there. Won't her partner expect to be with her too?"

"Long gone, so Debs tells me. You don't need to worry about him. Anyway, you said you're over Wendy, so what's your problem?"

"I have a feeling the problem might be more hers than mine. I'm certainly over her, but I'm just not sure *she* is actually over *me*."

Graham lowered the hand in which his dart was poised for a bull's eye while he considered that.

"She does ask about you quite a lot, and she doesn't talk about that other chap at all, so you might be right. I must admit I did wonder that night at the barn dance if he was just there to make you jealous. So maybe she is still keen on you. I'll ask Debs. She'll know."

"No! Please don't say a word to Debs. I think it would be better, though, if I just turn up to help with your move during the day, but don't do the social thing in the evening."

"But you'll be tired and hungry, and Debs and I will want to thank you for helping out. If you're not interested in Wendy, just be polite, sit on your hands and don't join in if she jumps on you for a snog!"

Neil groaned, knowing that Graham could hardly be blamed for his lack of understanding when no one had any idea about his feelings for Claire.

Something in Neil's expression must have changed at the thought of Claire, because he looked up to find Graham studying him with curiosity.

"You've got someone, haven't you?"

Neil had never been able to lie without going red to the earlobes, so he didn't even try on this occasion.

"There is a girl I'm fond of, yes."

"Who?"

"I'd rather not say. It's early days…"

"Does Wendy know her?"

"Yes."

"And she's got no idea that the love of her life, her future vicar husband, is getting up close and personal with another woman – one she actually *knows*?"

"Please don't say anything, Graham! We're deliberately keeping quiet about things for a while because of this exact situation. Everyone felt they had the right to an opinion when Wendy and I were together and, in the end, it was probably that as much as anything else that pushed us apart."

"Well, yes – and the fact that, delightful as Wendy is, she can be a pushy little madam."

"Not at all. She's a wonderful person, and I'll never be able to thank her enough for her kindness to me, but…"

"But now you've met the real Miss Right, the spectre of Wendy glowering at the two of you from the sidelines might be less than helpful."

"Exactly."

"But what am I going to say to Debs when you back off the moment Wendy comes anywhere near you on our moving day? She's sure to smell a rat!"

"I'll come up with a decent and truthful reason why I need to leave. I know! I have to prepare my sermon for St Gabriel's on Sunday!"

"Look, Neil, can't I just explain to Debs? She might be able to soften the blow for Wendy – you know, tell her what a lucky escape she's had in getting rid of you!"

"I'd rather Wendy knew nothing, for the time being at least."

Graham was suddenly serious. "I can't lie to Debs, mate. I don't want to."

"Of course not. But please, just say nothing. Let me make my own tactful excuse for having to leave."

Graham sighed heavily. "But you are still up for helping?"

"Definitely!"

"Friday night for the bike, and at my house first thing on Saturday morning?"

"I promise!"

"And will you also promise that I'll be the first to know the secret identity of your mystery woman?"

Neil grinned. "Maybe."

"Fine friend you are!" Graham was smiling too as he glanced down at his watch. "We're just going to have to agree

I won this darts match. I was thrashing you, of course, but after all this talking I've run out of time. Piles of marking to do. I hate teaching maths. Correction. I hate the kids I teach maths to, horrible little tykes!"

And as Neil watched his friend grab his coat and disappear with a wave, a twinge of foreboding sent a cold chill down his spine.

* * *

"That's all settled then," said Margaret, putting the lid back on her fountain pen. "You two will be married here at St Stephen's on April 15th at two thirty in the afternoon."

Peter and Val beamed at each other as they sat holding hands on the lumpy old settee in the vicarage sitting room, where Margaret usually met engaged couples as they made their wedding plans.

"What a happy occasion it'll be!" continued Margaret. "Not that the end of a marriage is ever a cause for celebration, but under the circumstances, Peter, as Glenda was the one who chose to break her wedding vows by going off with another man, you have behaved very properly."

"I feel as if I've lived under a yoke of unhappiness for many years," replied Peter, turning to gaze tenderly in Val's direction. "This wonderful woman's changed all that. Thank God for second chances. I can't wait for Val to be my wife."

As if no one else were in the room, Val leaned forward to plant a loving kiss on his willing lips.

"Just a moment, you two! There'll be time enough for that once you're married. Now, Peter, I can leave the music choice to the two of you, can I? You'll talk to Brian and Sylvia about hymns and anything you'd like the choir to contribute?"

"Certainly. And although you'll be taking the service, I'd like Neil to read the lesson, if that's all right with you. He's been a great friend through this."

"Then I'll leave you to ask him about that too. Right then, you lovebirds, off you go! Frank's got my lunch waiting in the kitchen."

* * *

Just as Frank and Margaret were tucking into crusty rolls stuffed with ham and salad in the vicarage, Neil was pulling up outside the Mayflower, a large residential care home run by a Christian organization. It was a fairly new development which had opened in stages over the previous two years. Residents who were able-bodied enough to have their own bed-sitting room with cooking and bathroom facilities were well settled in the largest wing, while those who were so frail that they needed twenty-four-hour nursing care had recently moved into the brand new block. There were also several rooms specially designed for the needs of patients suffering from dementia.

Over his months of visiting the Mayflower, Neil had come to look forward to meeting up with several residents he'd become very fond of. They were the Gaiety Girls, as they called themselves – four lively eighty-year-olds who were all game for a spot of "Knees Up, Mother Brown" whenever Tom, the only gentleman resident under the age of seventy, struck up the tune on the ancient piano kept in the far corner of the recreation room. Nothing pleased them more than a sing-song of everything from the Beatles to "songs from the shows", and over time the care staff had come to realize that if the noise became a bit too raucous for other quieter residents, the only way to stop the Gaiety Girls was to announce a session of Bingo in the front room, and they'd be off in a flash, leaving Tom to wonder where everyone had gone!

The Girls loved Neil. They mothered and smothered him. They hugged and fussed over him. They wanted to know all about what was happening at St Stephen's in particular and the town of Dunbridge in general. They were also the first to take their seats in the sitting room for the short Eucharist service that Neil led for the thirty or so residents who usually came along. Afterwards, accompanied by one of the nursing staff, Neil would wander along the corridors, popping in to say hello to residents who had not been able to come to the service themselves. He would sit beside them, chatting about everything from the weather and the menu at lunchtime to their worries about money, family and illness. Finally, he would take their hands and pray with them, offering them Communion if that was their choice.

He found the whole experience humbling and immensely moving. So many of the people he met there were stiff and racked with pain, often unable to walk or even get out of bed without help, and yet he'd learned to look beyond the frail body and muddled mind to glimpse the person they had been before illness and old age had claimed their health and contentment. Sometimes they would keep him for a longer chat, often astonishing Neil with tales of their youth or working life, and he would send up a silent prayer for them, knowing that there was a little of God in each and every one of them.

Two hours later, he was ready for the cup of tea that was always on offer in Matron's room. Shirley McCann came across as a no-nonsense, frighteningly efficient boss, especially when it came to the high standards she demanded of her staff, but it didn't take long in her company to see her softer side. She always made time for a soothing word to a troubled resident, or compassionate reassurance for worried family members.

That day, Shirley was plainly not alone: the sound of delighted laughter drifted out of her office as Neil came round the corner.

"Oh Neil, come and hear this!" Shirley giggled as he walked into the room. "Sylvie, tell him what happened!"

As Sylvie was a regular worshipper at St Stephen's, Neil knew her well, so he sat down in a high-backed chair and took the cup of tea Shirley handed to him.

"You know Joe in Room 8 up on the first floor? Sweet man, not all that old really – he's only seventy-five, isn't he, Shirley?"

Neil nodded. "The Geordie? Lovely chap. Great friends with little Irish Mary?"

"That's the one – and, of course, you know Mary too! Do you remember they arrived at the Mayflower on the same day and practically fell over each other on the front door mat? Well, you probably don't – but they struck up a friendship on that day and it's just gone from strength to strength. They're always together. You rarely see one without the other."

"So are they OK?" asked Neil, sipping his tea.

"Couldn't be better! In fact, yesterday was a bit of a red-letter day for them, because Joe finally plucked up courage to ask Mary to marry him!"

"My goodness! What did she say?"

Sylvie's expression softened. "It was really sweet. He got down on one knee and everything – and she said yes!"

"That's wonderful!"

"It really was. We broke open a bottle of Asti Spumante and they spent the whole afternoon making plans for their life together. It was very romantic!"

"So when's the happy day? Can I do the honours?"

"Well, the whole idea nearly came a cropper because when the bell was rung as usual to warn everyone that tea would be served in half an hour, Joe and Mary went back to their own rooms to freshen up before their meal, and that was when the doubts set in! Once he'd got behind his own door, Joe realized that although he could clearly remember asking Mary to marry him, he couldn't quite recall if she had actually said yes!"

"Heavens, what did he do?" asked Neil, his tea completely forgotten as the story unfolded.

"Well," said Sylvie, thoroughly enjoying her role as storyteller, "he couldn't stand the suspense a moment longer, so he headed off down the corridor to knock on Mary's door – and that was where I saw him. I heard everything. He blurted out to her that he was worried she hadn't actually given him a reply to his proposal, and Mary just burst out laughing. She threw her arms round his neck and said she was really glad he'd come, because she knew she'd said yes to someone – but couldn't remember who!"

* * *

Debs was a police officer. She was used to getting information out of people. Why hadn't he remembered that? Graham realized he was in trouble the moment he started telling her that Neil had volunteered to come and help him move the following Saturday. She said how nice that would be, because Wendy would really love it if the four of them went out for a pizza once the work was finished "just like old times". That was when Graham's expression must have changed enough for her to go into her "interrogating officer" mode.

"What are you not telling me?"

"Nothing. Neil won't be able to stay for the evening because he's busy."

"Doing what?"

"How should I know? Sunday's always busy for him. He's a vicar."

"This is Saturday."

"He's got to get ready for Sunday."

"That's never stopped him going out on a Saturday night before."

"Well, he's not coming for the pizza. That's it."

"Because he doesn't want to? Neil's always starving. Why wouldn't he want to go out for a pizza?"

Debs looked thoughtful as Graham tried to dig himself out of the hole he'd talked himself into.

"It's not that he doesn't want pizza. He just doesn't want pizza…"

"… with us!" finished Debs, a note of triumph in her voice. "Or, more precisely, with Wendy. Am I right?"

"Look, don't say anything to Wendy. He just feels it would be better if they weren't thrown together that way."

"Better for whom? Wendy would love to see him. She's got high hopes of them getting back together. Wouldn't that be a nice relaxing way for them to feel comfortable with each other again?"

Graham sighed. "That's not going to happen, Debs."

"Why not?" Debs's voice was sharp. "How can you be so sure?"

"Because he's got someone else!"

There! He'd said it – and instantly regretted his promise to Neil to keep that information to himself. Neil didn't know Debs. She could be terrifying!

"Who?"

"I don't know."

"Graham!"

"I don't know, I really don't – but I think it's all quite new because he's just taking things gently. They're not making it public for the time being, but he obviously feels very sensitive about the whole business."

"So he's really not interested at all in Wendy?"

"As a friend, yes, but nothing more."

"Well, Wendy's most certainly interested in him, although personally I think she needs her head examined!"

"Don't breathe a word about this to her, Debs, please. I promised Neil."

"She's my best friend. I'll have to ring her. She needs to know."

"Debs, please!"

Debs moved closer to Graham and took his hand in hers.

"Graham, I know you promised, but if it was me rather than Wendy, I'd want to know. I just don't want her to end up hurt because she's not emotionally prepared for the man she loves turning up with another woman on his arm."

"But she broke off with him!"

"Yes, but she didn't mean it! She was just teaching him a lesson. She's perfect for Neil. Anyone can see that. He's just too thick to work it out for himself."

Graham knew it was no use. There was no stopping her. He groaned loudly and buried his face in his hands.

* * *

After their meeting with Margaret, Val and Peter were feeling the need to celebrate, so they went for an early evening meal at their favourite country pub. Between courses they scribbled lists in Peter's notebook about guests for the wedding, possible venues for the reception, thoughts on the menu and colour schemes. They touched and giggled and gazed and held hands as they savoured the thought that they would finally become man and wife. They talked about where they would live, as their plan was to sell both their houses and move into a new home together. Val had already spotted a bungalow she wanted Peter to see later that week. They faced a future full of promise, excitement and contentment, and they couldn't be happier at the prospect.

Val was due to be on duty very early the next morning, so it was just after nine when Peter reluctantly dropped her off at her door with a lingering kiss that left them both longing for more. Throughout the five-minute car journey between her house and his, Peter's thoughts were full of love for the wonderful woman who was about to share his life. He realized now that he couldn't really remember ever being happy throughout the thirty long years he'd been married to Glenda, and by going off with her boss she had made it very clear that she too had been far from content. Glenda had reached out for her own happiness. Now it was his turn.

As he turned the car into his drive, he realized he must have left the light on in the lounge. He couldn't remember ever doing that before. Love must be sending him a little bit mad…

He turned the key in the lock and walked into the hall, not taking in at first what he was seeing: a mountain of boxes and cases piled up in front of the stairs. And just as, with horror, he began to recognize a few of the items strewn on the floor in front of him, he looked up to see a figure standing in the lounge doorway.

"I'm back," said Glenda. "This is my house every bit as much as it's yours. And may I remind you, husband dear, that we are still married."

"But Glenda, I don't understand…"

"It's over between me and Roland. What a worm that man turned out to be! I'm back, Peter – so you'd better take my cases upstairs and make me a welcome cup of tea!"

CHAPTER 9

"How's it going, Neil? Are you managing to get a word in edgeways with the terrifying Margaret as your rector?"

Balancing a cup and saucer in one hand and a digestive biscuit in the other, Neil turned to find Bishop Paul at his side.

"Yes, thank you, sir, I'm fine."

"Paul, please. Call me Paul."

"Paul," agreed Neil uncomfortably as he looked for a space to put his cup down. "Yes, it's going well. Margaret is a great help, very encouraging."

"I knew when we appointed her that she would be like a dose of salts for Dunbridge. The work there got a bit stale – Victor had been rector at St Stephen's for over two decades by the time he retired. The congregation was certainly dwindling before Margaret took charge."

"It's an interesting community," agreed Neil.

"And how do you find these archdeaconry get-togethers? It must be good to see your fellow students from theological college now you're all established in your roles as curate?"

Neil looked around at the company in the room with its mixture of familiar and new faces.

"We're all in such different parishes. Rob over there is

probably the one I know best, but he's in a busy inner-city church. It couldn't be more different from the rural community I've become part of in Dunbridge."

"Any regrets?"

Neil considered the question for a few seconds before answering. "Not really. Rob's naturally more confident than me. Large congregations and inner-city problems suit him."

"In my experience, it's no good going to a small town if all you want is a quiet life," replied Bishop Paul. "In fact, a small community often means that you get more involved in the lives of not just your congregation, but your neighbours who may never dream of coming to church."

"That's true," agreed Neil. "You may not approve, but I enjoy a pint of real ale now and again, so I make a point of popping into different pubs around the town just to talk to whoever I meet there."

"Do you wear your dog collar?"

"Usually, yes."

"What effect does that have?"

"A good one, on the whole. People come up and talk to me about their marriage break-ups, their money problems – and once in a while, their tussle with faith."

"Outreach and evangelism at its best," laughed Bishop Paul. "I thoroughly approve."

"I'm not sure some of the more formidable ladies of our congregation do. They're praying for my soul!"

"Well, that's a bonus!"

"I know. Honestly, I need all the prayer I can get…"

"Knees still knocking at times?"

"Definitely."

"Mouth dry before you start a sermon?"

Neil nodded.

"Terrified you're going to lose important papers, baptize a baby with the wrong name or forget to turn up to an important meeting that you actually organized yourself?"

"Yes! Who's been talking?"

"All of us. Every minister in the land has known that feeling at some time or other. The job's so complex. Being a spiritual guide is sometimes the least of your concerns among all the other jobs that need to be got through from morning to night every day of the week. You sort out your timetable only to find that two funerals land on you, or you've got extra parishioners to go and see, and your carefully planned schedule goes out the window. You end up constantly exhausted, overworked and overwhelmed – but that's ministry!"

"And that's what I've signed up for. I don't mind the relentlessness of it, really I don't. I just worry whether I'm capable of doing it well enough. I hate the thought that I might let people down through my inexperience or lack of confidence."

"Well, from what I hear, your confidence is growing daily. In fact, I've been getting very good reports of you…"

"Really?"

"Really, and not just from the church community either. Be encouraged, Neil. You're still in your training period, *potty training* as they affectionately call it. This is exactly the time for you to be finding your feet, making your mistakes and discovering your own strengths."

Neil fell silent as he digested this.

"And, dear boy," said Bishop Paul with real kindness in his voice, "I'm always available if you need a chat. In confidence, so you don't need to worry that anything you say will go further, but please feel free to come and talk to me any time."

"Thank you, sir."

"Paul."

"Thank you, Bishop Paul. I appreciate that, I really do."

"More tea, Vicar?"

Looking down at the cold tea in the cup he'd abandoned at the start of their conversation, Neil nodded.

"Don't mind if I do!"

* * *

Peter was at the house when Neil got home. Since the shock of Glenda's reappearance two nights before, when he'd listened to her demands for less than five minutes before walking straight back out of the front door, Peter had taken up residence in Neil's back bedroom while he tried to get his mind round what was happening. It seemed he could think of nothing else because, without even acknowledging that Neil had been away for the whole day, Peter took up their conversation as if there'd been no interruption at all.

"I'm not giving in to her! In every practical sense we're divorced. It's only the decree absolute to come through now, so she can't do this. She just can't!"

"Have you tried talking to her today?"

"There's no talking to that woman. I've had years of her talking *at* me rather than *with* me."

"Would it help for me to come with you? I could be a sort of arbitrator…"

"Have you met Glenda? She's not interested in anyone else's opinion but her own."

Neil nodded in silent agreement, remembering how terrifying he'd always found Glenda's presence.

"How could she do this to me, just when I have the first chance of happiness in years?"

"Does she know you're planning to marry Val?"

"I've not told her. Until now, since the day she left, there's been no contact between us except through solicitors. Mind you, Christine has probably mentioned Val to her. I know Christine's been keeping in touch with her mother, which is only right."

"How have Christine and her brother reacted to the break-up of your marriage? I know they've been very supportive to you, but have they got some sympathy with their mum too?"

"John's furious with her. From what he said, he wants to have nothing more to do with her. That would be a shame, because he and Celia have two great boys who could end up never really knowing their grandmother, especially with them living way up in Scotland. Christine's trying to stay neutral, although when I spoke to her husband Mark last night, he said that she's hopping mad at her mother's behaviour. She's ringing me when she finishes teaching this evening. I have to say she's been wonderful about the whole thing."

"And Val? How is she taking the news?"

Peter's smile was wry. "You know Val, always calm, always kind, always more worried about others than herself. This has been a terrible shock for her, though – for both of us."

"And what does your solicitor say? Can Glenda stop the decree absolute going through?"

"Not unless both of us agree to it, and that's not going to happen – but Glenda knows me well enough to realize the legal route isn't the best way to get to me. She knows how committed I am to my faith. She knows I take the vows I made in church much more seriously than the bit of legal wording on our marriage certificate. She's clever enough to challenge me on spiritual grounds. I promised before God to love and cherish her *until death do us part*, and she's still very much alive. As if I could forget it!"

At that moment the phone rang. Without even considering that it was Neil's phone rather than his, Peter rushed into the hall to pick up the receiver. Obviously the call was for him because half an hour later, when Neil passed him on his way to the kitchen, Peter was still deep in conversation. Before long, his head appeared around the kitchen door.

"Neil! Were you serious about coming along with me when I talk to Glenda?"

"Of course, if you think it would help."

"And could you make tomorrow lunchtime?"

Neil's mind raced as he tried to picture his diary. In the end, there was little more important than supporting a dear friend and parishioner at a time of need like this.

"Of course," he replied. "At the house?"

"One o'clock?"

"Fine. I'll make sure I'm free."

And, a man with a mission, Peter ran upstairs to his room and shut the door.

* * *

"Brought reinforcements, have you?" Glenda stepped back to open the front door so that Neil and Peter could enter. "Welcome to my home, Neil. I'd offer you a cup of tea, but Peter hasn't bought any milk."

"This isn't a social call, Glenda," said Peter stiffly, "and Neil is here simply as an observer. We need to talk."

"Nothing to talk about," said Glenda, leading the way into the lounge, where she sat down in the most comfortable chair. "Peter is my husband. This is *our* home. It has been for years. I've had a bit of a nervous breakdown, for which I deserve sympathy and understanding rather than condemnation, and now I've come back to the bosom of my family, where I belong."

"Not any more, you don't! Not since you walked out on me for that slimeball you worked with."

"Well, that's the first thing we agree on. Roland *is* a slimeball." Her eyes filled with tears. "He used and abused me. He promised me the world, then betrayed my trust."

"Saw through you, did he? Or did he simply find you as difficult to live with as I have all these years?"

"I understand your resentment, Peter, and find it totally understandable and forgivable."

Peter's gasp of shocked indignation was completely ignored as she raised her voice even louder, this time directing her attention towards Neil.

"But as you know, Reverend Fisher, this is a Christian family. We are a Christian couple who made our wedding vows before God. Those promises are not to be taken lightly, as I know you agree."

"It's not me who has to agree, Glenda," replied Neil. "This is Peter's choice. I know him well enough to know that he was deeply hurt by the way in which your marriage broke down. He hadn't seen it coming, so it was a dreadful, cruel shock. Christian marriage is based on love and commitment. It's difficult to see any love in the way you left him – and you can hardly describe yourself as committed to the ideal of Christian marriage when you went off to set up home with another man after what seems to have been a long period of infidelity about which Peter knew nothing!"

"If he'd been a more caring, more involved husband, he would have noticed. He would have seen my unhappiness and worked harder to improve our marriage."

"And if you'd had even a scrap of decency," interrupted

Peter, "let alone genuine love and concern for me, you'd have kept the vows you say are so important, and worked harder yourself to keep not just our marriage but our family together!"

There was venom in Glenda's voice as she spat back at Peter. "And if you'd been a real man, I wouldn't have had to look elsewhere for fulfilment!"

"But you did and I'm glad! Yes, it was a shock that you left, but a huge relief too. I'm glad you went. I'm glad this sham of a marriage is over and I want you out of my life once and for all! There's no place for you here."

Glenda's tone changed as she peered closely at Peter.

"Well, you would want me gone, wouldn't you, when you're already playing house with that soppy Val? Dull, boring, probably frigid – it's hard to imagine what you see in her, but I certainly know what she sees in you. This, for a start!" She flung her arms out towards the room they sat in. "She's after whatever she can get from you, and who can blame her when you think of that ordinary little box she lives in? Oh, she's got your measure, Peter. Years of running your own estate agency, a good pension – half of which, I'm pleased to say, the solicitors agree is due to me, along with fifty per cent of this house. But that's not the point, is it, Peter? Does she know how comfortably off you are? Have you told her about your little nest egg, the rather substantial inheritance you got from your father? Oh, you did happen to mention it! What a surprise! She saw you coming, my poor deluded husband. Do you think she actually wants *you*? She'd have to be completely without a brain in her head. Oh, but now I come to think about it, she *hasn't* got a brain in her head, has she!"

"That's enough, Glenda!" Even Neil was surprised by the force in his voice as he interjected.

Mascara lay in black smudges beneath her eyes as she turned towards Neil.

"I know. I'm sorry. This has all been so upsetting – to hear that my husband is planning to marry another woman when our marriage is not even over."

"That's just a legal technicality, Glenda," said Peter. "Our marriage was over years ago."

"Please don't say that." Glenda directed her tear-filled gaze towards Peter. "I know I've behaved unwisely. I know I've not always been the most accommodating wife. But I've changed. Everything that's happened in the last few months has made me realize what really matters: family, loyalty, marriage. I know how important those things are to you too. You're a decent man, Peter, and the honourable thing for you to do now is to accept that we must draw a line under the past so that we can build a new future – together, man and wife, as we were always meant to be."

At that moment the doorbell rang. Peter jumped up immediately and practically ran to the door. There was the sound of muffled voices before the lounge door was opened again – by Peter and Glenda's daughter.

"Christine!" smiled Glenda. "You've arrived at just the right moment to knock some sense into your stubborn old dad. You tell him! He'll believe it from you. Tell him that any decent man would stand by his wife, whatever difficulties they've both been through. Tell him how much it would mean to John and you to see us together, with the family reunited. Tell him!"

"Go and get your things, Mum," said Christine quietly. "You're coming home to Brighton to stay with Mark and me for a while."

"I most certainly am *not*!"

"You've asked for a reconciliation, and Dad's said no. Nobody blames him for feeling that way. So just get your things, and we'll try and get ahead of the rush hour on the M25."

"You've no business talking to me that way, Christine. I am your mother!"

"Then, just for once, behave like one. Show a bit of care for someone other than yourself, and leave Dad alone. You've ruined his life once. Correction, you've ruined his life for years. Let him find some peace at last."

"With that woman? He's got absolutely no right setting up home with a nobody like her!"

"He has a great deal more right than you had when you disappeared with Roland."

"I made a mistake. Perhaps if you'd all cared a bit more about how I was feeling, you could have saved me from making such a dreadful error of judgment."

"You made your choice, Mum, and for you in the end it was the wrong one. For Dad it was probably the greatest kindness you've ever shown him."

Christine moved over to perch on the side of the chair, putting her arm around her mother's shoulders.

"He loves Val, Mum, and she loves him – truly loves him in a way you never could. Let him go. Let him find his own happiness, just as we all hope eventually you'll find yours."

"How can I be happy without a man to look after me?" wailed Glenda.

"No *man* is ever going to make you happy. No one else can ever be responsible for *your* happiness because that's your decision to make. And I don't blame you for being scared. You've not lived on your own for years. Dad's always been there to organize things around you. But you're a strong and capable woman, Mum, you know you are."

"I'm not," sobbed Glenda. "I'm really not! What will be become of me?"

"Whatever you choose. We'll help you – John and me and both our families. You may worry about feeling lonely, but you're not alone. We love you and we're all there for you. We're not taking sides. We'll be supporting Dad too, in whatever way we can. But you've got to let go of him, Mum. That's the right thing to do."

Glenda's shoulders sagged, as if all the fight had gone out of her, and as mother and daughter sat huddled together, Neil caught Peter's eye, suggesting that it was time for them to leave. They slipped out of the lounge, then Peter collected all Glenda's belongings strewn around the house while Neil piled them into the boxes that were still where she'd dropped them in the hall on the evening she arrived. Then they loaded the lot into Christine's car just in time to see the two women emerging from the front door.

Glenda didn't look at Peter. She kept her eyes on the car as she walked down the garden path without a backward glance. Once her mother had climbed into the passenger seat and slammed the door, Christine turned to draw her father into a warm, loving hug.

"Thanks, Chris. This is good of you. I hope she won't cause disruption at home."

"I teach teenagers for a living, Dad. I can certainly cope with a stroppy parent having a mid-life crisis."

Peter smiled. "I'm sure you can."

"By the way, we'd love to come!"

For a moment, Peter looked puzzled.

"Our invitation to the wedding arrived this morning, and we'd all love to be there. You and Val will have a very loving marriage, there's no doubt about that."

Peter's emotional response was muffled as he hugged Christine to him.

"So just get on with that wonderful new life of yours, and leave Mum to me."

"Take care of her. She's not all bad, you know."

Christine nodded in agreement as she turned towards the car, driving quickly away before Glenda could change her mind.

CHAPTER 10

"Steady there, Frank! Shall I take those?"

Coffee in the church hall after the Sunday morning service was still in full swing. Neil was just hurrying out to St Gabriel's for their weekly service when he came across Frank, his arms still around a box of collecting tins, swaying rather precariously.

"Keep thinking I'm twenty years younger than I am," mumbled Frank. "Can't get up that fast any more."

"Right!" agreed Neil, taking the box out of his hands. "Take a seat and get your breath back for a while. Were you taking these over to the church?"

Frank nodded, clearly winded by his dizzy spell.

"I'll take them. I'm going that way. You stay put."

"Everything all right?"

Wendy suddenly appeared at Neil's elbow.

Frank shook his head dismissively. "Look, please don't fuss. I'm absolutely fine. These days the blood just takes a bit of time to get to my head, that's all. Margaret's always nagging me to slow down."

"Me? Nag?" said Margaret, catching the last line of their conversation. "Oh, for heaven's sake, Frank, what've you done this time?"

"Got up too quickly," explained Neil.

Margaret's expression darkened with concern.

"Yes, I do nag you about that and now you see why. Give yourself a few minutes, then I'll take you home."

Checking that the colour was returning to Frank's face, Margaret turned to Neil.

"You will remember to talk to David Murray after the service at St Gabriel's this morning, won't you? He's got all the details for that burial there on Thursday."

"Yes, David's as efficient as ever in his churchwarden duties, thank goodness. He assures me he's got everything in hand."

"He was saying," mused Margaret, "that he remembers Vera Dunton from when he was a boy. Her family farmed all the land backing onto St Gabriel's for ages, but the new estate has swallowed up most of that area now. From what her son Philip was telling me on the phone, I don't think Vera could have seen much of that. Her husband died about twenty years ago, and she's been living up in Gateshead near Philip and his family ever since."

"So now she's coming home?"

"There's been a Dunton family plot at St Gabriel's going back two centuries or more, so it's only right that it should be her final resting place. You still OK to do her service on Thursday?"

Knowing that Thursday was always Margaret's day off, Neil nodded agreement just as Wendy helped Frank up to join them. Margaret slipped her arm through her husband's, and the couple headed off, talking quietly together as they went.

"I need to get a move on," said Neil, still clasping the box of collecting tins. "I'm due at St Gabriel's in fifteen minutes."

"Are you going to the vestry?" asked Wendy.

"To pick up my robes, yes."

"I'm heading that way too. I need my box of kids' percussion instruments for school tomorrow."

Closing the door behind them, they stepped through the wrought-iron gate and started down the path through the graveyard towards the back of the church. Yesterday's icy March wind had unexpectedly given way to a warm spring morning, with a touch of sunshine peering through soft white clouds dotted across the pale blue sky.

Both Neil and Wendy found their eyes drawn towards the Clarkson family plot. Ever since Ellen's funeral, there had been a constant supply of fresh flowers beside the white marble headstone marking where she was laid. Neil's heart lurched as he saw the first flowers appearing on the daffodils thoughtfully planted by Claire as a touching annual reminder of the dearly loved little girl. Claire! His heart filled with love at the mere thought of her.

"I can never walk past here without thinking of that tiny white coffin being lowered into the ground."

Wendy's voice was almost a surprise as she stood close beside him, their arms touching as she continued. "I still can't believe we've lost her. Why does God let something so awful happen?"

"Perhaps we'll never know this side of heaven," replied Neil, his eyes still on Ellen's grave. "Every day we pray that his will be done, and we just have to trust in him, and that God is in everything. He's a loving God, our heavenly Father. We know that he understands our suffering, because he saw the suffering of his own son."

"It's very hard though," whispered Wendy, her head falling gently against his shoulder.

A bolt of alarm shot through Neil at the intimacy of the gesture.

"I never had chance to thank you for your kindness after Ellen's funeral," continued Wendy. "You're a very dear and special man, Neil. Oh, I know you don't love me any more. I understand that I'm just not good enough to be what you need…"

Looking down at the sadness in her upturned face, Neil felt a wave of sympathy wash over him.

"Wendy, don't think that. You're a wonderful woman. Whatever went wrong between us was most certainly my fault. Please don't think for a moment that you failed in any way…"

"But you don't want me."

"Wendy, I…"

"And I hear you have a new woman in your life."

Neil stared hard at her.

"I hope she's good to you, Neil. I hope she loves you as much as I always will, as much as you deserve."

Immobilized by the shock waves coursing through him, Neil stood helplessly as she slowly lifted her face up so that her lips met his for a few heart-stopping seconds before she turned on her heel and walked away.

* * *

The following Thursday morning Neil arrived at St Gabriel's in good time to make certain everything was organized for Vera Dunton's burial. Her coffin was due to complete its journey from Gateshead and arrive in the village of Minting around noon. He was glad that David Murray was on hand to help because, as churchwarden at St Gabriel's for the best part of thirty years, David took great pride in the welfare of both the elderly building and its dwindling congregation.

David was waiting in the porch when Neil arrived, and the two men wandered over to where the grave had been dug ready for Vera's burial.

"You knew her, didn't you?" Neil asked.

"She was a bit of a battleaxe, as I recall," said David, his eyes narrowing as he delved deep into his childhood memories. "I used to go past her house on the way to school, and she'd sometimes shake her fist at us if she thought we'd been pinching her apples or picking up conkers from under her horse chestnut tree."

"What was her husband like?"

"He never spoke to us much really, but, to be fair, it was a big farm to look after and there was only him to do most of the work. I always thought he had twinkly eyes though, and I think Philip got on well with his dad."

"You know Philip? You'll be meeting an old friend today, then?"

"Well, he was several years older than me, so I didn't know him well. He played rugby with my brother, and came to the house after matches sometimes. He got a job as a salesman, I think, and that's what took him away from the area. I only heard quite a while after his dad had died that he'd married and was up in the north-east. My mother told me that Vera found it so difficult trying to run the place on her own that a couple of years later she moved up to live next door to Philip and his family."

"What happened to the farm?"

"Well, that was a bit of a family scandal, really. It was mostly before my time, but my mum and dad said the whole village knew about it. Vera had always loved farming from the time she was a little girl, but Herbie, her brother, never really got on with farm work. That didn't go down well for the only son in a family who'd been farmers for generations. The story went that he ran away to sea when he was just a teenager and was in the navy for quite a while – but then, when his father died, he inherited the lot, even though he had no interest in it beyond what it was worth."

"Nothing for Vera, then, even though it was her husband who was keeping the farm going?"

"It didn't work like that in those days, did it? The eldest son always took over the family business. Any daughter in the family was expected to get married, and then it was up to her husband to look after her."

"So what happened?"

"Well, the first thing Herbie did was to sell off about half the property, including several big old barns with planning permission for them to be converted into houses."

"The ones over the back? Isn't that where Angela Barker lives?" asked Neil, thinking of the busy, well-known Barker family, whose members often came along to services both at St Stephen's and St Gabriel's.

"Interesting you should mention her. Angela and Keith had all sorts of trouble with Vera when they first moved into that barn."

"Why?"

"Vera hated them and made her feelings known in every way she could."

"Just because they were the people who bought the place?"

"I don't suppose it mattered to Vera who they were. Apparently she was furious that her father had left the farm to her brother when he plainly didn't want it, but when Herbie started selling off the land and barns, she was beside herself with anger. Her husband was carrying on doing all the work, keeping what was left of the farm running, while Herbie cleared off to do his own thing with all the money."

"Poor Angela. It obviously didn't frighten her and Keith off, though, I'm glad to say."

Just at that moment, they caught sight of the long, black roof of a hearse slowing down as it passed the low hedge along the front of the churchyard wall. The driver carefully manoeuvred the vehicle through the gate and up the path towards the door of the church where Neil and David were waiting to greet them. Three people climbed out of the front seats. Vera's son, Philip, appeared first, followed by his wife, Pat, while the driver, who introduced himself as Andy, made his way round from the other side of the car. Once Philip and David had reacquainted themselves after so many years, Neil got down to business.

"We're all ready. I suggest we have a short funeral service inside the church, then we can move over to the grave for the committal and blessing. Is anyone else likely to come?"

"There's none of Mum's family left in this area now. She was eighty-five when she died."

"There are four assistants from the undertakers in town – they're coming along in a quarter of an hour or so, to help with the actual burial," put in David.

"I see," said Neil, turning to the driver. "Have you got the paperwork?"

"Paperwork?"

"The green slip?"

Andy's expression was totally blank. "They didn't give me nothing."

"The green slip which authorizes the release of the body?"

Andy shrugged his shoulders. "Never said a word about no green slip."

Neil looked hopefully at Philip.

"This is the first I've heard of it." There was a note of

alarm in Philip's voice. "That's right, isn't it, Pat? They didn't give us a green form of any sort, did they?"

"Well," said Neil, his thoughts racing, "as far as I know, a body can't be released for burial unless it's been authorized. Usually the undertaker takes care of the relevant paperwork along with all the other arrangements for the funeral."

"This has been unusual, though," said Philip, "because we didn't organize a proper funeral near us. She's outlived the few friends she had, and she always said she wanted just a few words said down here at St Gabriel's before we put her in the plot beside my dad and her parents. She wasn't big on religion, if I'm honest, and she was never a woman to want a fuss."

Neil looked at David to find the churchwarden looking back at him with a matching expression of total confusion.

"I can't ring Margaret," Neil said, thinking out loud. "She's away at her daughter's today. I won't disturb her."

"Are you the undertaker?" David asked the driver.

Andy shook his head.

"Can we get your boss on the phone, then? He is the undertaker, I assume, so perhaps he can shed some light on this?"

"He's not my boss. He's my uncle. He's just giving me a few readies for driving down here today."

Pat started to sob quietly.

"Look," said Philip, his arm around her shoulders, "this is really upsetting my wife. How much does this bit of green paper matter? Mum's obviously dead. I can vouch for the fact that's her in the box because we only closed it up this morning before we left. That's the plot she wants to go in and we're all here, so let's just get on with it!"

"It's not as simple as that, I'm afraid."

"I need the loo," wailed Pat.

"It's been a long journey, love. Of course you do. Is there a loo here?"

"Not in the church, I'm afraid," replied David. "Look, can I suggest that you and your wife make yourselves comfortable in the pub just over the road there while we three try to get to the bottom of this? We'll make a few phone calls, then come and get you when it's clear for us to proceed."

"I could do with a wee too," said Andy moodily.

"You're representing the undertaker here today," said David sternly. "We need answers, if not from you, then from your uncle. You'll have to get him on the phone immediately to see if we can sort out this unfortunate muddle as quickly as possible."

An hour later, it became abundantly clear that the impossible had happened. Against all odds, Vera's body had been released and despatched for a burial at the other end of the country without the correct paperwork being completed. Philip and his wife blamed the mistake on the undertaker. The undertaker blamed it on them for wanting such an unusual arrangement. The bottom line was that, whoever was to blame, Vera was stuck in a box on *top* of the ground she really needed to be buried *in*.

"Who issues these release forms?" asked Neil.

"It's part of the death certificate, so a registrar does it."

"Where can we find a registrar quickly? Will we have to go to Bedford?"

A smile crept over David's face. "Perhaps not. I know a lady who is most definitely a registrar, although mostly retired these days, I understand."

"Where is she? Can we ring her?"

David turned to look beyond the end of the church grounds. "Right there. Angela's a registrar! I'm sure she is!"

Neil, who wasn't close enough to Angela and her family to know what professions they were in, muttered a quick prayer of thanks under his breath before hurrying after David, who was already striding ahead towards the gate behind the church. Several hundred yards beyond that, the path opened out to reveal a beautiful old barn. It had been lovingly converted into a spacious family home, the front of which was covered by a blanket of varigated ivy.

"She's probably not home…" worried Neil, but seconds after their ring on the doorbell, Angela herself opened the door. Inviting them in at once, she sat at one side of the kitchen table while they poured out their dilemma from the other. When they'd finished, her expression was difficult to read as she considered their problem. At last, she leaned forward, folding her arms on the table as she looked at them.

"Well, there are several things you need to know in answer to this. Firstly, yes, I am still a registrar. I've basically retired from being in the office all week long, and mostly just do the nice, glamorous stuff these days – weddings either at the office or in all sorts of other unusual places. I pick and choose the jobs really. But yes, as a registrar I can still sort out the release form you need. That is in my power."

"Great!" Neil felt his shoulders drop with sheer relief.

"I said it's in my power. I didn't say I was prepared to do it."

Neil realized that David was nodding his head with understanding as he looked across at Angela.

"There was never any love lost between you and Vera Dunton, was there?"

"She was a witch! There's no other word I can think of to describe that evil woman after what she put me through."

"Because she didn't want you to buy the barn?"

"She had no idea the barn had been sold until we arrived

to look around. I remember she came marching over when we were trying to talk to the architect, and started smashing the window of his van with a shovel. She was like a screaming banshee!"

"That must have been so frightening."

"That's an understatement. What followed was months of vitriol and spite. We moved in before the work was completely finished, and she was still furious with us. It would have been easier for me if Keith hadn't been working in London at the time. That's why we moved here: so that the kids could grow up in the country while he was near enough to get down to London fairly easily."

"So you spent a lot of time on your own here with the children?"

"From seven in the morning until eight at night every weekday, and I can tell you I lived in fear of her. I had visions of her creeping up on us and setting the barn alight with the children and me in it."

"Surely not?"

"Well, we'd have been hard pushed to find enough water to put any blaze out. We weren't connected to mains water for ages, but when the water supplier asked for permission to take a feed from the supply to her farm so it could be piped across to us under her land, she flatly refused. She chased them off with a shotgun! And because of that, we had to find thousands of pounds to get them to bring us a fresh water supply around a much longer and more difficult route. She knew I had a small baby and a toddler here, but she just didn't care. She was completely heartless."

"I think her heart had been broken," said David softly.

"Perhaps. If I were a kinder person, I might allow her that, but she robbed me of my peace of mind. She robbed us all of the delight and pleasure of building our family home here. She robbed my children of the chance to play freely in their own garden for fear she'd barge in to complain about them. She did everything she could to drive us away."

"But you stayed?" said Neil quietly.

"Yes, we did! We were determined not to let her beat us. This was our home, our dream. We weren't going to let a bitter old biddy force us out. She didn't feel any compassion towards us and I'm afraid I can't find even a trace of compassion in my heart towards her now."

"After all these years? Even now, you still feel like that?"

"Neil, I'm a Christian. I've been a Christian all my life. My family are regular worshippers here and at St Stephen's – and because of that, I'm ashamed at how I must come across to you right now. I know you're thinking you should give me the lecture about how Christians are supposed to turn the other cheek and love their neighbour, but when it comes to Vera Dunton, any spirit of Christian kindness deserts me. I have never hated anyone in my life except for that awful woman, because she put my family in danger, and we lived in fear because of her. We didn't deserve any of that and I can never forgive her. I just can't!"

"She's been living with her son up in Gateshead ever since she left."

"Did she make his life a misery too?"

"She was eighty-five when she died last week, a sick old lady who simply wished to be brought back home after her death to be buried alongside the parents she loved and the husband she adored."

Angela said nothing.

"Philip and his wife Pat have travelled down with her today."

She stiffened.

"Would you at least see them?"

"I'd rather not. Don't drag me into this, Neil."

"This is hard for them too."

"I remember him, actually, Philip. He used to come down and see her sometimes, before she moved up to be with them."

"How was he towards you?"

"Sheepish, mostly. I don't think his life was ever much of a picnic with her as a mother."

"Probably not, but he's done his best by her. He and his wife Pat have looked after her all this time."

Angela was silent for a moment.

"Where are they now?"

"At the Black Bull."

"Look, bring them over. This isn't their fault, but I don't want them to think it's all my fault, either, so I'd prefer to be honest and explain all this to them myself."

Within ten minutes, David had raced over to the pub, bringing back just Philip to Angela's home as Pat had been about to tuck into a meal she'd ordered in the pub. When Angela opened the door to him, Philip didn't immediately come in, but stood for a while looking up at the outside of the building.

"I remember this. I used to play in this place when it was a cowshed."

"Did you?"

"My dad would be in here before six in the morning, even on Christmas Day. And at the weekends, when I didn't have to go to school, he used to get me up so I could help him."

Angela eyed him with curiosity as he smiled at the memory.

"Actually I don't think I ever helped much, but he made me think my contribution was important."

"What was your mother's reaction to that?"

"They were good together, Mum and Dad. I remember how her face used to light up whenever he came in at the end of the day. It was as if, for her, the house wasn't a home until he was in it."

"I can't imagine your mum being like that."

Philip looked at her. "No, how could you? I remember you too. You had a couple of youngsters when you came here, didn't you? I thought she'd drive you away. That's what she wanted, but I told her how pointless it was to feel like that, because even if you did go, the barn would never be hers again."

"Did she really believe that could happen?"

"Perhaps. I think in the early days when Uncle Herbie sold off most of the farm, she was just so angry with him that she lashed out in all directions. You were in direct line of fire."

"Philip, she made our lives hell. You have to know that, because I'm struggling even now, after all this time, to find any sympathy towards her."

Philip nodded with acceptance and understanding. "I don't blame you for that."

From inside the hallway, David and Neil looked at each other helplessly.

"Come in, Philip," said Angela suddenly. "Come and see what we've done to your old cowshed."

It took more than a quarter of an hour for Philip to be shown round Angela's home. At each stop, he had a memory that painted a picture of his parents' tough life on the farm as he was growing up. By the time he and Angela reappeared in the kitchen, they were chatting like old friends.

Angela leaned against the Aga, her expression thoughtful. Philip came to stand close by her.

"I'm sorry," he said simply, "really sorry about how Mum treated you. I knew how hurt Mum was by what Uncle Herbie did. I think everything got mixed up in her mind, so she blamed you, even though you'd done absolutely nothing to deserve it. I watched how she struggled on after she'd lost Dad. She just couldn't cope on her own. It broke her heart when she had to move away. She never really settled up north, even though she was with us for more than twenty years. You probably won't believe this, but she did mention you. She said more than once that she regretted the way she'd been with you. She knew it was too late, but I think deep down she would have liked to apologize. So *I'm* saying sorry to you. To your family from ours – I'm sorry."

A single tear ran down Angela's cheek, and she quickly wiped it away. Then she reached out to clasp Philip's outstretched hand, and the two of them stood there for a while, both plainly moved by what they'd just shared.

"Right!" said Angela, abruptly pulling back her hand. "Philip, you go and get your wife. Neil, you head over to the church to set up for the service. David, you ring the local undertakers and get those four chaps here ready to help with the burial. I'll be along shortly with a green slip – and time to join you all in a prayer for Vera."

* * *

"Any idea who she is yet?"

Debs and Wendy were having one of their monthly nights out when they decided to let someone else do the cooking and went out for a meal while they caught up on the gossip.

"Not really," replied Wendy. "I don't think it's anyone at the church. No one's said a word and I've been watching his every move."

"So where could he have met someone?"

174

"Don't know," shrugged Wendy. "Another curate, maybe, when he's gone off for his potty-training sessions?"

"But why keep quiet about someone as suitable as that? I just can't see it, can you?"

"Perhaps not."

"What about the internet? Lots of people meet that way nowadays."

"Neil's a complete technophobe," smiled Wendy. "He'd never have the gumption to do something like that."

"So perhaps Graham's got it wrong. Maybe there isn't anyone else in Neil's life?"

Wendy took a mouthful of garlic bread while she considered that possibility.

"Neil didn't contradict me when I told him I knew."

"How did he seem?"

"Shocked. Guilty, even."

"So what did you do? Did you wish you hadn't mentioned it?"

"What I did…" said Wendy, licking the remains of garlic bread off her fingers one by one, "was to kiss him."

"You didn't!"

"I did."

"And what was his reaction?"

"I don't know. I didn't stay around long enough to find out. I believe in leaving my men wanting more."

"And does he?"

"Oh, yes," purred Wendy. "He may not know it yet, but he certainly does."

"Well, I've got a bit of news for you," said Debs, laying down her knife and fork as she leaned closer to Wendy. "I haven't told Graham yet, but I did a test this morning."

"A pregnancy test?" asked Wendy, her eyes wide with disbelief. Debs nodded.

"And? Are you?"

"I most certainly am!"

"Debs, that's brilliant. At least, I think it's brilliant, but how do you feel about it?"

"Well," said Debs, her expression becoming more serious, "I think it's wonderful. Not sure what Graham's reaction will be, though."

"It'll be the making of him!"

"I know that, and so do you – but I've got a feeling his initial reaction will be sheer panic."

"You can talk him round, though, can't you? I can see him being a great dad."

"So can I, but the important question is, can I see him being a great husband?"

"You want to get married?"

"Of course I do. No child of mine is going to come into this world out of wedlock. And if that sounds quaint and old-fashioned, well, that's just the way it is. Unless Graham agrees to put a ring on my finger, that's it. It's over and I'm off!"

≈ CHAPTER 11 ≈

"I love you."

Claire was standing by the kitchen window gazing out at the garden as Neil slid his arms round her waist, nuzzling his face into the soft skin of her neck. She turned immediately in his arms so that she could stretch up to draw him to her in a leisurely kiss that ended with him softly running his lips over her cheeks and chin and nose before kissing her again with deepening passion.

"For heaven's sake, you two!" grumbled Harry good-naturedly as he came through the kitchen door. "You're obviously mad about each other, so when are you going to come clean? You make a great couple. How about you just get on with it?"

His arm still resting across Claire's shoulders, Neil considered Harry's suggestion carefully.

"You know what it was like before, Harry. The trouble with church life is that everyone wants to know everyone else's business. I can't sneeze without half the members of the Ladies' Guild turning up with jars of Vick and homemade soup."

"Well," said Harry as he started to fill the kettle. "Are you sure of your feelings for each other or not?"

Claire and Neil looked at each other fondly.

"Absolutely," said Neil.

"Then I think it's time you came out. People know Claire well enough. She may not attend services, but she's well thought of and liked as the church gardener."

"Is it going to matter that I'm not signed up as a Christian, though, Harry?" asked Claire. "Neil's a vicar. Whoever heard of a vicar's partner not being a Christian?"

"It probably happens more often than you think," replied Harry. "Besides, isn't it more important that the relationship between the couple themselves is right? It's obvious that you love Neil, Claire. You're talented. You work hard. You run your own business. You're kind and caring, always the first to lend a helping hand – and you're a terrific mum to young Sam."

"In that case," smiled Claire, kissing Neil's cheek, "this man is just extremely lucky to have me!"

"Amen to that," agreed Neil, kissing her back.

"What about this Sunday morning, when Sam's in the Palm Sunday procession with the rest of his class?" suggested Harry. "Why don't the three of you just act naturally there, like the unit you really are?"

Neil nodded. "I think you're right. I know I'm being less than honest by keeping our relationship to ourselves – but it's felt so precious that we've just wanted to enjoy it for a while without having to take everybody else's opinion on board. But I agree with you, it's been long enough. So let's do it, Claire, shall we?"

Claire smiled her agreement before asking, "Do you have to make an announcement or anything?"

"I don't think so. We'll just start being ourselves when we're out together."

"What about Wendy, though? Would it be best to warn her in advance?"

Neil thought for a while. "I don't think so. We broke up a long time ago now. If she's still carrying a flame for me, I'm sorry, because I'd never want to hurt her – but you and I are together. That's a fact. Probably better that we don't rub her nose in it by making a big issue of the whole thing. I think we should behave in the same way around Wendy as we do with everyone else."

"Iris will be here by the weekend," commented Harry. "Are you going to tell her too?"

"You mean, Harry, that my mother doesn't already know, bearing in mind how many times she rings you each week?"

Harry grinned. "I might have mentioned it in passing."

"What did she say?"

"How long have you got?"

"She must approve of Claire," retorted Neil. "She's your great-niece!"

"Oh, your mother knows Claire comes from very good stock!" laughed Harry. "Seriously, though, she not only approves, but says she always knew you two would get together. It was, after all, *her* idea…"

* * *

It's the tradition in most Anglican churches on Palm Sunday morning for the congregation to gather at a central point in the town, so that they can re-enact Christ's entry into Jerusalem, when crowds welcomed him with cheers and waving palms. For Christians the occasion is very poignant, because they know that his triumphant arrival in the city was the start of a week of changing fortunes for Jesus: later he was arrested, tried, beaten, then made to carry his own cross up the hill to Calvary to be crucified like a common thief. Three days later, he rose from the dead, and the celebration of his resurrection at Easter is always the most joyful time in the Christian calendar.

Sam was a pupil at the church school attached to St Stephen's, where the youngest children had always enjoyed dressing up in biblical style to lead the procession of clergy, choir and congregation into the church for the Palm Sunday service.

Sam liked dressing up, but he would rather have been in his Spiderman outfit. The cotton shift his mother had made him for the procession looked far too much like a dress for his liking. The tea towel on his head kept falling off until Claire put a hair clip in it – and everyone knew only *girls* wore hair clips. All in all, Sam was a bit uncertain about the whole thing.

He felt a great deal better, though, once they'd reached the market square, and he could see that the rest of the boys from his class looked equally daft. That didn't stop them racing around playing chase until their teacher, Mrs Martin, blew a whistle and organized them into separate lines of boys and girls.

"Now, children, you need to remember that we're in the centre of the town, and people drive their cars around this square. They won't be able to stop if silly boys and girls decide to run out into the road, will they? So we're going to keep safe. Every boy take a girl's hand…"

"Euck!" shouted Sam, along with just about every other boy in the group.

"No talking, please!"

That delightful old showman, Boy George, had been volunteered to stage-manage the procession. Now in his eighties and the revered leader of the St Stephen's bell-ringing team, it only took a small glass of sherry to get him reminiscing about his long career in amateur dramatics.

Old thespians, even amateur ones, know old tricks, as the gathered crowd soon discovered when George pulled out a megaphone that looked as elderly as he did. It certainly worked, though, and George briskly snapped out instructions for the children to line up behind the pony – which had been hurriedly brought in as a substitute for the donkey, which no one had managed to find locally. On the pony, cunningly disguised as Jesus, was a girl called Jessica. OK, so Jesus should have been a boy, but it was *her* pony, and that was the deal.

"Right, the Boys' Brigade band is next, with the choir and music group members falling in behind them. Churchwardens, servers and clergy – you follow on, leaving the rest of the congregation to form the main part of the procession at the rear."

"How did Graham take the news?" whispered Wendy to Debs as they made their way towards their positions in the music group.

"Well, let me think – what emotions crossed his face when I told him I was pregnant? Disbelief, shock..."

"Wasn't he pleased?"

"It took him quite a while to get over being indignant that he'd been caught out. Then it finally began to sink in that he was going to be a dad – and I have to say, in the end, he was all right about that, really."

"So he's being supportive?"

Debs grimaced. "This *is* Graham we're talking about."

"You'll sort him out, though, won't you?"

"Perhaps."

"So what happened when you told him you wanted to get married?"

"He laughed."

"And then he came round to the idea?"

"No. He said he doesn't think marriage is relevant in this day and age, and doesn't want to be forced into an institution he doesn't believe in. That's why I said *perhaps* just now because that's my bottom line. If he doesn't care enough about me to make me his wife, I don't trust him enough to be the father of my baby."

"Oh, Debs, I am sorry…" Wendy stopped as she saw her friend's expression suddenly change as she stared at something in the crowd.

"Can you see what I see?"

Wendy followed her gaze to find a very homely tableau unfolding on the other side of the square. Neil was laughing as he knelt down to put Sam's headdress back on safely, while a smiling Claire was leaning over them both, her hand comfortably resting on Neil's shoulder.

"So that's how it is…" whispered Wendy.

"Right under your nose all the time…"

"She's so wrong for him."

"Of course she is!"

"People at St Stephen's won't like this," said Wendy firmly.

"But she's quite popular there, isn't she?" asked Debs. "Don't a lot of them use her as a gardener?"

"Not when I've finished with her, they won't."

Debs looked at Wendy. "Be careful. Don't do anything that might rebound on you. Wouldn't it be better just to let them think you don't care at all – you know, play for time?"

Wendy looked at her thoughtfully. "You're probably right. I can bide my time because I can assure you that before too long I'm going to sort that little madam out once and for all!"

* * *

The Easter service was packed and joyous. Neil had initiated the idea of keeping the large Christmas tree which had been decorated with sparkling lights in December. It was stripped of its branches and sawn in two, and the pieces brought back into the church on Ash Wednesday looking rough and bare, and fixed together in the shape of a cross. On each Sunday during Lent, the cross was hung with items relevant to the story – a purple cloth, a palm branch, a crown of thorns – until on Good Friday the church echoed to the sound of nails being hammered into its bark in a stark reminder of Christ's suffering and crucifixion. Then during the Easter Day service, people stepped up to fix fresh flowers onto the cross, often in memory of those they loved and had lost. The end result was moving and glorious, the dead wood covered with living colour. Afterwards the congregation of St Stephen's went home to their Easter Sunday roast, happily clutching chocolate eggs and greetings cards, which had been exchanged with many hugs during coffee in the church hall.

Later that afternoon Neil looked on in contentment at the group seated around the lunch table. They were all at Harry's house, although earlier Iris had insisted on throwing everyone out of *her* kitchen so that she could work her culinary magic without interference. The result was magnificent: a delicious prawn salad starter, followed by lamb roasted to perfection, with home-made ice cream laced with sweet strawberries that Claire had grown in their garden the previous summer. Iris had even tried her hand at making a traditional simnel cake, covered in toasted marzipan adorned by a circle of eleven marzipan balls – a reminder of the eleven disciples who stayed true to Christ after Judas had betrayed him. The cake looked wonderful, although the only one even to consider trying a piece straight after lunch was Sam, who definitely had a sweet tooth. Harry, Claire and Neil finished the washing up and collapsed into comfy chairs, content and replete.

Easter Monday dawned with blue skies and bright, warm sunshine. Iris wanted to look around a local stately home that was known to have a glorious garden full of daffodils and blossom at this time of year, so they all went together. To one side of the garden was an adventure playground and hedge maze to keep youngsters entertained, so Sam was in his element. Neil finally carried the exhausted little boy back to the car at the end of a wonderful, heart-warming day.

Most surprising of all was what happened once Sam was safely tucked up in bed. Neil was just heading to the kitchen when he met his mother in the hall on her way to join the others in the lounge.

"Do you know, Neil, I've had a really lovely day!" she said, in a voice which bore no trace of the sarcasm and spite that so often lay behind her words.

"I'm glad," he smiled back.

"Claire's lovely. You've got a good one there."

"I think so."

"Harry's relieved to see her happy at last."

"She's made me happy too; happier than I've ever been."

Iris nodded without comment, then stepped closer to put her arms around him. Neil couldn't remember the last time his mother had hugged him, and to his shame he certainly couldn't recall wanting to hug her since he'd been a very small boy. There they stood, mother and son, sharing a moment of togetherness at long last.

* * *

It was an equally glorious spring day when a sleek white Rolls Royce pulled up outside the porch of St Stephen's. Val stepped out into the sunshine to a ripple of applause from neighbours and friends who had turned out to see the arrival of the bride. She looked elegant in a full-length cream dress and brocade jacket, with a matching fascinator in her hair and a simple bouquet of snow-white lily of the valley. However, everyone agreed that it was the glow of complete happiness that was her most beautiful accessory. There was no doubting that Val marrying Peter was making the pair of them the happiest couple ever.

At the front of the packed church Brian struck up Mendelssohn's "Wedding March" on the organ, and Peter stepped into the aisle, his son John standing smartly at his side. Heads turned to watch Val, on the arm of her proud son Anthony, walking down the aisle to where Peter stood, his eyes shining in a face softened by love. He reached out to kiss her on the cheek as she joined him. Val handed her bouquet to Peter's daughter Christine, before the couple turned to face Margaret, who was smiling broadly as she introduced the proceedings.

Much later, Margaret would look back on that ceremony as one of the most meaningful she'd ever conducted. The love and delight of the couple as they took their vows was so touching that almost everyone in the church found themselves either reaching for a hankie or taking the hand of the partner with whom they had shared the same vows in the past. The choir sang John Rutter's arrangement of "The Lord Bless You and Keep You" while the register was being signed, and Wendy's solo performance of "O Perfect Love" had the older ladies sighing at the romance of it all.

Standing next to Claire in the second row, Neil felt her fingers tighten on his as the bride and groom emerged from the vestry to the strains of Wagner's "Bridal Chorus". Neil and Claire's eyes met in complete understanding. One day, this would be them. One day, they would be man and wife. One day soon.

* * *

The newly married Mr and Mrs Fellowes could have had their reception in the hushed, carpeted surroundings of the local hotel, but that wasn't their choice. They had met through St Stephen's. The Christian fellowship of St Stephen's had supported Val through her husband's death, and Peter through all the upheaval caused by Glenda's disappearance. It was, therefore, an easy decision for them to throw elegance to the wind in favour of a grand buffet and dance in the church hall to which all congregation members were invited. Warmed by their generosity, the congregation responded generously themselves by fully supporting Beryl's suggestion that the church community's gift to the couple should be their wedding breakfast. The magnificence of the resulting buffet was the talk of Dunbridge for many years to come.

Once the meal was over and the hall darkened, the small band began by playing the couple's chosen first dance number, the Jim Reeves song "I Love You Because". Faster songs followed, but this was a night when romance was in the air, so many slower melodies were played to entice couples out onto the dance floor to smooch and sway together.

Neil had never been one for dancing, but when Claire took his hand and led him out onto the dance floor, he stepped into her embrace, heads touching, fingers entwined, as they let the music sweep over them. They didn't notice that just about every member of the Ladies' Guild was watching the two of them carefully, noting the obvious affection between them. They didn't see the elbows nudging neighbours to draw attention to what was going on in the life of their popular young curate. Whether there were grumbles of disapproval or smiles of encouragement, all were lost on Neil and Claire, who only had eyes for each other.

They were also blissfully unaware of the mixture of sadness, longing and bleak hatred in the heart of the figure watching them from a darkened corner of the hall. So engrossed was she in peering at the couple that Wendy didn't notice Margaret moving across to stand alongside her.

"They look good together, don't they?"

Wendy didn't take her eyes off the dance floor as she answered. "She's so wrong for him."

"He doesn't seem to think so."

Wendy turned to look at Margaret. "We both know Neil has a lot to learn, especially about relationships. I don't think growing up with a mother like Iris has taught him much in that area. Do you?"

Margaret nodded. "That's probably true, but I think Neil is very much his own man."

"He's naïve and gullible. How can he possibly think it's proper for an ordained priest to choose as his partner a woman with such loose morals that she got herself pregnant by a man who couldn't wait to disappear off to the other side of the world rather than stay with her?"

"That, surely, says more about the man than her. I don't think anyone doubts that Claire is an excellent parent to young Sam."

"She's an unmarried mother. Neil's an Anglican minister, committed to the Christian teaching that sex should only ever be part of a loving marriage. That way children like Sam would have the security of knowing their parents respected each other enough to marry and create a proper home together before bringing them into the world."

"And that same Christian teaching," responded Margaret, "tells us that ours is a loving God who recognizes our human failings and yet still holds his arms out to us in understanding and forgiveness."

"Yes, God can forgive. He has the power and the right to do that. We don't. Neil doesn't. Surely, as a priest and moral leader, he should uphold the ethos of our Christian faith, not endorse wrongdoing by blatantly embracing it – like that!" Wendy spat out her final words in the direction of Neil and Claire, who were still totally oblivious as they continued to sway in time to the music.

"You've been hurt, Wendy," said Margaret, putting a comforting arm around the younger woman's waist. "Badly hurt. I know you were – are – deeply fond of Neil. You saw a future with him – *your* future as a vicar's wife, a role which you would have filled superbly. You weren't alone in thinking that you would make wonderful partners, because just about everyone else at St Stephen's thought that too."

"Except Neil, apparently."

"Well, that's where we all got it wrong. Your relationship with Neil made perfectly good sense, but we don't fall in love with our heads, do we? It's our hearts that lead the way. And that…" Margaret nodded in the direction of Neil and Claire, "… is where his heart has taken him."

It might have been a snort of disgust that Margaret heard from Wendy then, but more likely it was a sob of pure misery from the way her voice was shaking when she next spoke.

"But the problem isn't just that she's not a Christian. Surely that's bad enough. But she openly admits she doesn't even believe in God! How can Neil accept that? How can he possibly think he could share his life with someone like that?"

"We don't know he's planning to share his life with Claire. This could be a very short-lived affair. We who love him simply have to stand alongside him and support him as we can."

"I can't bear to see them together..."

Hidden by the darkness of the room, Margaret could tell Wendy was crying.

"I know, love, I know – but you have your own life to get on with, and I believe, with all your gifts and talent, you have so much potential for happiness and fulfilment ahead of you."

"Not without Neil..."

"Well, that's up to you. Be everything you can be for *yourself*, not someone else. Maybe, in the end, Neil will be the man for you – but just maybe there's someone else completely different in your future, with whom you will find much greater contentment. Let Neil go, Wendy. Save yourself the pain. Just let him go."

Shaking her head miserably, Wendy couldn't answer. Instead, she gave Margaret's arm a grateful squeeze before heading towards the exit.

* * *

"I've made a decision," announced Iris a couple of weeks later.

Neil was about to leave the house to visit a bereaved family and help them plan a funeral for the following week.

"Is this a decision that takes a lot of explaining?" he enquired. "Or could it wait until I get home later?"

"No," said Iris, "this really won't take long. It's very simple. I've decided to move to Dunbridge!"

Neil was already heading towards the front door, but her answer stopped him in his tracks. His mother living permanently here in the town that was both his home and work place? How did he feel about that?

His thoughts were interrupted when he turned to look properly at Iris's face. He was used to her customary expression of belligerence and self-righteousness, but at this moment she actually looked quite nervous, and anxious to hear his response.

"Well, that would be nice," he said slowly. "What's brought you to that decision?"

"Loneliness," she said simply. "I'm lonely in Bristol. I don't really know my neighbours. I used to enjoy playing bridge, but two members of the club have recently died, and I've got no time for most of the other ladies who go there. My brother David has his own family. He doesn't need me. I feel useless, without purpose and very alone."

"I see," said Neil, still uncertain how he felt about this revelation.

"On the other hand, Neil, I think perhaps you *do* need me."

She must have caught sight of the gleam of panic in Neil's eyes, as she continued, "Oh, don't worry. I don't mean you aren't perfectly capable of doing your job. Actually, much to my surprise, you're becoming rather good at it. You'll never make a fortune, of course, and you would have been much better off as an accountant, like your father…" She lifted her hand to stop Neil as he spluttered an objection. "But, in spite of what you think, I do recognize you have your own life to lead, and you no longer need your mother trying to wipe your nose all the time. You'll probably learn better from making your own mistakes."

"Have you thought about where you might live?" asked Neil, hoping she wasn't thinking of moving into 96 Vicarage Gardens with him.

"No, I need to do a bit of house-hunting. I did notice a bungalow for sale in the next street up, Ransom Road – number 60, I think it is. It actually backs onto Harry's garden. I've made arrangements to take a look at it later this week."

"Have you spoken to Harry about this?"

"It was Harry who suggested it."

"Really?"

"Harry Holloway is a very wise and wonderful man," said Iris softly. "He's a good friend to me."

"He is," agreed Neil. In all honesty, he had often worried about whether Iris was in danger of becoming an overpowering burden that the gentlemanly Harry suffered politely.

"And I'm a good friend of his," added Iris.

"Yes?"

"We're not quite the same generation, but we come from the same era. We have a similar approach to manners and family and relationships and priorities. We laugh at the same jokes. We remember the same song words. We have a lot in common."

"I can see that," was Neil's careful reply.

"We're companions," continued Iris. "We like one another. He brings out the best me, and he says I do in him."

"Right."

"Harry's dreadful at looking after himself, especially now his health is such an issue, and I'm dreadful at being on my own with no one to look after – so…"

"So you plan to keep each other company?"

"Precisely."

"And Harry suggested this?"

"He did. He insists he's coming with me to look at that bungalow."

"Well, that seems settled then. What about your own house in Bristol?"

"I put it on the market two weeks ago."

"You mean, you knew before you came that this was what you wanted?"

"Absolutely. I was considering the possibility of living here when I left before Christmas, but thought I should go home and think it all through in the cold light of day. And my life there *is* cold. It bears no comparison to the warmth and friendship I've found here."

"You know, Mum, I'm only a curate in this town. I've got one, maybe two years to go before I take on my own parish – and that could be anywhere!"

"Then you'll just have to move on, Neil. I understand that, and it's only right and proper. Wherever you move to will become your home – but this is mine. I want to make my home in Dunbridge. I like the smallness of this town. I like the fact that when I walk through the market square, people recognize me enough to say hello. That's why I want to stay here."

Neil moved closer to put his arm around her shoulders. To his surprise, her news was beginning to grow on him.

"And who knows?" she continued. "You might need me sometimes. I'd like to be helpful."

"You are, Mum. You always are."

A wave of fondness came over him, and he did something that previously would have embarrassed him and infuriated her. He really hugged her. And, wonder of wonders, she hugged him back.

* * *

On the last Thursday in April, as they returned from Evening Prayer, Margaret suggested that Neil pop into the vicarage to collect some papers he needed for the morning. It was a beautiful evening, with shards of golden sunlight breaking through reddened clouds to create an almost magical sunset.

Margaret was in good humour. They'd had a busy but productive day when they'd found themselves acknowledging that the fellowship and Christian purpose of St Stephen's was going from strength to strength. The church was beginning to take its place as a focal point for all sorts of events and activities within the town.

"Just the way it should be," commented Margaret, as she swung open the front gate. "Churches were built to be communal meeting places not just for worship, but for everyday life. It's good to see that start to happen again in St Stephen's."

Pulling the key out of the front door lock, she took off her coat as she headed up the stairs.

"Those papers are in the back room, Neil, and Frank's probably in the kitchen, if you want to say hello."

Thinking it best to find the notes he needed first, Neil went to search for them among the piles of papers of all sorts and ages that were balanced rather precariously on the large dining table in the centre of the room. It was at that moment that he heard a scream that chilled him to the marrow.

"Neil!" It was almost unrecognizable as Margaret's voice, shrill and shrieking. "Neil! Oh, God, no! Neil!"

In no time at all, he was racing up the stairs two at a time.

"It's Frank," she wailed. "I think he's dead!"

CHAPTER 12

Frank had probably been dead for an hour or more before they found him. That was the opinion of the local GP, Dr Jones, who was summoned by the ambulance team and police. Margaret had refused to leave the room, in spite of the suggestion by the emergency officials that she might be more comfortable downstairs while they got on with what had to be done. With help from the ambulance man, Neil had finally managed to prise her off the floor where, for more than half an hour, she'd been sitting cradling Frank's head on her lap. Eventually she allowed herself to be helped up and led across to the bedroom chair on which Frank's favourite jacket was still neatly hanging.

While Neil pulled up another chair beside her, Margaret simply sat, glassy-eyed and deathly pale, staring at her husband's body as the doctor pronounced him dead. The exact cause would have to be determined at the post-mortem. At that point, Neil felt a shudder go through her as she sat, trembling and wordless, beside him. Her hands were cold, so Neil laid his large hand over hers in a futile attempt to offer her the warmth of his loving care along with a measure of physical warmth.

She didn't respond as the doctor gently examined her, but when he delved into his bag to draw out some medication

194

to help calm and settle her, her hand moved with surprising speed to knock the offered pills away.

"I don't want those," she whispered. "I don't want to sleep."

"You've had a terrible shock, Margaret," said Dr Jones. "These are just to help you relax a little."

There was disbelief in the sharp look she shot at him. "I just want to know what happened," she said, her voice thin and choked. "What happened to my darling? What caused this? Was he in pain? Was he lying there in agony and fear, not able to get hold of me? Was I too busy, the way I'm always too busy, to be there when he really needed me? Was he calling out again and again, and I didn't come? Is that the last memory he had before he… before he…"

The doctor looked at her steadily as he answered. "I can't be sure what caused his death, but providing you don't hold me to it, I could probably make an educated guess. This looks to me like a ruptured abdominal aortic aneurism – a break in the main blood vessel to the heart. If that's the case, Frank would have known very little about it after the initial rupture."

"But why? What would have caused that?"

"His age, maybe? He's in his late sixties now, isn't he? Or his diet, perhaps?"

"We eat well. Frank's the cook. He's always going on about us needing a low-fat diet now we're not getting any younger!"

"His lifestyle? Was he stressed, do you think?"

"Never. I'm the one constantly climbing the wall with stress. He's the calm one, taking everything in his stride."

"Well, the post-mortem will answer a lot of those questions," continued Dr Jones, "but honestly, this condition isn't unusual in a man of his age. In the end, there probably isn't one single trigger for something like this. It just happens."

"Well, it shouldn't have!" There was vehemence in Margaret's voice. "This shouldn't have happened to Frank. He's the sweetest, kindest, most wonderful man in the world, and he doesn't deserve this! He doesn't!"

"We're ready to move him now," said the ambulance man standing beside Frank. "Is it OK for us to take the body, Doctor? Have you finished your examination?"

"Where are you taking him?" demanded Margaret. "He belongs here. I didn't say you could take him. He wants to be here…"

"Margaret," said Neil softly, tightening his clasp on her hand. "They have to move Frank to make him more comfortable. You don't want him to stay on the floor as he is now, do you?"

Thoughts seemed to be churning in her head.

"He could lie on the bed. That's our bed. He wants to lie there…"

"They need to find out what caused this, Margaret. They have to take him to the right place to do that."

"The mortuary, do you mean? It'll be cold there. They'll open him up, won't they? I don't want to know what happened if it means they have to cut him open. I can't bear the thought of them cutting him open…"

With an almost animal-like wail of pain and despair, Margaret practically slid off the chair as she rocked to and fro, sobs racking her body, tears running through her fingers as she covered her face with her hands. She cried and cried for so long that she wasn't even aware that the ambulance team had gently picked Frank up and laid him on a stretcher so they could carry him out of the room and away from the house.

"I need to ring her daughter," Neil whispered urgently to the doctor. "Could you stay with her for a minute while I do that?"

Once he'd located Sarah's number, Neil so dreaded the thought of breaking the unbearable news that he almost hoped she wouldn't answer. But she did. Her voice sounded bright and friendly and welcoming – pleased, but slightly curious, to hear from Neil out of the blue. Moments later, all Neil could hear was her shock and dread as she tried to take in what had happened.

"I'll come as soon as I can. Hang on, I've got Edward here. Martin's not home yet. He won't be home until about seven…" Her mind was plainly racing with all the logistics. "I'll ring him. I'll call him straight away. We'll come together. I just need to sort out Edward. Maybe my neighbour can help? I'll ring her. I'll ring my neighbour. Oh God, I can't believe this. Dad always seemed so fit and well. I can't take this in…"

Neil hesitated about whom to call next. He knew without any doubt that the person who would be the best company for Margaret right now was her dear and trusted friend, Cyn Clarkson. Should he call her, even though her own emotions were still raw from her little granddaughter's death? Was that fair to Cyn? He thought about her, the strong matriarch of the Clarkson clan, the organized, welcoming churchwarden, and he knew instinctively that Cyn would cope with this tragedy with the same practical good sense and compassion with which she approached everything. He was floundering in his own grief and shock. Cyn would get beyond that. She would know what Margaret needed right now.

And so it was that, an hour later, Neil wearily made his way back up Vicarage Gardens, knowing he simply couldn't face the emptiness of his own house. His knock on Harry's door was answered by Claire. She had no idea what had happened, what he had gone through, but she simply opened her arms to draw him in as he collapsed against her.

* * *

Sarah and her husband arrived later that night, and the next morning when Martin had to leave again for work, Sarah stayed on with her mother until Frank's funeral a fortnight later.

Neil called in at the vicarage every day, hoping to see a sign that Margaret was regaining some of her usual character and temperament, but she remained hollow-eyed and pale, saying little, eating nothing, and wide-eyed and sleepless both night and day.

He'd thought she would want to play a full part in planning Frank's funeral, but her withdrawal from reality made him wonder if she even knew it was going on. When Sarah announced that she'd made arrangements for the couple's previous parish priest, Richard Cole, to come out of retirement to take Frank's funeral service, Neil was awash with relief. Normally the job would fall to him, and he feared it would be impossible for him to lead this service without breaking down himself, especially as the service would be deeply emotional for everyone associated with St Stephen's community. Whoever led the service had to be capable of a professional detachment that would put the needs of others first when it came to channelling the grief of so many who loved Frank. Neil knew he was not that man. His own sense of loss was too overwhelming for him to feel detached about anything.

In fact, he felt that any skill he'd acquired over his theological training and two years as a curate was completely inadequate in the face of this shocking tragedy. He had often reassured grief-stricken relatives while planning funerals at St Stephen's, and he knew he'd learned most about that from Margaret herself. She had always seemed to know exactly what to say and how to respond when she was faced with other people's confusion and sadness. Shouldn't he be the one to offer the same sort of Christian support and reassurance to Margaret herself in her time of need?

One afternoon several days after Frank's death, he sat down beside her with his Bible on his lap. Margaret stared out of the window, silent and withdrawn as usual.

"Margaret," he said quietly, "shall we pray together?"

She didn't move except to close her eyes as he carried on.

"We could start by reading the Bible – some of the passages from the gospel that reassure us of God's eternal care and love for us, especially at times of great sadness like this."

At first he thought she wasn't going to respond, but then he found himself almost holding his breath as she slowly, very slowly, turned her head to look properly at him.

"There is no God," she said. "If there was, Frank would still be with me."

And with that, she closed her eyes again to shut out both Neil and the world in which she no longer had any interest.

* * *

Margaret came to the funeral. Supported by her daughter and son-in-law, she walked stiff-backed behind the coffin as it was carried down the aisle. It was odd to see her so soberly dressed in black from head to toe, when her usual garb was colourful and even flamboyant. No colour today, not in her clothes, not in her skin, nor in her dull grey eyes.

She got to her feet for the first hymn, "The Lord's My Shepherd" – Frank's favourite, so Sarah said – but she didn't even attempt to join in with the words she knew so well. She sat down then, staring straight ahead as Sarah stood up to read the poem that begins "Do not stand at my grave and weep", before the Reverend Cole gave an outline of Frank's early life. He'd been a long-distance runner when he was a young man, apparently a very successful one. *How surprising,* thought Neil, who would never have thought that of the older Frank he'd come to know. Frank had been in the army for seven years, and was in the Catering Corps. *No wonder he was so good at rustling up meals at a moment's notice,* mused Neil. Frank had met Margaret at a Spanish-language evening class they'd both joined because they'd been thinking about taking one of the new package holidays to Spain. In the end, they went to Spain together – for their honeymoon.

Throughout it all, with Sarah on one side and Cyn on the other, Margaret registered no expression on her face. Even when Peter Fellowes got to his feet to give a moving, funny, touching tribute to Frank on behalf of all who'd known and loved him at St Stephen's, Margaret's eyes were dry when practically everyone else in the church was reaching for a tissue.

And then it was over. On the organ, Brian started to play a poignant arrangement of "Abide with Me" as the pall-bearers gently lifted the coffin off its stand, hoisting it onto their shoulders to start their slow march down the aisle and out of the church. Family members and close friends filed out behind them to follow the hearse to the crematorium. It had been agreed that Neil would stay behind to host the wake in the church hall, so his last sight of Margaret was a glimpse of her pale, expressionless face as she was helped into the car to make her final heartbreaking journey at her beloved Frank's side.

Nearly an hour later, Sarah and her husband Martin briefly came back to the church hall to thank everyone for their sympathy and support. They explained that Margaret was exhausted and emotionally drained by everything that had happened, and that they planned to take her back with them to their home in Beaconsfield while she regained her strength and health.

The following morning Neil watched as Margaret climbed into the back of Martin's car. She said nothing. She reacted to no one around her and her eyes stayed firmly fixed ahead of her as the car drove slowly down the drive and away.

* * *

"This has been a sad business, Neil, very sad," said Bishop Paul as they sat together in the front pew of St Stephen's a couple of days later. "It's hard to imagine Margaret without Frank. He was a splendid man."

"Surprising too," added Neil. "There was so much about him I didn't know until I heard the tribute to him at the funeral. In fact, the more I learn, the more I realize how little I knew either of them, really. On the face of it, it always seemed that Margaret was the strong one in the partnership, but their relationship was much more complex than that. I remember her telling me once that their marriage was very passionate, and that Frank was her rock."

Bishop Paul nodded thoughtfully. "Proof yet again that it's all too easy to make assumptions about other people's lives and feelings. Years in ministry have taught me that."

"Well, that's the other thing," continued Neil. "What about Margaret's ministry? Will she want to come back to it?"

"From the point of view of the church, she must have as much time as she needs before making any decisions about her future. In other situations similar to this, I've been aware that getting back to work has been a significant step on the path to recovery. After all, the working life of an ordained minister is spent reassuring others of the presence and power of God, and it's exactly that message they need themselves as they cope with their own grief and bereavement."

Neil stayed silent as he wondered if he should share with Bishop Paul Margaret's shocking revelation that she no longer believed in God. Better not to mention it. It had only been a matter of days since Frank's death. Margaret's mind was traumatized. Healing would come in its own good time.

"So what do you think?" The bishop's voice broke into Neil's thoughts. "Are you up to the job?"

Neil looked at him in confusion.

"Margaret's job? Can you cope without her, for the time being at least, until her return?"

"I don't know," stuttered Neil. "This is a busy parish. There's always been more than enough work for two people, let alone one."

"I'll try to arrange whatever support I can for you. Not easy, though. Everyone's stretched and I haven't got spare pairs of hands in ready supply."

Neil didn't reply. His mind was busy trying to imagine coping alone without Margaret.

"There is Hugh, of course," continued Bishop Paul. "He's only about ten miles away. He's retired from his own church now, but I know he'll be more than willing to help out with your services at any time. And do you know Rosemary, the non-stipendiary industrial chaplain? I'll put you in touch with her too. She'll probably be able to lend a hand from time to time."

"Right."

"And you have a good team here. They'll rally round, I'm sure."

Neil thought about Peter, Val, Cyn, the Lamberts, Boy George and all the other stalwarts at St Stephen's.

"Yes, they will," he agreed. "We'll keep things going and pray for Margaret's safe and healthy return."

"And I'm always on the end of the phone, Neil. Just ring at any time if you've got a problem or simply need to chat things through."

"OK," replied Neil, hoping he didn't come across as shell-shocked as he felt.

Bishop Paul reached out to touch his arm. "I know this is tough for you, Neil. I don't underestimate the responsibility that's being laid on your shoulders. You're not yet two years into your curacy, and this is neither ideal nor fair. It's just what it has to be until we know more from Margaret. I'm sure that when she's feeling stronger she'll be longing to get back to where she's loved and where she belongs."

"I hope so."

Bishop Paul looked at his watch. "I must go."

"Of course. Thank you for making time to talk to me like this."

"We're on the same team, Neil: God's team. He'll see us through. Now, before I go, shall we pray together?"

And as Neil bowed his head, he thought he'd never needed God's love and strength more than he longed for it now.

* * *

It was gone nine in the evening when the phone rang as Neil sat poring over the piles of paperwork on his desk.

"Neil, it's Graham. Got a minute?"

"For you, definitely! I'm surrounded by so many bits of paper, my eyes are swimming."

"Can I come round?"

Neil laid down his pen, alarmed by the note of worry in his friend's normally confident voice.

"Of course. I'll put the kettle on."

"Any beers in your fridge?"

"A couple."

"Get them out. I'll see you in ten minutes."

True to his word, a quarter of an hour later Graham was sitting on Neil's settee, pulling the fob off a can of beer.

"Debs is pregnant."

"Oh!" said Neil, not quite sure whether that was cause for celebration or commiseration.

"It's a bit of a shock." Graham took a swig from the can. "To put it mildly."

"How is she?"

"Throwing up first thing every morning, but basically fine, I think."

"Well, that's a relief."

"I didn't see this coming. I knew the pill didn't agree with her, but we were always careful – well, I thought we were."

"So this wasn't planned then?"

Graham shrugged.

"So how do you feel about the prospect of becoming a dad?"

"Shocked."

"But has the shock worn off enough now for you to think it through a bit more?"

"Yeah, and I'm coming round to the idea. Debs and I are solid. We always planned to stay together. We wouldn't have bought the house if we hadn't thought that, so kids would probably have been on the horizon at some time in the future anyway."

"But this has all happened quicker than you thought."

Graham gazed down at the can in his hand before he went on. "The thing is – what happens now?"

"Have the two of you talked about it?" asked Neil.

"Well, we're living together in the house. We're set up. We've got enough room. So what if we have a baby there in a few months' time? I can't see there's a problem."

"Well, that all sounds OK."

"Debs says she wants to get married."

"Good!"

Graham snorted dismissively. "You would say that, wouldn't you! You're a bloomin' vicar!"

"You're not keen on the idea, then?"

"Look, mate, no offence or anything, but most marriages I know end in disaster. What's the point of signing a bit of paper promising to share everything and stay together when you know you can just walk away if it all goes wrong?"

"It may not go wrong. If there's enough love and commitment between you, the kind of love and commitment you need if you're bringing a child into the world…"

"I'm committed! I love her! I just don't see why we need to spend all that money getting married to prove it."

"It doesn't have to cost a lot of money. You could keep it simple."

Another snort from Graham. "Have you met her mother? She's not going to let her little darling get married without a great big production."

"It's not her mother who's getting married. It's you and Debs considering this, and you can choose to keep it as simple as you like."

"Neil, you're not listening. There's *nothing* I like about the whole idea of getting married. I'm not interested. I don't want it."

"Even if it's important to Debs?"

"I'm not just being bolshy. It's not aimed at her. It's nothing personal at all. I just don't agree with marriage."

"I guess it feels personal to her. It's all tied up with whether you love her enough to recognize her need for some formality in the arrangement between you, especially if children are going to be involved."

"Now you're beginning to sound like her. I thought you were my mate, so you'd understand. If you can't get over the job you do long enough to listen to how I feel about this, then I might just as well go now."

Graham made to stand up.

"Sit down," said Neil, grabbing his arm. "I am listening. I hear what you say. You've got every right to feel the way you do about marriage, but Debs has the same right. She obviously feels differently about it. The thing is, with the baby coming, the two of you are going to have to reach a decision about this, one way or the other."

"She's already decided. She says if I'm not prepared to marry her, it's over between us. She means it too."

"Can you risk losing her over something like this?"

"I think she's asking too much. She thinks I'm not giving her enough. Stalemate!"

Neil sat back to think for a moment.

"Would it help to talk to someone, a relationship counsellor perhaps?"

"I don't know. Maybe. I can't really see how a stranger could help."

"They take a detached view, and help you to listen to what the other's really feeling."

"I think we've made our feelings abundantly clear."

"Graham, you could lose Debs and your child over this. If a bit more conversation might help, isn't it worth a try?"

"It's not me who has to try. It's Debs who's being stubborn. She's made it clear it's her way or no way! What kind of relationship is that?"

"I'm so sorry, Graham, I really am. I can recommend

an excellent counsellor, if the two of you think it's worth a try. Other than that, I'm not sure what to suggest. Is there anything *I* can do to help?"

Graham sighed heavily. "Probably not. I just needed a sympathetic ear, I suppose."

"You have that. I'm always here to listen. I just wish I could do more."

"Well, it's only the two of us who can do that, isn't it? And if I can't change, and she can't either, that's the end. And you know what, mate? I'm gutted by that, really gutted."

* * *

"Over here, Neil!" called Barbara. "The playgroup stall's over here!"

Neil pushed his way through the crowd milling around the brightly coloured tables in the church hall until he and his precious cargo reached Barbara.

"Four sets of face paints!" he panted, breathless from the run he'd just made back to the vicarage on a mission to find exactly where Margaret kept their extra supplies.

"Thanks, Neil. We've been run off our feet this morning. We're used to the girls queuing up to have their faces painted, but all the boys have been coming along too so we can make them look like their action heroes. I blame television and those dreadful computer games! They all want to be Spiderman or Transformers these days. Whatever happened to being a good old-fashioned cat with whiskers, or a pirate with a bit of a beard and an eye patch?"

Neil laughed as he perched on the table to look around the hall. "It's going well, isn't it? I must say, whenever the Friends of St Stephen's organize these Bring and Buy sales, they always do a good trade. It looks as if the money's rolling in today."

"Sorry!" called Barbara over her shoulder as another little boy came up to have his face painted. "Spiderman needs me!"

Neil went over to say hello to Beryl and her team on the tea and cake stall before wandering around the tables, stopping to chat to familiar faces here and there as he made his way round the hall. Suddenly he felt a hand on his arm. Peter Fellowes stood beside him, close enough to whisper in his ear.

"We've got a problem. Do you see that woman with the wheeled shopping bag over in the corner there?"

"With the red jacket?" asked Neil.

"Do you know her?" asked Peter.

"Don't think so. Should I?"

"You might have to get to know her. She's been slipping bits and pieces into her bag at each stall she visits, and to my knowledge she's not paid for any of them."

"Oh dear!"

"It's not as if we're charging much. I don't suppose anything here is over 20p."

"Would you like me to go and have a quiet word?"

"I think you should," said Peter.

Neil started to make his way closer, keeping the woman in his eyeline as he went. Almost immediately he saw her lift the lid of her wheeled basket just wide enough to drop a knitted cardigan inside before shutting the flap again and moving on. Within seconds, Neil was at her side.

"Hello," he said kindly. "I wonder if I could just have a peep in your basket? I think you might have accidentally dropped a cardigan in it before you had chance to pay for it."

He realized she was younger than he'd initially thought, probably only in her early twenties, when she spun on her heel to look at him, her face flushed with guilt.

"No, nothing!"

"Would you mind if I take a look, then, just in case you've picked something up without realizing?"

The woman immediately stepped defensively in front of her bag, then thought better of it, and headed at speed towards the exit. Her progress was hampered by the heavy, rather battered old basket, and Neil was soon ahead of her, barring her way. He was about to say something challenging to stop her in her tracks, but his heart softened at the sheer fear and panic he saw in her face.

"Don't worry," he said softly. "You're not in trouble. I'm just wondering if you're OK. Have you got time for a cup of tea?"

It was plain the woman didn't intend to respond. She meant to bolt out of the door as fast as she could. But Neil's kindness – and the mention of tea – seemed to change her mind. Uncertainly, she allowed herself to be drawn back into the hall as Neil gently led her over to a corner table next to the tea and cake stall. Peter Fellowes was hovering curiously.

"Peter, could you get this lady and me a cup of tea, please? And a cake or two?"

Fortunately, the woman couldn't see the exasperated look Peter shot at Neil, but the churchwarden seemed to get the message that Neil thought he was dealing with more than just common theft here.

"I'm Neil, by the way. We've not met, have we?"

The woman kept her eyes down, plainly unwilling to talk.

"I'm the curate here at St Stephen's. Have you ever been inside the church?"

"No," was the muffled reply.

"It's a lovely building. We think so anyway," continued Neil, his mind racing to find other small talk that might get the conversation going. "Do you have another church you like to go to?"

"No."

"Oh," replied Neil. He thought he detected what sounded like an Eastern European accent as the woman started to talk again.

"Not now. Used to."

"Where was that? Here in Dunbridge?"

"London."

"So what brought you to this area?"

"No reason. I got on train. Came here."

"When was that?"

"A week?"

"So where are you living?"

She shrugged without replying.

At that point, following Peter's instruction, Beryl bustled over to their table bringing a pot of tea, two mugs and a plate of dainty sandwiches and cakes. The woman's eyes grew wide with longing as she stared at the spread.

"Here you are, love!" chirped Beryl breezily. "Enjoy!"

The woman didn't need any further invitation as she reached out to grab a sandwich in each hand, stuffing them into her mouth as if she hadn't eaten for days.

"She's starving…" Beryl mouthed silently, catching Neil's eye from where she stood behind the woman's chair. The two of them looked on as the woman demolished practically the whole plateful, hardly stopping for breath. As the food disappeared, Neil picked up the pot to pour two mugs of tea, pushing one of them over towards her as she ate. She shovelled in two sugars and gulped down a whole mugful as quickly as the piping hot tea would allow. It wasn't until she'd finished the lot that she seemed to become aware that Neil was still sitting beside her.

"Will you tell me your name?" he asked.

"Why?"

"Because we're having tea together, and I've already told you my name is Neil. It would be nice to know who you are."

She considered for several seconds before lowering her voice to answer.

"Maria."

"Maria. Nice to meet you. Do you have another name too?"

"No," was the short reply.

"When did you last have something to eat, Maria?"

She didn't answer.

"And you live in Dunbridge?"

Another shrug.

"You've got friends or family here, have you?"

Suddenly, she was pushing back her chair, grabbing for the handle of her wheeled basket.

"Must go…"

"Where?"

"Just go…"

"Let me take you. Where do you live?"

She was struggling to get to her feet.

"Maria?" Neil's voice was still soft, his expression gentle and curious as he looked at her.

Slowly, she sat down again, burying her face in her hands.

"You haven't got anywhere to stay, have you?"

She shook her head miserably.

"Where have you been sleeping?"

"Little house at railway."

"In the builders' yard?"

She nodded again.

"Where is your home, Maria? Where are your family?"

"Romania."

"And do you have any friends in this country?"

"When I came. No room for me. I left."

His heart lurching with sympathy for her, Neil's mind was racing as he thought about what to do next.

"Would you let me help you?"

She said nothing, as if she was beyond hoping for help from anyone.

"In the next town, there's a place called a hostel, where someone who needs help like you can find a bed to sleep in," explained Neil as slowly and clearly as he could. "The people there can help you. I'd like to ring them. Will you let me do that?"

Panic flashed across her face again.

"Police?"

"No."

"They tell police?"

"If you have done something very wrong, they might have to, but that's not what they want to do. They need to know about you – where you come from and why you're here. They will ask why you have no home, why you're hungry and why you were stealing clothes from us here today."

Maria said nothing, as if she was too tired to protest.

Neil beckoned to Peter, then stood to give him a brief explanation of Maria's situation before Peter disappeared towards the church office where they kept the twenty-four-hour number of the homeless hostel.

Almost an hour later, Jim from the hostel arrived at the hall. Several months previously, Jim had come over to speak at a Sunday morning service at St Stephen's. The organization he worked for had a Christian ethos, and most of the team members there gave their services as an expression of their own faith. Many of the residents who passed through their doors would never have known that, though. Whoever needed their help, and whatever they were able to offer, the team did what they could.

"Thanks, Jim," said Neil, while Beryl helped Maria to her feet, laying a warm coat from one of the stalls over her shoulders.

"That's OK. I'm glad you called."

"It's good that she found her way here and we noticed her."

Jim turned to smile at him. "What does it say in the Bible about us not always recognizing Jesus when he's right here with us in the form of someone who is hurting, hungry, dirty or shouting the odds? When we walk away without doing anything, we never know who we're turning our back on, do we?"

And as Maria looked over her shoulder to give Neil the slightest of nods, Jim put his arm around her and led her out towards his car.

⇋ CHAPTER 13 ⇌

C laire's step-father David came down with her mother Felicity for a short break over the late holiday weekend at the end of May. The couple enjoyed the fact that, with only one connection, they could hop on a train from Dunbridge straight into London. That meant they could catch up on exhibitions and shows that rarely made it up country as far as their home town of Scarborough. Claire was fond enough of David to think of him as her dad. She had no memory at all of her real father, who'd been in the navy when he married Felicity back in 1980. All too late, Felicity had discovered that Trevor lived up to the sailor's reputation of having "a girl in every port". Soon after Claire was born, he disappeared up to Scotland to join the other woman, who understandably thought he was all hers, as she already had two children by him.

Felicity had brought up Claire alone until she met David, a financial advisor she'd come into contact with through her work as an account manager for a local insurance company. Claire was nineteen and living independently when the couple married in 2005, and only twenty-two when she met Ben, Sam's father.

On the second evening of their visit, Felicity called Claire up to their bedroom, where she had laid out some papers on the bed. Scrutinizing them carefully, Claire realized that she was looking at details of a savings account opened in Sam's name, into which generous payments had been made every month since August the previous year.

"What's this?" demanded Claire.

"It's from Ben. I told you he intended to start making regular payments for his son."

"*My* son! Sam is *my* son!"

"His too, Claire. You have to acknowledge that."

"Just as he acknowledged his son when he disappeared back to Australia without a word the moment he knew I was pregnant? He gave up any rights he had towards Sam then!"

"He hasn't given up on his responsibility, though, as these payments make clear."

"I don't want his money!"

"Maybe you don't *want* it, but I know you *need* it – and why not? You have a son to bring up on your own. Children cost money."

"Ben doesn't even know him. How could he, when he lives five thousand miles away? He's nothing to us; nothing!"

"Well, the way he's set up this account, he's given you the option either to change the arrangements so that you can administer the account yourself and use it as you need to, or you can simply leave it in Sam's name so it provides him with a nest egg for when he's older."

"And what's the price we have to pay for that? Does he want photos of his son, so that he can drool over them and show them to his friends so they can see what a wonderful dad he is? Is he going to start asking for Sam to spend time over there with him – a stranger Sam doesn't know from Adam? This is blackmail, Mum, and I don't want anything to do with it!"

"Well," said Felicity, her voice calm and reasonable, "you can't stop him placing his money wherever he wants to – and this account is most definitely set up in Sam's name, there for him any time he needs it. You can't stop that, and why should you? You've made your feelings and terms very clear. I've passed that on to Ben as clearly as I can whenever he's been in touch…"

"What do you mean, in touch? I know you showed me that one letter from him a while back, but just how often have you been in touch with him?"

"Every three months or so over the past year and a half."

"I had no idea it was so often. How could you, when I've made it perfectly clear how I feel about him knowing anything about my son?"

"I don't mean to upset you, Claire, but in all conscience I believe it's the right thing to do."

"And what else have you sent him, along with your opinion of how I feel? Photos? Stories about my son that he has no business knowing?"

"Occasionally, yes."

"So why didn't you send nice little photos and stories to my real dad as I was growing up, then? When it was *you* in this position, you didn't want to share anything about your child with the man who'd walked out on *you*, did you?"

"The difference," answered Felicity stiffly, "is that your father not only never asked about you, but moved house without ever letting me know his whereabouts. I can tell you that regular payments from Trevor would have made life a great deal easier for both me and you. I didn't have that option. You do – and for Sam's sake I think you'd be wise to get off your high horse and allow Sam the extra benefits his father's money can buy."

Claire fell silent, her cheeks flushed with anger, but seconds later she softened as she saw the genuine concern behind the curtness of her mother's words. Without a word, Claire stepped into Felicity's arms, which tightened around her.

"Sorry," muttered Claire, her voice muffled by her mother's shoulder.

"I'm sorry too. Sorry that you ever had to go through all this on your own. I understand you feeling betrayed. Ben behaved appallingly. But he seems to have matured over the last six years, at least enough to realize that bringing up children is an expensive business."

"So you think I should just take the money for Sam's sake?"

"I do. Detach your own feelings from this. Do it for Sam."

"Nothing else though. You don't tell that man anything! Promise me."

"I promise that from now on I will pass any letters on to you. You decide what you want to do with them."

The tension in Claire's body softened as she snuggled further into her mother's shoulder.

"I love you, Mum."

"I love you too, my darling, very much."

* * *

Graham and Debs never did go to the counsellor Neil offered. It quickly became clear that the couple were both so entrenched in their own opinions that neither the love between them, nor their baby due in a few months' time, could sway them enough to prevent their relationship plummeting to disaster.

As regularly as his extra-busy workload would allow, Neil met up with his friend in the evenings, growing steadily more concerned by Graham's increasingly gaunt face. His body seemed to be shrinking, along with his confidence that there was any way at all to save his failing relationship.

Debs looked little better. As her pregnancy advanced, she gradually stopped attending rehearsals for the church music group, preferring to sit in a pew at the back on the few occasions she came along to services.

One Sunday, when the later service at St Gabriel's was being taken by Hugh, the retired local minister, Neil suggested to Debs that they didn't join the rest of the congregation for coffee in the hall, but instead put the kettle on for the two of them in the church office, where they could have a quiet chat.

Reluctantly, Neil had to admit that just as he could see the logic in Graham's argument, he also had real sympathy with Debs's point of view.

"I'm a Christian, Neil. Oh, I know Christians aren't supposed to start living with the man they love, and get pregnant by him before they're married, but there you are; that's what's happened, and I've got to deal with it. It would be hypocritical to pretend I regret any of that. I've loved Graham since we were kids. I couldn't wait to set up home with him. I'm proud to be having his child. I just can't live with him any more."

"Do you still love him?"

"Very much. But after everything that's happened, I wonder whether he loves me – or actually knows me at all! I think children should be brought up in a family where the parents are married. And I think that marriage should be blessed by God, because we need God to be part of it if we're going to have any chance of making it work for the whole of our lives, till death do us part."

"Why does Graham have such a downer on marriage? Do you know?"

"His father ran out on his mum when he was quite young."

"Well, that must have made a very painful impression on him."

"And several of the teachers he works with are either having affairs or getting divorced."

"That won't help either…"

"But that's not going to happen to us! We've known each other all our lives. There's no one for me but Graham. He might have taken a very long while to realize it, but he's always been my man."

"And I know he loves you. He talks about nothing else."

"So why doesn't he realize how important this is to me? Now I'm going to have his baby, we need to be married. It's a simple fact. It's the right thing for all of us. Why can't he understand that? And even if he does have some illogical reason to hate the whole idea of marriage, why is he prepared to put our future together in jeopardy rather than have a reasonable conversation with me so that we can try to work it out? I just don't get it…"

"He does seem very set against the idea – but more than that, he seems to think that if the two of you do get married, it would have to be a big fancy affair that really isn't him at all."

"It doesn't have to be that way, Neil. You know that."

"But what about your mum? Graham thinks she'd never let you get away with anything less than the fairytale wedding."

"That's ridiculous. He can't blame Mum for this. There's no one to blame but him."

And so it was that on one Friday evening two weeks later, Neil kept Graham company in the Wheatsheaf while Debs moved out of the home they shared. Wendy and her brother Darren helped her to strip the house of the furniture she'd bought, and all the bits and pieces that added a woman's touch to the place. When Graham walked back in at eleven that night, he realized the four walls he was left to live in were simply a house, no longer a home. Neil watched helplessly as the big man slumped down on the stairs, doubling up in pain as he sobbed.

* * *

The month of June was manically busy for Neil, especially with marriage ceremonies for couples who realized that the old porch gate outside St Stephen's would provide a picturesque backdrop for the wedding photo they would eventually choose to take pride of place on their mantelpiece. Pastoral visits to elderly parishioners who couldn't get to church, regular services at residential care homes, chaplaincy at the hospital and the hospice, along with confirmation classes and parish business meetings, not to mention morning and evening prayers – they all combined to more than fill his time, and that was before he got anywhere near the constant stream of paperwork and arrangements needed to run a parish as complex as St Stephen's. Peter, Val and Cyn were absolutely wonderful, each taking on as many extra responsibilities as they could. Cyn had even offered a home to the dreaded Archie, Margaret and Frank's grumpy cat, whose opinion of Neil had clearly not changed since their first meeting when the huge feline had taken an instant dislike to the nervous young curate! But even with all the support he received from many members of the congregation, in the end Neil knew they were just kindly volunteers, whereas he was the one in the paid job. His curacy seemed to have disappeared into the ether. To all intents and purposes he was the vicar, and in that role he was very alone.

True to his word, Bishop Paul kept in close touch, and over the weeks that followed Margaret's move, Neil came to realize that the bishop had meant what he said about always being available if Neil felt out of his depth or in need of advice.

"Have you heard anything from Margaret?" Neil ventured to ask during one of their frequent phone calls.

"I've rung her daughter several times, but I've only recently managed to get a word with Margaret herself," admitted the bishop.

"How was she?"

"Not very chatty, but she did sound a lot better than when I last saw her."

"Do you think it would be appropriate if I went to see her?" asked Neil. "I'm not sure what the protocol is here, but I'm very fond of her. We've got to know each other well over my time here."

"Of course you can go, if you'd like to. In fact, that's probably an excellent idea, because you're more likely to get an honest response from her than I am."

"I could go next Monday, on my day off."

"With my blessing, Neil – and feel free to claim the cost of your mileage, because I consider this a diocesan duty. Ring me, won't you, on your return?"

It was with some trepidation the following Monday that Neil found himself turning his car into the spacious drive of Sarah and Martin's home in Beaconsfield. Sarah had the front door open before he'd climbed out of the car, giving them the chance for a quiet word before he went into the house.

"How's she doing?"

"Physically much better. She's eating more now, and sleeping reasonably well. But it's not her physical health that's worrying me most."

"What does the doctor say?"

"That grief takes its own time; that he'd expect nothing more from someone who's just been widowed after forty years."

"Does she miss Dunbridge? Because I can tell you we all miss her! We're longing for her to come back."

Sarah hesitated before she spoke again.

"Look, come on in. She knows you're here. She's in the front room. I'll bring you both a cup of tea."

There was real welcome in Margaret's face when she saw him, and she got up from her armchair to put her arms around him and hug him closely. Her body was trembling, and he wondered if she was crying. He just held her without saying anything until she seemed a little calmer.

Sarah came in carrying a tray laden with a pot of tea, bone china mugs and a jam sponge cake.

"I'll leave you to it, then," she suggested tactfully, closing the door behind her.

"You're looking so much better, Margaret," Neil began. "How are you feeling?"

"Lousy," she replied. "Drained. Empty. Lost. Alone. The list of adjectives is long. Do you want them all?"

Uncertain what to say, Neil leaned forward to pour tea for them both before he continued.

"It all happened so suddenly – such a shock…"

She nodded, taking the cup he passed to her.

"We were going to retire in five years' time, you know. We'd got it all planned. We both loved life in ministry – Frank as much as me – but we always thought it would come to an end with enough time for us simply to enjoy each other's company for our remaining years. I feel robbed of that. It's not just my darling husband I've lost, but all the dreams we had together.

I have no life without Frank. I'm nothing, nothing at all."

"You wouldn't think that, Margaret, if you could see how much you're missed at St Stephen's. I feel like a headless chicken without you there, and everyone in the congregation tells me they feel exactly the same. We need you. We need your spiritual strength and your way with people, and the warmth you bring to every situation. When are you coming back? Please say it's soon!"

She looked down at the cake, and cut two slices before putting one on a plate that she passed to Neil.

"Sarah made this. I can't make cakes. Frank was a wonderful cake-maker."

Neil smiled. "He certainly was!"

"I'd like to learn to make cakes like Frank," said Margaret, as if her thoughts were far away.

"That would be good. Beryl would value any contribution you feel like making to her cake stalls."

"And I'd like a little garden of my own – and Archie. I miss Archie. Is he OK?"

"Cyn's taking care of him at the farm."

Margaret chuckled to herself. "I didn't think you'd volunteer to offer him a home!"

Neil took a bite of cake, pleased to see Margaret do the same.

"I'm not coming back, Neil. I can't. Too many memories. I can't go back to that house where Frank – where Frank…"

Neil quickly put down his plate to take her hand.

"Well, then, perhaps you should consider going into ministry in a less demanding church, with a smaller house and a little garden that Archie would enjoy?"

Margaret shook her head. "No. That's not for me."

"I know Bishop Paul would do everything in his power to find the right place for you, somewhere you'd feel supported and cared for. Ministry's been everything to you, Margaret. You bring so much to the life and faith of others."

"I'll never be able to do that again. I wonder now how I ever did."

"Margaret, I—"

She cut him off in mid-sentence. "It's gone, Neil – any certainty I had about what I believe."

"Look, you've been through so much. You need more time…"

"No." She put her hand up to stop him. "You don't understand. I believe in nothing. I have no sense of God, because if such a being existed, if there truly *was* a God who was all-seeing and loving, then I would know it now – and there's nothing, nothing at all."

"But you've heard so many bereaved relatives speak this way in the first wave of grief and shock. You've reassured them through it. You've reminded them of the promise in the gospel that Christ has gone before to prepare a place in his house for those we love. You know that we come from God and we return to him. You know that! You believe it with such passion that you make others believe it too!"

"Not any more. I have an overwhelming sense of guilt that I expected other people to believe that in *their* grief, when I now know I can't believe it in my own."

Shocked to the core by what he was hearing, Neil's hand instantly lifted to cover his mouth. Margaret gazed at him, noting his distress.

"I'm sorry. I know that's not what you want to hear."

"I don't think you're well yet, Margaret. You need a chance to get your strength back…"

"That's true. I might rediscover my strength – but not my faith. I'll never believe again."

Neil drew a deep breath, and minutes passed as each sat with their own thoughts.

"You should go," Margaret said at last.

"No, I don't have to leave yet…"

"You should go," she continued, "to tell Bishop Paul my decision. Tell him I'm sorry, but I won't change my mind."

Neil nodded dumbly.

"And Neil?" There was sorrow in her eyes as she looked at him. "I know this lays a great deal on your shoulders, and that's unfair on you. I also know that you'll rise to the challenge brilliantly."

He shook his head dismissively. "I'm struggling, if I'm honest. Everyone's trying to be helpful, but there's so much only the minister is allowed to do."

"And you've got the work of two ministers to cope with. That's tough, Neil, and I'm sorry I've been the cause of that."

To his surprise, Neil felt tears pricking his eyes. Margaret looked calm and resigned – so different from the energetic, charismatic character who had inspired so many at St Stephen's, the dear friend and mentor he'd come to love. In that moment, he wasn't sure who he felt more sympathy for: the parishioners who would miss her inspirational presence, or Margaret herself in whom the flame of faith had gone out. *Not for long*, he prayed. *Dear Lord, be with this lovely, sad, wounded soul. Stay near her. Protect her. Help her to find her way back to you…*

Their conversation was over. There was nothing more to say. They stood to hold each other in a silent embrace that said so much. Then he left, and as he turned to see her standing in the bay window, his heart ached for her.

* * *

225

Iris had been staying at his house for little over a week when she made her announcement.

"Well, I've done it! I've signed the papers on number 60!"

Neil nearly choked on his mouthful of casserole.

"But you haven't sold the house in Bristol yet, have you?"

"In the end, my neighbour decided to buy it for his daughter. He approached me privately, so there's no estate agent involved. It's all going through very quickly, I'm glad to say. I've been in that house for more than thirty years, since your dad set up his accountancy firm in the area. If it had dragged on because no one liked our home enough to buy it, I would have found that very distressing."

"But I didn't realize the people here in number 60 had actually agreed to sell!"

"I heard today. They've been waiting to know whether they'd got the house they're after – and they've just heard it's all going through. It's a short chain, including two cash buyers, and one of them is me! My solicitor says we could complete in a matter of weeks."

Neil drew a sharp breath, trying to take in the speed with which his childhood home was being sold, and his mother relocated. Her face was flushed with excitement, though, and he realized that his feelings were irrelevant compared to the tremendous upheaval she was facing in order to start a new life in Dunbridge.

"How can I help?" he offered with a smile. "What about packing up at the Bristol end?"

"Virtually done. I've been going through cupboards and drawers for months, getting rid of lots of bits and pieces I should have taken to the charity shop years ago."

"You'll need a removal company…"

"I've got one organized. They'll pack the boxes properly

for me too, so there'll be some burly men on hand to do all the lugging about."

Neil grinned at her. "You've got everything sorted, then!"

Her grin matched his. "I can't wait, Neil. The house I'm buying backs right onto Harry's beautiful garden, so I'll have that wonderful view every morning when I draw back the curtains."

"And Harry's OK with all this…?"

"He's the one suggesting where I should go for nice curtains and reasonably priced carpet!"

Neil chuckled. "Always practical, that Harry."

"And you don't mind, Neil? You're not worried that it's going to cramp your style having your mother in the next road down?"

"Honestly, I'll be too busy to notice!"

"Well, that concerns me too. Perhaps I can cook the occasional evening meal for you, just to make sure you get round to eating something decent every now and then. I want to help, you know. I'm very proud of you, Neil. Your father would be too."

Neil could hardly believe what he was hearing. Surely this couldn't be his mother, who'd nagged him incessantly from the moment he was born?

"Mind you, you need to wash that car of yours! I've been telling you that for days. No one's going to trust a vicar who arrives in a filthy car!"

Thank God, thought Neil. If his mother completely lost her bite, he might not recognize her!

* * *

Claire was worried about Neil too. She knew he was overwhelmed with work, but then it wasn't difficult to appreciate how tough it must be for a young, relatively inexperienced curate to take on all the challenges and responsibilities of a busy parish like Dunbridge. And it was even harder to do it all without the guidance and support of an established rector like Margaret. She feared, though, that the cloud of depression that seemed to be hanging over him was prompted by more than just overwork. It was less noticeable when he was in the full flow of his role as a minister, but very obvious to her at times when he was able to drop the mask of efficiency and simply be himself, either at home or in the company of those with whom he felt most comfortable. Then he seemed to wear an air of detachment, as if he was so deeply lost in his own thoughts that the world beyond was hardly touching him.

He would appear to be watching television, and yet she could see his mind was focused on images that certainly weren't on the screen. Sometimes he lost his way mid-sentence, apparently unaware that the meaning of what he'd been saying had been abandoned. Dark circles under his eyes betrayed his lack of restful sleep, even though his lids would close with exhaustion whenever he sat still for more than two minutes at a time. It was as if there was a sadness right at the heart of him that he chose not to articulate, and which she couldn't reach. He was shutting her out in a way that seemed totally oblivious rather than deliberate. She had to get to the bottom of it, not just for them as a couple, but for the sake of the wonderful, wounded man she loved.

It took a few days to tie up all the loose ends on the arrangements she resolved to make, but at last came the evening when everything was in place and she was ready to tell him about what she'd organized. With surprise, she realized she was a little nervous. Recently, there had been hardly any evidence of the easy-going Neil she loved so much.

He'd just finished a phone call in the upstairs office in Vicarage Gardens when she came up to join him, carrying two cups of coffee.

"Are you done now?" she asked, putting down the cups so that she could massage his stiff shoulders. "You look all in."

"I've got one person ringing me back, but I imagine that won't be till the morning now."

"I don't know how you cope with all this paperwork when it means you have to spend so much time locked up indoors," she said, her fingers skilfully making their way along his tense muscles. "That's why I love working outside. Fresh air always seems to blow the cobwebs away."

He sighed as the knots in his neck started to loosen. "Mmm, I envy you."

"You could do with a bit of fresh air yourself."

He shrugged. "Well, I suppose I get the odd gulp of that when I run from one meeting to another."

"Just imagine how lovely the Derbyshire Dales must be right now."

He closed his eyes as if he were picturing the roll of the hills and the feel of the wind on his cheeks.

"I can dream, can't I – but it'll be a long time before I get there again."

"No, it won't. We're leaving on Wednesday. It's all booked."

He turned sharply to look at her, not taking in what she was saying.

"Everything's arranged. Hugh's stepping in to cover your services for a couple of days. Peter and Cyn are taking care of all the other arrangements while you're away. You need a break, Neil. You're exhausted. It's no wonder, when you've been through such a tough time lately. So I'm taking you away for a while. It's all organized."

"But I can't go!" exclaimed Neil, his hand ranging over the pile of papers strewn across his desk. "Just look at this lot! No one can take all this over. There are too many loose ends."

"Nothing that won't wait for a couple of days."

"Claire, I can't…"

"You're going, Neil, because if you don't, I think you'll be ill, and I love you too much to let that happen."

His shoulders slumped then, as if he hadn't got the energy to argue. He rested his head back against her, and she leaned over to kiss him on the lips.

"So," she said softly, "you have tomorrow to dig out your walking boots, and we'll set off first thing on Wednesday morning. OK?"

"OK," he agreed, although there was no enthusiasm in his reply. Claire knew he really didn't think it was OK at all.

* * *

There was barely a breath of wind as they reached the peak. They'd taken their jackets off and tied them around their waists by midday, lifting their faces to the sun as they stood, breathless and triumphant, with the long climb behind them.

"Coffee?" Claire's voice broke the silence as they stood gazing out at the view.

"Love one!" replied Neil, taking off his backpack as he spoke. "I could murder a sandwich too!"

He looked over at a familiar flat rock just yards away from where they were standing.

"I was here last year, you know, just after my ordination. I left my car keys on that rock over there, and got right back down to the car park before I realized. Had to climb all the way back up again to fetch them."

Claire's face lit up with amusement. "So had you been having a picnic here?"

"No, I might have left the keys up here, but I'd made the daft decision to leave the sandwiches down there so they'd be a bit of a reward when I got back! I wasn't thinking straight, was I?"

Claire spread out the cups and packs of food on the rock before settling comfortably on her jacket, which she'd laid on the grass. Her expression was thoughtful as she watched Neil doing the same.

"So what *were* you thinking about?"

"You. Wendy. Harry. I'd just been ordained. You remember, everything was so muddled at the time…"

She nodded before taking a leisurely bite of sandwich.

"Do you feel less muddled now?"

He looked across at her.

"About you, most certainly. I knew I loved you last time I was here. I just wasn't free to feel that way and it was tearing me apart. So much has been in turmoil since then, but there's one thing I'm absolutely certain of. I love you, Claire. I'll always love you."

"You must admit, though," said Claire carefully, "when it comes to being the partner of an Anglican minister, Wendy's much better material than I'll ever be. I'm an odd choice for you in lots of ways. Faith's fundamental to the man you are, and if I can't share it – well, I worry that it could cause a lot of tension for you in the future."

"But you're never dismissive of what I believe. You're open-minded. You support me in your own way."

"But I'm full of questions. That might get you down, especially if, in the end, I can't accept the answers that make absolute sense to you."

Neil looked out over the rolling hills stretching away towards the horizon.

"I think," he mused quietly, "we all hear God's word in our own way, Claire, according to who we are and what we've been through. Christianity makes absolute sense to me. Christ is a real presence in my life – always has been – and now it's my pleasure and duty to help other people find him for themselves. But I can only help. I can only tell them what I've discovered in my own life. Their experience might be completely different from mine."

He turned to look at her before carrying on.

"I think God touched you on the night of Harry's illness, and that for the first time you got a sense of his presence."

She nodded. "I don't know what it means, though. Was it real? It was a frightening night. We were both pretty emotional. I prayed for Harry when I've never, ever prayed before. Was that God? Was my prayer answered, or would Harry have got better anyway?"

"I think," he replied, "that finding faith is one very small step on a journey of discovery that lasts a whole lifetime and possibly beyond. That journey may take us down different theological paths, and it's possible that people may never attach whatever faith they feel to any religion at all – but we all take our own path. I've chosen mine, Claire, but I respect you in yours. I'd worry if you were instantly sure, if you suddenly embraced everything I believe, just because you love me. I want nothing more from you than your honesty – and your love. I need your love most of all."

She leaned across so that their heads touched, her fingers winding around his before speaking again.

"And do you feel the same about Margaret? That she has to be free to make her own journey?"

She sensed a change in him as his body tensed.

"Margaret's always been a Christian, deep in the heart and soul of her. Her certainty and sense of vocation has been a real inspiration to me."

"And now? What now, when she seems to have lost that certainty?"

He looked troubled, not able to answer immediately.

"I can't understand how that could happen," he said at last. "I've heard Margaret so often bringing real comfort and encouragement to people who've been bereaved, reminding them of God's presence and love..."

"But in the face of her own grief, she's found that wasn't reassurance enough."

"That's what I don't understand. More than ever before, this was when she could have leaned on God, because surely he's with us most of all when we're facing despair and confusion. She believed that. She inspired others with her belief..."

"But losing Frank's turned everything upside down for her," interrupted Claire. "She's bereaved, Neil, and that's probably as much a physical condition as an emotional one. She's not well, and may not be for quite a while to come."

"And the Margaret I knew used to say exactly that when we met people whose grief was raw. They sometimes said that any faith they had was choked out of them by the trauma of losing someone they loved, and she would talk them round. I've tried to remember every word she said and how she put it across, because I know I'm going to need those skills in my own ministry."

"And now, because her faith has slipped away from her, are you worried something similar could happen to you?"

"Yes. I'm ashamed to say I am. Who knows what would happen to me if I lost *you*? We honestly don't know how we're going to react until awful things like that actually happen to us, do we?"

"So Margaret's decision is threatening your own sense of certainty, then?"

"Honestly, Claire, I'd like to say quite the opposite, because at the moment my life is a constant prayer, asking for strength and clarity. One minute I find myself feeling absolutely confident in what I believe, and then the next I remember the change I saw in Margaret, and my head's full of questions."

"That brings us back to my previous question. Are prayers answered? Is there some power, that you call God, who listens and responds? Do you feel he's listening to you now?"

"I'm praying for that all the time, and yes, I believe he is. I'm praying that he is."

"Is all this what's been bothering you since you came back from seeing Margaret?"

Pain flashed in his eyes as he looked at her.

"It just never occurred to me that a deeply held faith like Margaret's could be shattered in this way. I can't imagine that ever happening to me, but then I didn't think it could happen to her either. Who knows what challenges might come my way in the future? What if the unthinkable happens, and I end up losing my faith just like her? I'm an Anglican priest. My whole purpose is to bring other people to Christ, but if I lost the certainty in what I've always believed to be true, how could I fulfil that purpose? I couldn't. I'd be a failure – and more than that, without God at the centre of everything I do, I'd be totally and absolutely lost, adrift in a sea of confusion and darkness."

"With me right beside you," said Claire gently. "I'll always be right there beside you, just as I am now. And whatever comes your way will come my way too. We don't know, do we, what lies ahead? That's what makes life such a wonderful adventure.

What's happened to Margaret happened to *Margaret*. Your life, your understanding of God, your relationship with me and everyone else you love – they're unique to you. And if challenge comes – as I'm afraid, my darling, it often will – we'll pray about it together. We'll face whatever comes our way as the loving couple that we are."

For several moments Neil seemed too overcome with emotion to say anything, but when he did, he started by looking down at their linked hands.

"I don't want you to be my partner, Claire."

Her eyes widened with shock.

"That's just not enough for the way I feel about you. You're my world. Your love for me makes sense of everything, and I love you more than I can put into words. I'm offering you myself just as I am, inadequate as I feel in so many ways. Would you be willing to take me on and sort me out? Will you accept me: my heart full of love, and my promise to adore you for the rest of my life? Will you be my wife?"

ᴤ CHAPTER 14 ᴥ

News of their engagement was greeted with delight by Harry and Iris. The old man's eyes looked suspiciously shiny as he hugged first Claire and then Neil, with the stern warning, "You'd better look after her!" Iris seemed genuinely moved too, announcing rather grandly that she knew all along this would happen – as if their decision to marry was all down to her careful planning!

"So, is it common knowledge? Are you going to make an announcement about it?" asked Harry.

"I'd like us to get the ring first," said Claire, sliding her arm around Neil's waist. "It'll feel properly official then."

"We've decided to go shopping on my day off next week," explained Neil. "Perhaps we'll organize an engagement party after that. It's all so new we haven't really decided yet."

"No thoughts on a wedding date either, then?" asked Harry.

"As soon as possible," replied Neil as he planted a kiss on the tip of Claire's nose.

"Euck! You're kissing again!" piped up Sam, who'd just come in from the garden. "You two are always kissing!"

Laughing, Claire stooped down to put her arms around her son. "That's because we've decided to get married, Sam.

How do you feel about Neil being your proper daddy from now on?"

Sam looked up at the two of them, his face suddenly serious.

"Cool!" he said at last. "Can I have an ice cream?"

* * *

Ice creams were in plentiful supply the next day, the Saturday of St Stephen's Summer Fayre. The combined committees of the Friends of St Stephen's and the Ladies' Guild had been in overdrive for weeks, planning the theme and decoration of each stall, not to mention cooking, icing, painting, sewing, sticking, hammering, cajoling, bossing – and occasionally squabbling – in preparation for the big day.

There was relief all round when the day dawned with glorious sunshine in a clear blue sky. Claire was out early in the morning collecting stock and setting up her plant stall with a colourful array of bedding plants, flowering shrubs and vegetables, all of which she'd grown herself. Neil had been detailed to table-lugging and chair-moving duties, so he was hot and red-faced when two familiar figures walked hand in hand into the church hall.

"Hello, mate!" Graham and Debs wore matching beaming smiles as they made their way towards him.

"Well," laughed Neil, "aren't you two a sight for sore eyes! It's great to see you back together."

"Couldn't bear it without her," said Graham, "and I will never be without her again ever. That was the worst fortnight of my life!"

"So..." mumbled Neil, uncertain how much to say. "What are your plans?"

"We've got a booking to get married on Tuesday morning at the registry office."

"That's great news! Congratulations, both of you!"

"Bit of a surprise, though, eh?" asked Graham, his expression becoming more serious.

"I guess you've talked everything through and reached a compromise."

"Well," said Debs, "that's what we've come to talk to you about."

"Are you free on Tuesday morning?" asked Graham.

"Probably not," grinned Neil, desperately trying to recall his diary for the coming week, "but nothing I can't rearrange if necessary. How can I help?"

"Be my best man?"

"That's *absolutely* necessary! I'd be honoured to."

"It's only a very small affair: just our mums, Debs's dad and a couple of really good friends. We don't want any more than that."

"No speech needed, then?"

Graham grinned. "Just get me and the ring there, that's all I ask."

"And I have a request too," added Debs, "a rather unusual one."

"Ask away!"

"I know there's complete mayhem in the grounds here today, but does that involve the church too?"

"No. Thankfully that should remain a sanctuary of peace and quiet this morning, and with all the jobs I'm supposed to be doing in the grounds and office right now, they'll never think of looking for me there. Come on!"

So, like naughty children escaping from an unwelcome chore, they slipped out of the back door of the hall and into the church. The interior was bathed in warm rainbow hues as bright sunlight poured through the Victorian stained-glass windows. Graham's pace slowed as he took in the scene.

"Have you ever been in here before?" asked Neil curiously.

Graham shook his head. "Only in the company of eight hundred little monsters during the occasional school carol service that I couldn't wheedle my way out of. It didn't look quite the same then."

"This way!" called Debs. She was already past the screen and walking into the sanctuary, where she leaned against the choir stalls nearest to the altar and waited for the men to join her.

"Sit down, Graham," she invited, "and you too, Neil, please."

Obediently, the two men slid into a pew.

"It's hard for you, Graham," she began, "to understand what this place means to me. I've been coming here all my life. I've sung in these choir stalls since I first learned to read music when I was about eight years old. For as long as I can remember, I've been a member of the choir for almost every service – Christmas, Easter, Harvest, Remembrance, Palm Sunday and all the rest of the special occasions in the Christian calendar. We've sung to welcome babies at baptism, and at so many wonderfully moving marriage ceremonies, like Peter and Val's a few weeks ago, and at heartbreaking funerals like the one for little Ellen at the end of last year, when just about everyone in the church was in floods of tears. This is the place people come to mark the important moments in life – where they're free to express their feelings, in fellowship with whoever's there to share that moment with them. I can't begin to think of going through the most significant change in my life without coming here to lay everything before God."

"I get what you mean, Debs," said Graham, "I do. I know you'd like to have the big wedding here, and I know that's not just for your mum, in spite of everything I've said about her in the past. It would mean the world to you, I realize that – but..." He stopped mid-flow, unable to continue as he looked helplessly around him.

Debs finished his sentence for him. "But this just isn't you."

Graham shook his head sadly. "No, love, it isn't. I'm many things, not all of them much good, but I've never been a hypocrite. I don't belong here."

"You didn't think you belonged in a marriage either," she said softly, "but you've agreed to that."

"Yes, I have. Being without you for those two weeks made me realize I could never be without you again – you and our baby. If you doubted my commitment before that, you won't ever need to give my love and loyalty a moment's thought from now on, because I'll sign up to anything to keep us together.

"The oddest thing happened during that time when you were gone. Something you'd said kept playing on my mind – about how, if we weren't married, even if we all lived under one roof, you'd have no choice but to put your surname down on the baby's birth certificate rather than mine – as if you couldn't trust me to stay around if I wasn't prepared officially to give both of you my name. How could we ever truly be a family if I had one surname and you two had another? That was when I realized I actually *wanted* to marry you. I want us to be a proper family. I honestly can't wait to marry you, Debs. But not here, not in this way. Not with this place full of people all dressed up in big hats with the choir singing tired old words that don't mean anything to me. As much as I love you, I can't – I just can't."

"I know." Debs lightly touched his hand, her expression full of love as she looked at him. "I can't ask you to go through all that when I know how much you'd hate it, but I still can't get away from what I feel marriage really is. For you, it's the official piece of paper we'll get at the registry office on Tuesday. For me, it's much more important to know God is in it with us; that he will support and bless us in our life together. *That's* what will make it a true marriage for me."

Graham looked at her forlornly, fearing the worst as she continued.

"But, you see, I don't think God needs the big hats, the full church and words out of a book either. He's with us now, in this empty church, and he sees and knows us just as we are: Debs and Graham, in love, expecting our first baby, standing together at the start of our married life. Will you stand with me, Graham, here and now, in our ordinary Saturday-morning clothes, in this church that means so much to me? Can we say what we really want to say, make our own promises to each other right now in the presence of God?"

Neil was the first to move, quietly taking his place in front of the altar as he invited the two of them to join him. Debs was still standing uncertainly in front of the stall where Graham sat for several heart-stopping seconds before he stood to take her hand, holding her close as sudden tears glistened in her eyes. With his arm around her shoulder, they walked slowly over to where Neil was waiting.

"God is here." Neil's voice was intimate, barely above a whisper. "His Spirit is with us, and we ask for your blessing, Lord, on Graham and Debs as they come before you now at the start of their married life together. You know their hearts. You know the love they have for each other. You see the joys and the challenges they have ahead of them. Bless them, Father, and accept the vows they want to make to each other now in your presence."

To his surprise, it was Graham who spoke first, his eyes fixed on Debs as he turned towards her.

"When I look at you, Debs, so strong and beautiful in every way, I wonder what on earth you see in me. I mean, just look at me! I'm a mess of a man: disorganized, not remotely ambitious, irresponsible, overweight. The list's endless. And yet, through all the years we've known each other, you've seen something in me I never knew I had – especially these last months, when I finally woke up to realize that the woman of my dreams has been right under my nose all the time.

"You bring out the best in me. You've helped me see what I could and should be. You've taught me to love, to belong, to share everything I am with another person. With you, I've finally recognized what really matters in life, and that's you, *us*, the two of us together with our baby, and the family home we're going to build together.

"I'll get things wrong, Debs. I'll drive you mad at times, and I'm sure we've got some humdinger rows ahead of us. But I promise you I'll love you deeply and faithfully for the rest of my life."

Beyond the window, the sun had moved across the sky so that the shadow on Debs's face brightened as she started to speak.

"I don't think it was just chance that we grew up as next-door neighbours. I think God planned it that way. He intended us to be together because we're good for each other. Remember how you taught me to ride a bike without stabilizers? And how you were always around to sort me out when I was thinking of doing something daft, like walking on the railway-bridge wall, or jumping in the river when I couldn't swim?

"You protected me too. Remember those girls who were pushing me about at school? You helped me with my maths homework. You were absolutely right when you talked me out of being a beautician, because it would never have suited me, and then it was you who pushed me through my police entrance exams. You were always there for me, Graham, always.

"But I hope I was there for you too. Do you remember when you were in your punk phase and gelled your hair into three different-coloured spikes? It was me who sorted you out again before your mum saw it. And on your birthday when you thought it would be a good idea to take all your clothes off in the market square? I was the one putting a coat round you and getting you out of sight as the police car was coming round the corner!

"And then there were all the disasters you had with girls. You just kept getting it wrong. But then of course you would, because for as long as I can remember, I knew I was the only girl for you. We belong together. We always have. We always will. Marrying you is everything I've ever wanted, my darling. I'll make a home for you and our children, and it'll be full of love and laughter. I'll work alongside you, and we'll build a life of contentment and fulfilment for us as a family."

Not even trying to conceal how moved he was by her words, Graham wrapped both his hands around hers as she went on.

"But life's not always easy, is it? You and I are both strong characters, stubborn, selfish sometimes, wanting it our way or not at all. We both know there'll be bumpy times ahead. That's why I need us to be here. God has to be in this marriage with us, because we've got no hope of making it work on our own. We need his grace and presence with us every step of the way. We need his guidance and forgiveness when we get things wrong. We need his love and comfort so that we can love and comfort each other.

"So here I am, humble, hopeful, trusting that God will answer my prayer as I stand with you now. Father, bless this dear man who has my heart. Bless me, especially as you know how often I can get things wrong. Bless us. Bless our marriage. Bless our family. Be with us always."

Neil stretched out to lay one hand on each of their heads as a shaft of golden sunlight suddenly beamed through the window to encircle the three of them.

"Those whom God has joined together, may no one put asunder. May he defend you on every side, and guide you in truth and peace – and may the blessing of God Almighty, the Father, the Son and the Holy Spirit, remain with you always. Amen."

* * *

By that evening, everyone was sure this was the best Summer Fayre they could ever remember. Blue skies certainly brought in the crowds, who came determined to have a good time. They cheered the children's acrobatic display, jived to the jazz band, sang along with the barbershop quartet, looked on indulgently as toddlers climbed onto the miniature merry-go-round, munched hungrily on hot dogs and mustard – and cleared Claire's plant stall within the first two hours. When it came to cakes, Beryl knew from past experience that she had to come prepared. In the church office she'd left a stash of enough baked delights to replenish the cake stall three times over before the goodies finally ran out.

The tombola was a great favourite, especially with Harry, who won a bottle of sherry with his first ticket. It was instantly confiscated by Iris, who reminded him sternly about the diet he was supposed to be sticking to after his heart attack. Iris herself was very sniffy about whoever had donated to the bric-a-brac table an opened but hardly used bottle of 4711 eau de cologne, presumably not having the good taste to realize what a treasure it was. She happily parted with 30p for it, knowing she had a bargain.

It was while Neil was taking the weight off his feet for five minutes with a cup of tea and an iced bun as he sat at a table prettily laid out with a checked cloth and jug of summer flowers, that Peter and Val came over to join him.

"Did you notice who's popped back for a visit?" Peter asked, nodding in the direction of the lucky dip. Peering through the crowd, Neil suddenly saw her: Maria, the Romanian girl who had arrived hungry and homeless at their last Bring and Buy sale. She looked up at that moment and stared straight at them, her face breaking into a shy smile. It was then that Neil realized she wasn't alone. Jim from the homeless hostel was standing beside her. He spotted them and took Maria's arm as they made their way over to say hello.

"Welcome, Maria!" smiled Neil. "How are you getting on?"

"Good. At the hostel, they are very kind."

"She's doing really well," smiled Jim. "In fact, I can't imagine how we managed without her. She's always making beds and cleaning up after everyone. A bit of a treasure, that's our Maria!"

"I'm glad. That sounds wonderful. So what happens now? How long can Maria stay with you?"

Maria's attention was already distracted as she looked at all the activity around her.

"I do like the look of those," said Val, noticing the longing with which the young woman was gazing at some necklaces sparkling on the hand-made jewellery stall to their right. "Do you want to come and see, Maria?"

Once the two women were out of earshot, Jim answered Neil's question.

"Hers is a bit of a sad story really – all too typical, I'm sorry to say. She was sent over by her family to join a cousin who was supposed to put a roof over her head and help her get a job. The cousin turned out to be a complete waster, not remotely interested in working, let alone looking after a rather naïve, scared young woman. He sent her out to get some bread one day, but left the flat and slammed the door behind him the moment she'd gone. She waited in the street for two days, but he never came back. So there she was – hungry, homeless and completely alone. She stayed in London for about a week, eventually keeping warm by just hanging around all day long in Kings Cross Station. One day when she thought no one was looking, she slipped into a train that seemed to be out of service, because it looked a lot warmer and more comfortable than the seats on the station forecourt. She lay down on the seat, so I suppose the guard didn't notice her when they closed the doors and took the train up the line. By the time Maria woke up, the train was standing in a siding just outside Dunbridge – you know, that bit of line where they hold the spare rolling stock ready for the morning rush hour."

"So that's how she ended up living in a hut at the builders' yard down by the station!"

"And she only had the clothes she was standing up in, so she had no choice but to try and help herself to anything she needed. She didn't have any money and her English is pretty basic, as you know."

"Does she want to go home?"

"I don't think so. It seems they only sent her over here because there was nothing for her there."

"And she's not illegal?"

246

"Romania's in the EU. Movement between countries is unrestricted."

"So what'll happen to her?"

"Well, that's where you might come in. It didn't take us long to see that she's a very capable young woman, hardworking and anxious to make friends in spite of her shyness. We'd like to work towards getting her into her own accommodation and able to support herself. That's obviously a long way off, but it would be a good start if we could organize some voluntary work for her, where she can get experience of working with other people in a caring environment where the only language spoken is English."

"That's a good idea."

"So I wondered if there was any way she could help here? She's a good cook. She's got five younger siblings, so she's used to being with children, and I believe she's basically honest. I know you caught her stealing from your Bring and Buy sale, but..."

"She had no choice," finished Neil. "I thought that straight away. Look, leave it with me and I'll talk it over with the team here. Can I give you a call in the week?"

Jim shook his hand gratefully. "I'll look forward to that, Neil – and thanks!"

Much later that afternoon, as the crowds thinned out and the sun dropped lower in the sky, a weary Claire came to find Neil. He was carrying away the final couple of tables to stack them in their usual place under the stage in the church hall. In the churchyard, the last of the banners had been taken down, and Barbara had organized a competition for her cub pack to find the champion at picking up litter. The boys were whooping around with enthusiasm, enjoying themselves too much to realize they'd been duped into tackling the job that everyone else hated.

Sighing with exhaustion, Neil put the tables he was carrying down on the grass, wrapped his arms around Claire and kissed her soundly.

"Where's Sam?"

"Harry and your mother took him home. He's loved every minute of this, but I don't think it will take much rocking to get him to sleep tonight. A quick bath and bed, I reckon!"

"Ooh," sighed Neil, "that sounds nice!"

"Apparently Iris has cooked us all one of her famous casseroles."

"Oh joy! Butter beans!"

"Except these are *my* butter beans. I can vouch for their excellent quality."

"Well, that makes all the difference," he grinned at her. "I will learn to love them because I am madly in love with the woman who grows them…"

He leaned forward to kiss her again with a tenderness that took her breath away, and as they stood locked in an embrace that blocked out the world around them, neither of them saw Wendy coming round the corner of the church, her expression reflecting a conflict of emotions: shock, then sadness and finally blatant hatred.

* * *

Debs looked lovely as she stood beside a spruced-up Graham at the register office the following Tuesday morning. To Neil's delight, the service was taken by Angela Carter, whom he'd last seen at Vera Dunton's funeral.

The marriage service was short and to the point, which perfectly suited the wishes of the couple and the very small group who were there to wish them well. Graham's mum looked on with pride, surprised to see that now her son had tidied himself up a bit he looked strikingly like her ex-husband, who'd had no contact with the two of them since their divorce. Debs's mum, Jackie, looked every inch the mother of the bride in her feathery hat, dress and matching jacket, all in a tasteful shade of mint green. Brother Darren was plainly bored throughout the whole proceedings, unlike his dad, Don, who seemed the most genuinely emotional of all of those who watched Debs and Graham make their vows that morning.

In his role as both witness and best man, Neil stood slightly behind Graham, in line with Wendy who was bridesmaid. Wendy had carefully avoided any eye contact with him from the moment they arrived – not that Neil had noticed.

The rings safely placed on the right fingers, the groom was given permission to kiss his bride, to a ripple of applause from the small gathering around them. The registers were duly signed, and once the group had found a patch of grass beneath a cluster of trees at the back of the building, cameras started clicking.

They were going on to an Italian restaurant in town for a wedding lunch, but Graham knew that Neil had to excuse himself because his workload was so pressing. Remembering everything the three of them had shared that week, Graham shook Neil's hand warmly.

"We're off to the Cotswolds for a week…"

"Nice place for a honeymoon," agreed Neil. "In fact, we might even think of going there when Claire and I get married…"

"What? You dark horse, you! When did that happen?"

"I asked her when we were walking in the Derbyshire Dales. We've not had time to get the ring yet."

"Well, congratulations to both of you! Debs, did you hear that? Neil and Claire are getting married!"

Angry with himself for not realizing Graham would blurt out the news immediately, Neil accepted the congratulations that echoed around him, knowing that among the crowd was Wendy, who would probably be less delighted than the rest of them. He looked over in her direction, only to catch a glimpse of her back as she hurriedly left the room.

"Drink at the Wheatsheaf on Monday week, Neil?" called Graham. "I'll let you win at darts."

"Will the wife let you out?"

"She will, because she knows I'll always come back."

"Good luck, then, Graham. You too, Debs! Enjoy yourselves – and God bless!"

* * *

It was almost midnight when Wendy sat back from her computer screen with a small sense of triumph. She'd found him! She'd thought so immediately from his Facebook entry, which gave his name and the details of where he lived in Australia, but it was the photo that confirmed it. Even though the picture was small and difficult to see clearly, she couldn't help thinking that Ben Stone had aged quite well from the rather gangly, blond young man she remembered from his visit to Dunbridge years before.

Thinking for a moment about exactly what she wanted to say, she started to type.

> *Hello! I think you might be the Ben Stone who*
> *spent several months in Bedfordshire, England,*
> *about seven years ago now. Am I right? If*

> *so, hello from me, Wendy Lambert. I was the*
> *dark-haired girl who never could quite beat you*
> *whenever we met at the squash club on Tuesday*
> *nights. Do you remember? How are you? It*
> *would be great to hear your news. And if it is*
> *you, isn't it time you paid us a visit again? It's*
> *been far too long. Mark me up as a friend if you*
> *fancy getting in touch.*
> *Regards, Wendy Lambert.*

Reading the message several times just to make sure it sounded right – friendly, intriguing, inviting – Wendy took a deep breath, then clicked the SEND button.

* * *

"It's perfect, Mum. I can see you really settled here."

Iris had survived the upheaval of the move from Bristol the day before, and now she stood enjoying an early morning cuppa in the kitchen of her new home in Ransom Road. She was looking remarkably fresh and pleased with life. There were boxes piled up in every room, but within the hour Peter and Val would join Neil and Claire to get things straight throughout the house. They all knew Iris would be in her element, issuing orders and trying pieces of furniture first in one room then another until she was finally satisfied – but Neil could forgive her that, because he couldn't remember ever seeing his mother so energized and contented. Initially he'd had real reservations about her moving from the house his father had taken her to as a bride thirty-two years earlier, but it was plain that her decision to buy in Dunbridge had brought out the best in her. She was busy, happy and surprisingly rather pretty, with her cheeks flushed by a mixture of excitement and sheer hard work. She even seemed to enjoy the experience of Neil drawing her into a heartfelt bear hug, as he did often these days. That was something the old Iris would definitely have thought rather distasteful and distinctly unnecessary.

By six o'clock that evening, when Val and Peter finally left, the house was transformed. Pictures had been hung, ornaments unwrapped, dusted and placed on shelves and mantelpieces, plants lined up on window sills, cupboards neatly arranged, beds made up and table lamps glowing with soft light. They all stood back to admire their handiwork as Harry and Sam arrived through the new gate, which Harry had installed to create a direct shortcut between his kitchen and hers.

"Thank you," said Iris, glowing with satisfaction as she looked around her. "You've all been so kind. Thank you!"

"This is for you!" said Sam, handing Iris a bunch of freshly cut garden flowers that Claire had gathered for him to bring as a house-warming gift. Having duly delivered the flowers, Sam looked around with interest. "Have you got Sky TV here?"

"I will have," replied Iris, "and if ever your grandad insists on watching snooker, and you think it's boring, you can come and join me over here. I quite like a good cartoon."

Sam nodded approvingly before stopping in front of the row of photos stretched along the mantelpiece.

"Who's that?"

"Me on my wedding day."

Sam peered closely at the photo.

"You look weird. I don't like your hair."

"It was all the fashion at the time."

"Who's that man?"

"That's Neil's father, Robert. We'd just got married when that photo was taken."

"At St Stephen's?"

"No, in a place called Bristol. Have you ever heard of it?"

"No."

"It's nice. I liked living there, but I'm going to enjoy being here even more."

"Where's Robert now? Why doesn't he live with you?"

"He died, Sam, nearly eighteen years ago."

"Oh. Like Grandad's wife. Her name was Rose. You really miss her, Grandad, don't you?" Sam looked pointedly in Harry's direction.

"I do," replied Harry.

Sam turned to Iris. "And do you miss Robert?"

"Yes, Sam, very much."

Sam's thoughtful gaze took in both Iris and Harry.

"Well, you're both old now and you're friends, so that's all right. Oh, Mum, that stuff in the oven is smelling good. Do you think it's ready yet?"

"Probably," said Claire. "Shall we go over and eat?"

"It's pasta, my favourite and I'm starving!" announced Sam, and with a mischievous grin, the small boy darted back towards Harry's house.

"Madam," said Harry, bowing towards Iris as he offered her his arm. "Seeing as we're all alone in the world and young Sam thinks we're *very* elderly Billy-No-Mates, would you care to accompany me to the dining room?"

As the two of them wandered arm in arm down the garden path, Claire planted a peck of a kiss on Neil's cheek, taking his hand so they could follow Harry and Iris through the gate. At that moment a memory flashed through Neil's mind. He recalled how fiercely Iris had fought to stop him becoming a priest and taking up his curacy in Dunbridge. How curious life was – and how wonderful it now promised to be...

* * *

There it was! The moment she clicked on Facebook, Wendy spotted his message.

> *Wendy, how great to hear from you! I have*
> *really fond memories of Dunbridge. That was*
> *a very happy trip for me. Funny you suggesting*
> *I should pay a visit sometime. Recently that's*
> *exactly what I've been thinking myself. Perhaps*
> *you could give me some advice on how best*
> *to organize it? Love your picture, by the way.*
> *You've not really changed at all, except you're*
> *prettier, of course! Thanks so much for getting*
> *in touch. Ben X*

Wendy didn't hesitate in tapping in her response.

> *So come as soon as you like! It must be winter*
> *there because we're enjoying a glorious summer*
> *here. You're welcome to stay at my flat if you*
> *need somewhere to base yourself. Just let me*
> *know when you're arriving, and I'll meet you*
> *at the airport. Don't think about it. Just come!*
> *Love, Wendy.*

And as she pressed the SEND button, Wendy realized that after all the miserable months she'd been through, things were *definitely* looking up!

Neil's misadventures continue in:

IF YOU FOLLOW ME

"...ambitions and emotions run high..."

Also by Pam Rhodes:

WITH HEARTS AND HYMNS AND VOICES

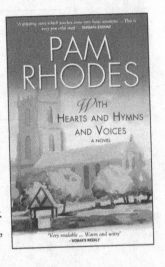

When the BBC *Songs of Praise* team decides to broadcast a Palm Sunday service from a small idyllic Suffolk village, not everyone is happy.

The vicar, Clive, is amiably absent-minded, but his practical wife Helen gets on well with the television team – perhaps a little too well, where the charming, enigmatic Michael is concerned. Charles, the Parish Council chairman, is deeply opposed and resents the enthusiasm of other villagers – including his wife Betty. As the outside broadcast vehicles roll in, the emotional temperature rises…

"Very moving, very powerful intimate moments... I really did enjoy it."
– Lynn Parsons, BBC Radio 2

"Very readable... Warm and witty."
– Woman's Weekly

"Ambitions and emotions run high..."
– Family Circle Magazine

"A gripping story which touches some very basic emotions... Captures wonderfully the two extremes of village life... This is very powerful stuff."
– Barbara Erskine

ISBN: 978 1 85424 975 3 | e-ISBN: 978 0 85721 074 6